T0307563

THE DEADLIEST GAME

THE DEADLIEST GAME

A NOVEL

HAL ROSS

Copyright © 2013 by Hal Ross

FIRST EDITION

All rights reserved. No part of this book may be reproduced in any form or by any electronic or mechanical means, including information storage and retrieval systems, without permission in writing from the publisher, except by a reviewer who may quote brief passages in a review.

Library of Congress Cataloging-in-Publication Data

On File.

For information, or to order additional copies, please contact:

TitleTown Publishing, LLC
P.O. Box 12093, Green Bay, WI 54307-12093
920.737.8051 | titletownpublishing.com

Distributed by Midpoint Trade Books
www.midpointtrade.com

Printed in the United States of America

Interior design by Jane Perini, Thunder Mountain Design
Cover Design by Elizabeth Lewis

FOR

DALIAH AND DYLAN

HONORABLE MENTION

THE WOMEN IN MY LIFE:

My wife Francine

My agent Claire Gerus

My editor Caroline DeLuca

My publisher Tracy Ertle

My sister Sylvia

And in memory of my mother Grace

PROLOGUE

It was an unusually warm day for April, but the weather did nothing to brighten Khalid Yassin's mood. Three years of living in New York among the infidels had just about drained his patience. Three years of plotting, organizing, ensuring that nothing was left to chance.

Now, he drove his late model Lincoln into the lot on 31st Street, handed his key to the parking attendant, and started off on foot.

Yassin was a tall, muscular man in his early forties. His brown hair was combed neatly. Armani sunglasses shaded his eyes. He was fortunate for someone born in the Middle East in that the lighter color of his skin allowed him to easily pass for an American.

He paused in front of the Macy's Herald Square entrance nearest to 34th Street and took everything in, from the vehicular to the pedestrian traffic, noting that both were equally congested. Often he could sense when danger lurked; after all these years, it had become second nature to him. And yes, something was there now, just below the surface, vague but perceptible. A face in the crowd, that of a young man he'd seen once too often.

He waited but not for long. Knowing he could not afford to delay, he removed his sunglasses, opened the door for an elderly woman with silver-gray hair and followed her into the store.

A cacophony of noisy chatter greeted him. Why did Americans have to talk so much? Was it their egos, he wondered, their need to be heard? *Yap, yap, yap.* He thanked Allah that soon he'd be through with these despicable people, once and for all.

The majority of shoppers were women. Some were pretty, three or four were pregnant. A handful hurried by. Others were casually strolling up and down the aisles. The fact that so few wore head coverings also grated on his nerves.

Yassin proceeded to the Louis Vuitton boutique on his right, where three sales clerks were poised for action—one Hispanic and two black. Looking at his watch, he saw it was already eleven o'clock. But where was his contact? He moved out of the boutique toward the center aisle of the store, hoping his expression didn't betray his anger.

Five minutes passed before he caught sight of the woman, rapidly approaching. She was an attractive Egyptian in her mid-thirties. He had recruited her because of her sympathy to the cause. He met her halfway and indicated the time. "What happened to eleven o'clock?" he demanded without preamble, pronouncing each word deliberately.

The woman paled. "I'm sorry. I was called into a meeting. Please, come this way."

He followed her back toward the Louis Vuitton boutique. She stopped at a counter clear of customers. Then she removed a key from her sweater pocket and opened the glass showcase to retrieve a large purse. "I'll get this wrapped for you," she said, turning away.

He stood by the counter, not seeing anything untoward, yet remaining alert. Had he a choice, he would take as many casualties as possible right now. But the need for control prevailed.

When the woman came back, she explained that his special package had arrived yesterday, by courier. "I put it inside the purse," she said carefully, clearly intimidated by him. "As you had instructed."

"I knew I could count on you," Yassin said, tossing her a small compliment. Then, testing her, "Did you tell anyone?"

She met his eyes reluctantly. "No one."

"Your husband?"

"No one," she repeated.

"Maintain your silence," Yassin said, his voice a steely monotone. He placed his hand on her arm and could feel the tension there. He squeezed a little too forcefully before letting go. Then he pulled out an envelope from his inside jacket pocket. He was about to pass it to her when he suddenly winced.

Damn shrapnel. The wound in his right arm had never healed properly. Too often Yassin forgot that certain movements caused the pain to flare. He rubbed the sore spot by habit, knowing it wouldn't do a bit of good.

His memories flooded back to that morning several years ago, when he had stepped into an Israeli trap and barely escaped the ensuing gun battle. But he had gotten away. And for one purpose only: to see his current mission through to completion.

Now, he handed the woman the envelope in such a way that the transaction was concealed. "Five thousand dollars," he said. "As we had agreed upon."

"Thank you."

"Keep this to yourself."

"I will," she assured him, her voice weak, practically a whisper.

• • • • •

Instead of heading out of the store, Yassin walked in the opposite direction. Within seconds, the same onlooker he'd noticed earlier drew his attention. The boy was in his late teens, gaunt, almost emaciated.

Yassin purposely picked up his pace, passing dozens of displays of perfume and cosmetics. This was doubtless the rival group keeping tabs on him, he decided, prepared to do everything in their power to undermine his efforts. Sunni versus Shiite; Muslim against Muslim—a conflict without end, hurting their cause time and again. If it wasn't the Pakistanis, it was the Iranians; if it was not the Egyptians, then it was the Afghans; faction upon faction of al-Qaeda, interfering rather than cooperating.

Before Osama bin Laden's death, they were disorganized; afterwards, it was pure chaos. In fact, the idea of sleeper cells was a wonderful concept were it not for the petty jealousies that turned them into rivals instead of comrades in arms. Why else were they seeing such failures as the Boston Marathon, where instead of hundreds of deaths there had been less than a handful?

Yassin carefully removed the knife he kept hidden in the sheath in his pants pocket. Then he paused and surveyed his surroundings. A slightly overweight, middle-aged blonde passed by and gave him a flirtatious look. He was tempted to use the knife on her, to teach her a lesson.

Now, when he looked back, the boy was gone from sight, obviously aware that he'd been noticed. But Yassin waited to be sure. He kept watch a few minutes longer.

Finally, he slipped the knife back into his pocket and walked out of Macy's. When traffic cleared he dashed across 34th Street against the light and positioned himself in front of a shoe store. There was no reflection in the window to cause alarm.

Satisfied, he returned to his car. He paid the attendant and drove off, realizing that he could not be too cautious. His long, arduous journey was coming to an end. Nothing could interfere with his plans. The hatred he felt would only be assuaged by accomplishing his goal. He wanted to make them pay. The Americans: lovers of Israel. And pay they would.

• • • • •

Yassin crossed the George Washington Bridge, arriving at his Long Island destination close to an hour later. A dirt road led past a vacant farmhouse and into a large gated property. More than one sign warned that the area was private and that trespassers would be prosecuted. Security cameras were locked in place. He pressed a remote switch on his sun visor. The gate slowly opened, allowing him to pass through.

Yassin drove for nearly a quarter of a mile before reaching the entrance to what appeared to be an old country estate. Off in the distance, at least a tenth of a mile away, sat a sprawling, two-story house. There were no sightlines to a major road. Just row upon row of pine trees, sufficiently mature to block the view. There was no barn or stable, only the house, and here—closer to him—a guard station. He could see five or six men loitering in front.

There was one other car, a cream-colored Ford, already parked close by. He pulled up next to it. He turned off the ignition and took the purse from Macy's in hand. No sooner had he opened his door and stepped out than he was greeted by a man close to his own age. He was bearded, wearing a plain robe and *kaffiyeh*.

"*Asalaam alaikum*," the man said.

"*Walaikum asalaam*," Yassin replied.

They embraced more like brothers than friends. They kissed each other on both cheeks, then patted shoulders before pulling apart.

"Is everything prepared?" Yassin asked.

The man nodded.

Yassin handed the purse to him, already anticipating his reaction.

The man opened it and removed a metal container that was less than two inches thick. "Wait here," he said.

• • • • •

Fifteen minutes later the man returned and pointed toward the house, drawing Yassin's attention. He checked his watch and began to count down aloud: "Five, four, three..."

The explosion that followed after the count reached one was controlled, yet fierce. A brief light flashed in one room—in the top left-hand corner.

Yassin was pleased. Everything he'd been told about this new form of *plastique* was obviously true. It was pliable enough to be hidden in a small space, yet powerful enough to cause the damage he required.

The other man led the way to the house.

Yassin took a moment to adjust to the dim lighting. When his vision cleared he could see signs of decay: patches of rust around the kitchen sink, beige wallpaper peeling, doors hanging off their hinges. The staircase they took to the top floor was splintered, making the climb precarious.

The higher floor was brighter, helped by a skylight. They passed a bathroom, two bedrooms, then paused at a third.

The man opened the door wide.

The lower part of the stick figure's body was still strapped into the toppled-over chair. A thick cord was tied around its waist. Some distance away lay the straw head, neatly decapitated.

Yassin shivered with excitement. Once more he was reminded of his loss, of the vow he had made to exact revenge. He moved forward, retrieved what was left of the shredded head, and began twirling it in his hand.

In his mind's eye he visualized real victims, American infidels all, their brain spatter staining the walls and ceilings of their homes, minute bits of bone scattered across numerous floors, the smell of blood, distinct and metallic in nature, permeating each room.

PART ONE

APRIL • MAY

CHAPTER 1

In retrospect, Blair Mulligan realized he should have tried anything to stop him. Even put a bullet in his head … if he owned a gun and knew how to use it. Instead, he watched as John Dalton pushed his way past his secretary, entered his office, and took a seat without being asked. "Thanks for seeing me," he said. "This won't take long."

The first thing Blair noticed was his eyes—two black orbs, void of emotion. "You didn't leave me much choice," he told him, sounding far less authoritative than he would have liked.

"It'll all be explained, Mr. Mulligan." John Dalton's voice matched the chill in his eyes.

Blair indicated the stack of paper on his desk. "I don't mean to be rude, but I really don't have time for whatever it is you're selling."

"Relax, relax," Dalton said. "I thought you guys in the toy industry were a fun-loving bunch."

"Oh, we are," Blair countered dryly. "It's a barrel of laughs here in Toyland. Now, what was so important that you barged in here without an appointment?"

"Mr. Mulligan, please. Are you always this uptight?"

Blair was caught between impatience with this intruder and his multitude of concerns. How could he explain to an outsider the intricacies of his convoluted industry? Where nothing remained constant. Where this year was already old news, and he was far into the planning stages for the next.

He again waved at the paper pile on his desk. "If I don't get through this crap today, I won't come out from under. *Capisce?*"

"Mr. Mulligan, your government needs you," Dalton said, removing a laminated I.D. card from his wallet and handing it over.

Blair had to admit that the man's identification seemed authentic: it bore a Federal Government seal with a picture of the agent in color, bearing enough of a likeness to pass. The only problem was, Blair wouldn't know one government bureaucracy from the other.

"BIS," Dalton said, as if that explained everything. And, after a pause: "Bureau of International Security."

"Never heard of it."

"Most people haven't. And that's the way we like to keep it." Dalton was wearing a dark suit of worsted wool and a slate gray tie. Not the most comfortable outfit for a warm April day in New York. His black attaché case resembled a computer bag with enough room for two computers. He dove into it now, removed a three-by-five, black-and-white photograph, and handed it over.

Blair blinked in recognition, unable to hide his surprise.

"Jeremy Samson," Dalton said, as if the man in the photo needed an introduction.

Blair and Jeremy had gone from being business associates to good friends over the past eight or nine years, and Blair couldn't, for the life of him, figure out why Jeremy would be involved.

"Mr. Samson is a gentile living in a Jewish land," Dalton continued. "He likes to boast of being an honest businessman. But the truth of the matter is, he has some excellent Arab contacts in mighty high places. You and he meet in Tel Aviv two or three times a year, conduct your affairs, usually spend at least one afternoon playing golf, sharing a Mediterranean dinner together, some wine for you, a Coke for him. He manufactures a number of your products—crafts and puzzles, for the most part—skims a little off the bottom line without you being the wiser. After all, what are friends for? Yet you still believe that relationships in the land of milk and honey are no different from those you cultivate back home. Only problem is, it doesn't stop there. Like many in Israel, Jeremy has his finger in a myriad of pots, not the least of which is his connection to subversive powers. Those anxious and willing to bring the United States to its knees. As a matter of fact, ever since September 11th…"

Blair didn't like what Dalton was insinuating. Not one little bit. "And the reason you have come here today?" he interrupted.

"Ever since September 11th, we have become far more vigilant about business being conducted in foreign countries. You are in a position to do your government quite a bit of good."

Blair held up his hand. "My government happens to be Canadian."

"We know about your background and where you were born, Mr. Mulligan. But you've got your green card now. And we are convinced you would be more than willing to help your adopted country."

Blair finally smiled. "And what exactly is it that Big Brother expects of me?"

"Do you mind if I smoke?" Dalton asked, reaching into his pocket.

"It's a no-smoking building."

Dalton removed a pack of Marlboros, then a matchbook and miniature pillbox made of tin, his portable ashtray. He lit his cigarette and took a long drag. He held it for what seemed forever, then exhaled. His eyes appeared oblivious to the smoke curling beneath their lids. "I don't want you for an enemy," he said as if he were placating an imbecile. "Let's play nice, Mr. Mulligan. It'll be easier for everyone in the long run."

Blair's anger intensified. "It would be easier if one, you didn't smoke, and two, you stated your case, then left."

"You'll be going to Israel later this month."

An alarm bell went off in Blair's head. "How do you know where I'll be traveling to? And when?"

"We are the government, Blair. We—"

"I know, I know," he stopped him. "You know everything."

"Precisely."

"Well, how does my going to Israel have anything to do with the U.S. government? And how is Jeremy Samson involved?"

"If you give me a minute, I can explain. You'll understand far more if you listen instead of constantly interrupting."

"Maybe I don't want to understand," Blair muttered softly.

"What's that?"

He looked up. "Nothing. Just get on with it, please."

Dalton's voice became even more pretentious, if that were possible. "A few years ago, the United States government was conducting…"

The sound of Dalton's cell phone going off caused Blair's cheeks to turn crimson. It wasn't just a tinkle either, but a volume that could only have been programmed to annoy. He wanted to rip the phone out of Dalton's grasp, even as the man flipped it open and raised it to his ear.

• • • • •

Blair arose from his desk and walked out, leaving Dalton to his privacy. He moved down the corridor to the small company kitchen and poured himself a decaf, freshly brewed less than an hour ago.

From this vantage point he had a clear view of his showroom. Over a thousand square feet of toy products—from radio-control cars to dolls—most with electronic components. As usual, he was filled with pride when acknowledging his success in New York. A rare accomplishment for a kid from a poor Canadian family.

A career in computer sales after graduating high school had led to a chance meeting with a toy distributor based in Montreal who was seeking a sales manager. Blair assessed the risks and decided to take the plunge.

Their business grew and became profitable. One of the companies they represented specialized in children's games. The owner of that company, a New York entrepreneur advancing in years, was anxious to bring in someone young enough who could manage and eventually take over his business. Months of discussion led to an agreement that changed Blair's life. And here he was, ten years later and at the age of thirty-five, president of Toys and More.

But success had not done much to build Blair's self-esteem. To his way of thinking, he wasn't the best looking man: face a little too narrow, lips thinner than he would have liked. But his blue eyes helped, along with his thatch of hair that was more sandy than brown. Still, he didn't delude himself. In sales, his good-enough looks and pleasant-enough personality had managed to get him this far. Not that there weren't days when doubts loomed up and he envisioned his success vanishing. And returning to the poverty of his youth frightened him more than he wanted to admit.

"Mr. Mulligan?"

Blair put down his cup as Dalton stepped into the kitchen. He looked even more formidable now that he was standing. His bearing was erect, his cold eyes penetrating. "I'm all done," he said without apology.

There was something in his voice Blair hadn't noticed before. An accent of some sort. Something foreign. "I'd like to know if you're expecting any more phone calls," he said.

Without responding, Dalton turned and headed back to Blair's office.

• • • • •

"You going to tell me what this is about?" Blair asked once they were seated, the feeling building that he was no longer in charge.

Dalton smiled briefly. "It's rather simple," he said. "A few years ago, while conducting covert operations, we happened upon an extremely damaging document. It made a mockery of the relationship some reputable American businessmen had with companies in the State of Israel. What it was telling us was that those with terrorist affiliations had infiltrated many of these organizations. That they were ready to use clever subterfuge, deploying soldiers of fortune far removed from themselves. And your friend, Jeremy Samson, was not only involved, but leading one of these factions."

The pause that followed felt ominous. Blair refused to believe a word of what was said. Jeremy was one of the most down-to-earth men he had ever known. His friend would not have had the motivation to join a covert movement, let alone to lead it.

He sat up straighter. "You're making a mistake," he said. "Plain and simple, you have the wrong person. I appreciate you coming to see me today, but I'm afraid you've wasted your time." He stood and held out his hand.

Dalton ignored the offer to shake but stood himself. "It's no mistake," he said. "Jeremy Samson claims to live an honorable life. But we know better. The man is corrupt and we need your help to bring him down. I guess I haven't made myself clear: your government isn't asking; we are *telling* you. The option of refusal does not exist..."

CHAPTER 2

Blair waited until John Dalton left. When he exhaled it surprised him. He hadn't been aware he'd been holding his breath. The man did something to him. Made him feel uncomfortable. But what could a government agent do to him? he wondered. Hold a gun to his head? Force him to cooperate against his will? He strolled out of his office and into the corridor, and headed toward his showroom.

Spotlights recessed in the ceiling revealed areas divided into sections. One was painted a vibrant blue, another a brilliant red. A third was green and a fourth black. Each section had its own signage and particular decor. Some ran for eight feet, others as much as twenty-four.

Dozens of glass shelves displayed the toys that supported Blair's livelihood. Closest to him, for instance, was a baby doll that weighed exactly the same as a newborn child. He took her in his arms and smoothed out her life-like hair, thin strands that were soft to the touch.

It dawned on him that even this doll represented a potential crisis. Phthalates was the latest buzzword in the toy industry, one of a long list of ingredients that was considered hazardous to a child's health. It had been a key component in plastic toys for the past hundred years or so. A fact conveniently omitted from the various stories in the press blanketing the world. To the reader it would seem as if phthalates had just this minute popped out of the blue.

Blair was a staunch believer in safety. But recently his patience was running thin. His industry had always submitted to the most ardent scrutiny. Today's world, however, sought scapegoats for consumer fodder. Blair wondered if it was more to sell newspapers, more to raise television ratings, than an altruistic sense of duty. Too many families had both parents working. Assuaging their guilty consciences was a priority above all else.

He now stopped to admire a series of construction toys, mostly comprised of magnets. They had sold over thirty million dollars worth of the product worldwide. Until they were confronted by Mattel's recall, soon followed by Mega Brands', and others. Suddenly, anyone's magnet product—including his own—was tainted. The consumer became confused, then angry. If it was manufactured in the Orient, they didn't trust it. Goodbye, potential growth. Goodbye, vast sums of investment capital.

Pausing for a moment, Blair frowned as he checked the other areas of his showroom. Was there one division that was unaffected in the last few years? Everything he sold was proprietary. A quarter was created internally, while the majority was licensed from some of the leading design-houses in the industry. Royalty payments alone reached into the hundreds of thousands of dollars per year.

He examined his line of radio control vehicles. Once again, sales had been running smoothly. Until the "Big Recall." Lead paint soon became foremost on every consumer's mind. Another dip in sales, and more important, in profit. The recall scare had made the Chinese government overreact. After embarrassing them, the toy industry ended up paying a high price. Revised testing procedures became a requirement. Working conditions were improved, and the cost of labor went through the roof.

In recent years, over thirty-eight hundred toy factories had either been shut down, or voluntarily went out of business. The pressure placed on those factories that remained was unsustainable.

Naturally, retailers around the world—caught up in the frenzy of media reports—instituted their own revamped testing procedures. Although more or less identical, few shared these tests with their competitors. And it was the toy manufacturer who was asked to cover this prohibitive bill.

Blair counted the number of strikes that were piled against him, from the phthalates scare, to the magnet and lead recalls, to the increased cost of redundant testing, to the rising cost of labor.

If that weren't enough, most major retailers, especially in North America, refused to accept price increases on existing products, thereby leaving the manufacturer to absorb the often fatal hit to his bottom line.

Mattel and Hasbro were strong enough to stop the slide had they sufficient backbone. But the almighty "order" still ruled these behemoths, and the fear of not meeting annual sales forecasts was all that mattered.

Blair had known the toy industry most of his working life. Seeing his livelihood jeopardized rankled in the worst way. If it were a case of his own ineptitude, at least he could say he had tried but failed. Knowing there was nothing he could do about the current situation only added to his frustration.

• • • • •

He approached a locked cabinet in the near corner of his showroom. He opened it with a key he kept with him at all times. Then he removed a bubble-wrapped package.

Only one thing could save his company from going under. One product, actually. And this was it.

Many boasted about America's brain thrust in Silicon Valley. Others praised the Japanese and the Germans. But quite often it was a high-tech company in Israel that was the creator or partner in the development of whatever technology happened to be du jour. Blair learned long ago, thanks to his friendship with Jeremy Samson, to not take lightly the talent and ingenuity of the people in Jeremy's adopted country.

Because of them, Blair now believed he had a unique opportunity. Many who worked in his business harbored the desire to come up with the next big thing, the one toy that would set the world back on its ear. Much of the industry was a crapshoot, however, with a fickle core of retailers and an even more fickle consumer.

Inventors were constantly coming out of the woodwork. Time and again they would show up at Blair's door with something they'd not only created but went ahead and produced, at an exorbitant cost.

"Why didn't you wait?" he would ask. "Why didn't you build a hand-sample and seek out meaningful feedback?"

Invariably, the answer would be the same: they were so certain of success they thought there was no point in being cautious.

This craving for the "big score" bore true in the toy industry largely because product was varied and ever-changing. Blair checked what he was now holding in his hands and felt a buzz, that indefinable something. Every instinct, every bit of his experience, told him he was looking at the next craze, the next multi-million dollar winner, the one product that consumers would be talking about for years to come.

To become a partner in this venture, he had invested all of the profit his company had earned since its inception. And Hillel Electronics were not easily convinced that they needed him ... not until Jeremy Samson pointed out the diversity of the retail environment around the world, and how going it alone without an expert would be foolhardy at best.

At equal risk to Blair was what he had planned for the initial launch. A multi-million-dollar advertising campaign. And a midnight introduction in September with only the top three retailers participating.

On the negative side, he could not avoid the fact that the video game business was rapidly imploding. Annual sales in the U.S. alone, by some estimates, had dropped by more than half. But Blair understood that, as with toys, anything new and innovative could act as a shot in the arm and revitalize what appeared to be a dying industry.

His product was lightweight and compact. It was only slightly larger than the portable units produced by Sony and Nintendo. Better still, it had a triple fold-out screen that offered a viewing space almost twice the size of either of its predecessors. It used the latest micro DVD technology, in 3D, without needing special glasses. Its colors were brilliant. Its memory capacity was far beyond anything released to date. It surpassed the kilobytes found in Microsoft's home unit and it outperformed it. All in a case that was compact enough to be transportable, yet diverse enough to be used on TV screens, connecting in seconds, wirelessly.

And that wasn't all. What really set their unit apart was the fact that it was also a cell phone and touch-screen PDA. It would come with over a dozen apps built in. Thousands more would be made available through the Internet.

The plan called for it to retail at the incredibly low price of eighty dollars, leaving a very meager profit. But they were using the razor blade/razor philosophy. They hoped the consumer would come back for the "blades," which in this case were their mini DVDs. Many would take virtual reality to the next level. Each would sell for thirty dollars apiece. Each would be so unique, Blair felt certain his potential audience would bite and bite big.

Picking up the handmade sample—but remaining mindful of its fragile state—he turned it on and watched the screen come alive.

There were two mini joy pads, one on each side, so the left-handed or ambidextrous player was accommodated. It had a fairly good stereo speaker system for something of its size. Plus an input jack for headphones.

He pressed *play*. The mini DVD that was supplied with the unit flashed a rainbow of colors. Then the name they had chosen leapt out.

It began as a spec in the top left-hand corner. It continued to build until the entire screen was covered: *CYBER-TECH*.

Blair hit the game-select button. He chose *Warzone*, and was soon transported into a *Star Wars* scenario. War ships of the dark side were preparing to attack the poor citizens of a not-so-far-off planet closely resembling earth. Being the good guy, he scored points for each enemy spaceship he was able to bring down. Once into it, it was impossible not to become addicted. This was what 3D, color, and superior graphics could do. Blair could imagine kids and probably their older brothers and sisters, even their parents, getting hooked.

"*Hoo-boy!*" he shouted out loud as pieces of debris came "flying" toward him. He got to feel silly after a while, blinking his eyes and dodging imaginary obstacles.

CHAPTER 3

When his cell phone rang, Blair glanced at caller I.D. and his mood brightened still further. He shut the game and set it down, quickly answering with a terse, "Who's calling me during the day?"

"Daddy?"

"Who?"

"It's me, Daddy."

"Who?"

"Me. Sandra."

"I don't know any Sandra."

"Yes, you do."

"No, I don't."

Pause. "C'mon, Daddy…"

Blair laughed. "Okay. Just fooling. What's up, kitten?"

"Did you remember this weekend?"

Blair thought his six-year-old daughter's voice was the sweetest instrument in the world. "What weekend?" he said, wanting to lead her on.

"This one."

"This one?"

"Uh-huh." Not only was her voice soft and lilting, but oh-so-grown-up.

"What about this weekend?"

"Did you already forget, Daddy?"

"Forget what?"

"Your promise."

"What promise is that?" he asked.

"You said you would take me to the fair at the shopping mall."

"I couldn't have promised."

"You did, Daddy."

"I did?"

"Uh-huh."

"Well—if you say so."

"I do."

"Okay."

"You will keep your promise?" Her voice rose.

Blair smiled to himself. He visualized his daughter's beautiful blue eyes, the spitting image of her mother's; God help him. And her curly, blond hair. Not nearly as curly as when she had been an infant, of course. But still special enough to draw attention wherever she went.

"Kitten," Blair said to her now, "when it comes to you, I promise to keep my promise."

"Then you're still taking me?"

"Of course, I am. What time did I say I would pick you up?"

"Umm, I don't remember, Daddy. I think you said early."

"Good. Then early it will be. Nine o'clock, sharp. You won't stay up too late the night before, will you? We can't have you chasing the boys around the neighborhood."

His daughter giggled. "All right, Daddy. I won't chase the boys."

"Do you promise?"

"I promise." She disconnected.

Blair sat staring at the phone, unable to wipe the silly expression from his face.

CHAPTER 4

It was after lunch when he stood from his desk. Blair had removed his red floral tie but still wore his navy suit jacket. He liked to think of himself as the last of a breed, dressing in business attire no matter the day of the week or what he might have on his agenda.

Now, he approached the window. The view of 37th Street west of 8th Avenue was not the most glamorous. And he was reminded of what had brought him here.

A number of years ago, many toy companies were headquartered in a set of sister buildings, at 200 5th Avenue and 1107 Broadway. The world came to them and it was a tradition of sorts. When the owners of both buildings announced that the properties would be turned into condominiums, indecision took hold. Shortsightedness led to alternatives that weren't viable. Goodbye toy buildings, goodbye to a central area to meet buyers, to review product, to discuss business. And goodbye to tradition. Instead, Blair and his competitors went their separate ways. No one seemed able to reach a consensus as to what building, in which location, could best accommodate their needs. So here he was, situated in a place chosen mainly for its proximity to the Javits Center, which happened to be the current home for New York Toy Fair.

• • • • •

For much of the afternoon, the visit from John Dalton, the government agent, crept into Blair's subconscious and prevented him from concentrating on his work. He should have been more forceful, he realized, made it clear, in no uncertain terms, that he didn't appreciate the intrusion, that he was not going to cooperate. Instead, as usual, he'd acted meek and indecisive. And the truth was hard to digest.

Born in a poor Montreal neighborhood, Blair had shared a bedroom in a rented flat with his sister. His father was a competent carpenter but unskilled at business. The man had worked day and night to barely eke out a living. His mother worked in retail and also kept long hours.

It was his sister, older by seven years, who nurtured him, who taught him her cardinal rules: to respect anyone of authority, to think before speaking, and that turning "the other cheek" said more about a person than protecting one's honor.

Blair wished he could have grown up tougher, into someone quicker on his feet. Maybe then a man like John Dalton wouldn't intimidate him, wouldn't be able to keep him so off balance.

• • • • •

He left work at five o'clock and took a taxi home, located in the least tony area of the Upper West Side.

His one-bedroom condo was small yet adequate. A den/living room. One and a half bathrooms. The largest room in the apartment was the kitchen, where a quarter of the space was filled by an off-white, rectangular table made of marble.

Blair kicked off his shoes, hung his clothes in the closet, then made himself a sliced turkey sandwich. He sat down in the den and began to dig into some recent editions of *Time*. He noticed a number of references to Homeland Security, the FBI, and the CIA. There was nothing on BIS.

He turned page after page, convinced he would find some reference, somewhere. There was too much space devoted to politics, and too many reports on the economy. His reading got to be depressing after a while. The fact that the turmoil in the Middle East and violence in Africa was getting increased attention did not improve his mood. Neither did the too-frequent reports of multiple murders by lone psychopaths.

Whenever he came across the mention of a government agency, Blair slowed his reading. What was it John Dalton had said? Few people were aware of his organization, which was the way they liked to keep it? He suspected that part was true. Up to a point. Nothing was ever completely hidden from the press. There should be something here, he was convinced. And it made him even more suspicious to not be able to find it.

Finally, bleary-eyed after forty more minutes of searching, he gave up.

John Dalton's agency was part of the U.S. government, he decided. It didn't much matter how clandestine the agency was.

CHAPTER 5

The phone calls started the following morning, and they were relentless. For the rest of that day and into Friday morning, Blair ignored them. Then his secretary ran in just after lunch to say that she couldn't stand it anymore. Blair told her to put John Dalton through the next time he called.

When his phone buzzed some fifteen minutes later, he threw darts at the receiver before jamming it to his ear. "John, what do you want?"

"*Shalom.*"

"Jeremy? *Shalom* to you, too. Sorry, I thought you were someone else."

"Obviously. Who's John?"

"Someone you don't know."

"I can see that. You in some kind of trouble, Blair?"

"No, no. Nothing I can't handle. Where are you, your office?"

"Why not?"

He looked at his watch. "At 7:30 at night in Tel Aviv?"

Jeremy chuckled. "You know me, a workaholic."

"Sure you are," Blair said. "When there's no babe hanging onto your arm. What's up?"

"Speaking of babes, this young lady I know is going to be in New York and I gave her your number. You don't mind, do you?"

Blair shrugged self-consciously. "You know I mind. Why do you even bother to ask?"

"To prevent you from remaining a hermit for the rest of your life."

"Jeremy—"

"No. Don't give me your usual crap. You can't keep sitting at home, pining for your ex."

"Pining?"

"Yeah. It means…"

"I know what it means, Jeremy."

"Look, you have to get a life. It's time."

Blair pictured Jeremy, sport shirt opened halfway down his chest, form-fitted to an athlete's body of well over six feet. Curly red hair. "I've got a life," he said half-heartedly.

"Yeah," Jeremy said. "Some life. Listen to me, buddy. If and when this girl calls, you better see her. I told her you were not only handsome but rich. She sort of likes that in men."

"Uh-huh. I bet she does."

"Take her out. She's hot-looking." He paused. "Promise?"

"Jeremy—"

"Promise?"

"Is that the only reason for this call?"

"Of course, it is. Outside of women, what else is there?"

"Don't have her call me, Jeremy. I will not go out with her."

"Serious?"

"Very serious."

"Okay, *boychick*. But you'll be sorry. Bye."

It was amusing to hear Jeremy use the odd Yiddish word. Blair put the receiver down and leaned back in his chair.

• • • • •

The phone rang not long afterwards and he picked it up without thinking.

"I need your answer," John Dalton said.

Blair gripped the receiver, tempted to disconnect. "You were just here a few days ago."

"And I didn't mean to imply that we would wait forever."

Why was it, Blair wondered, that the man's voice always tweaked a warning in his head?

"Mr. Mulligan?"

"Yes?"

"What's it going to be?"

"You need an answer today?"

"Yes. Right now. What we are asking for is not unreasonable. Help us this one time and you'll never hear from us again."

Blair was tempted to tell him how much he resented his barging into his office, resented the fact that he would accuse his close friend of treason.

"Well?"

He simply wasn't good at this sort of thing. A sigh escaped his lips. "My answer is no," he said. "Please stop asking."

CHAPTER 6

On Saturday, the second Mandy opened the door, Blair felt his blood pressure rise. The fact that more than two years had passed since their divorce hadn't made a bit of difference. She was five-foot-nothing, with long blond hair, dressed in a white, flimsy T-shirt and tie-dye jeans, which had holes at the knees. She looked more like a teenager than a woman of thirty-three. His attraction, however—which would always be there, he supposed—was tainted by her deception.

"Blair," she said. She kissed his cheek, but it seemed an afterthought.

His attempt at a smile failed.

"I'll get Sandra," she said, quickly turning away.

Mandy was working at one of the cosmetic counters at Saks when Blair had come to purchase a gift for his sister. Mandy served; he paid. The following day he went back for her phone number.

A few weeks later, after dating every second or third night, they were driving through Central Park when Mandy instructed him to pull over.

"I know the perfect spot," he heard her say, coaxing him out of the car.

Her "spot" was located behind a bridge embankment, barely hidden from sight. She tugged until he joined her. The ground was hard and cold. She covered them both with her coat.

For months this went on. The more exposed the location, the better. Beneath a park bench. In movie theaters. In airplane washrooms. During their second year together, it was a topless beach in Bali.

Gradually, Mandy's story came out: how she grew up an only child, her father prone to violence, her mother using the bottle as a crutch. In her teenage years, Mandy had been apathetic toward boys. It was not until her early twenties that she had discovered her need for sex on the wild side. It was the only way she could gain release.

When Mandy announced she was pregnant, Blair was distraught. He had been looking for ways to break off their relationship. The sex had been exciting, but he was too much of an introvert to ever be comfortable with it.

Still, he married her, feeling he had no choice. And although Sandra was born not nine but ten and a half months later, his love for his daughter overshadowed the truth and he was happy to live with it.

Too soon they were celebrating Sandra's first birthday, then her second and third, which was when Mandy began to go out with "the girls." A few hours each night became four or five. Occasionally, she wouldn't come home at all. Whenever Blair asked, she had a plausible excuse. She had too much to drink so she stayed over at a friend's house. Or her car broke down. Or she fell asleep.

Blair wanted to believe her. Sandra meant the world to him. For his daughter's sake, he was determined to keep his marriage together. Even though an inner voice teased, of course, reminding him that he was being played for a fool.

Still, he would have gone on ignoring the warning signs, but close and even distant acquaintances began hinting of Mandy's infidelity. When he finally confronted his wife, instead of denying it, she advised him to move out. "It'll be much easier for Sandra if she could live here with me."

Blair was dumbfounded. And hurt. The ensuing court battle was bitter and pointless. By some Machiavellian twist, the judge found no one to be at fault.

His lawyer at the time, Andrew Sciascia, was in his mid-forties, pot-bellied and balding, a man born of privilege on Long Island's Gold Coast. Despite the outcome, the two had become friends. And this was Blair's one salvation from the entire divorce proceeding.

• • • • •

"Daddy!"

The sound of Sandra's voice quickly brought Blair back to the present. Nothing caused his heart to kick-start like seeing his daughter. As he bent down to give her a hug, he was filled with something he'd never been able to describe. Infinite joy, of course. But something more.

Sandra was wearing gray leggings, and a burgundy sweatshirt with her favorite Disney Princess, Ariel, stenciled on the front in color.

"How are you, sweetie?" he asked. He gently tousled her mop of blond hair.

"I'm fine. Is this Saturday, Daddy?"

"It sure is."

"So, are you taking me?"

He kissed her forehead, then held her at arm's length. "Of course, I'm taking you."

"Oh, goodie. I'll get my coat." She pulled away. "Don't you go anywhere," she warned, sounding like an adult.

"I won't," he said. Then he stood and turned to his ex. "Still going out with that proctologist?"

"Frank's not a proctologist," she said angrily. "An ophthalmologist has nothing to do with your bum."

"Well, he's an asshole, isn't he?"

"Blair!"

"What do you see in the guy," he forged ahead, unable to stop. "His wallet?"

"Frank isn't like you, okay? He's considerate. He does things for me."

"Oh yeah? How? By screwing you on the front porch so all the neighbors can watch?"

Her complexion went from normal to scarlet. "I hate it when you talk this way," she said.

Blair was hating himself. But standing this close to her, remembering her betrayal, simply drove all reason from his mind.

• • • • •

"I'm ready, Daddy."

His daughter's big blue eyes were sparkling with anticipation. He took hold of her hand and guided her outside.

He helped Sandra into his car, the one luxury he allowed himself, a white BMW-525i. He attached her belt in her special seat and went around to the driver's side, pretending not to notice as she waved goodbye to her mother.

"All set?" he asked.

The smile she flashed was glorious.

Flushing Meadows in Queens had not been Blair's first choice for a home. But Mandy had insisted and, as usual, he had given in. Why sweat the small stuff, was his way of reasoning. So now Mandy was left with the house she always wanted. And he was the owner of a bachelor pad on the Upper West Side, which he didn't want at all.

For the next ten minutes his daughter regaled him with the events of her week. She was in first grade now and, among other things, was learning how to print her name and draw pictures. Suddenly, as if she had forgotten, she removed a lottery ticket from her coat pocket and handed it to him.

"What's this?" Blair asked, emphasizing his surprise.

She grinned. "A present for you."

"For me?"

She giggled, relishing his delight. "All for you, Daddy."

"How come? It's not my birthday."

She paused. "I know that," she said. "It doesn't have to be your birthday to get a present."

He unfolded the lottery ticket and pretended to study the numbers. He'd been purchasing them on a regular basis ever since moving to New York. "Win 4." "Take 5." "Win 3." He gave his daughter's arm a squeeze. "Thank you so much, darling."

"Mommy helped pay for it," she confessed.

"*Really?*"

She nodded. "Really, Daddy. But it was my idea."

"I know it was, snookums. You are a generous girl."

It was only a few minutes after ten by the time they reached the mall, yet it was difficult to find a parking spot. The temperature was on the cool side, barely in the fifties, but that did not keep the carnival from drawing a large crowd.

Luckily, after the second time around, he found a space and pulled in.

The rides were the sort only a child could enjoy. From a miniature Ferris wheel to bumper cars to a variation of the loop-de-loop. Then they were seated next to each other on something called the Laugh in the Park.

After each ride, Sandra would hold her arms outstretched wide, and say, "Hugs and kisses, Daddy?" And they would hug and kiss.

Soon Blair's nose was starting to run from the cold. How a guy from Montreal could be this sensitive to the least drop in temperature was beyond him.

Lunch was a non-stop affair. It lasted from 11:30 to well past 1:00. There were hot dogs with French fries—only they called them super fries—soda pop and pink cotton candy, a candy apple, and a chocolate bar. He couldn't help wondering where his daughter put it all.

It was in between the first and second, or second and third dessert, he couldn't remember which, when Sandra turned to him, and with wide, innocent eyes said, "Daddy, why do you hate Mommy?"

A freight train rumbled through Blair's brain. "I don't hate her," he said. "Why would you think that?"

She shrugged, tiny shoulders practically swallowing her neck. "I don't know."

"Has Mommy told you that? That I hate her?"

Another shrug. "If you don't hate her, then why can't you live with us?"

He coughed to buy time. "I would love to live with you, darling."

"That's not what Mommy says."

The wind had picked up by this time and the temperature felt like it had dropped another ten degrees. He was trying to come up with something clever to say, something that would not traumatize his six-year-old girl, when she went back to eating her dessert, their conversation seemingly forgotten.

But not by Blair. He didn't think Sandra was making up a story. And he realized he would have to investigate. Sooner rather than later, he would have to get to the bottom of what she had just told him.

CHAPTER 7

When he walked, he walked proud. It wasn't exactly strutting. It was his American walk—blending in, as he was trained.

Yassin was wearing Western-style clothes, jeans and a black sport shirt. He turned west onto 47th Street from 5th Avenue and slowed his pace. He began to stroll along the north side of the street.

He found it ironic to be here, on Diamond Jewelry Way, commonly known as the Diamond District. "*Jew* Way" was more like it. Everywhere he turned he seemed to spot another Hassidic Jew, with his *payot* slithering down his cheeks, and the *tzitzit* or fringes of his *talit* drooping beneath his black topcoat. Old and middle-aged, a few in their twenties, each wearing a *yarmulke* or oversized black hat. Most carrying a briefcase.

Hatred began to roil in his gut. He imagined millions of dollars traded on this street on any given day. Hundreds of thousands of dollars of profit earned by the very people he despised the most.

Look at them, he thought as he slowed his pace. *Look how they take so much for granted.* It galled him the way they went about their daily lives, as if they had everything to live for.

Two were coming toward him now. They were in their mid-sixties, perhaps older. He picked up his pace, waited until they were parallel, then jabbed an elbow into the shoulder of the one closest to him.

An "oomph" escaped the man's lips.

Yassin regretted not turning around. But he savored the moment nevertheless. He kept his head facing front as he proceeded further west.

Shop after shop drew his attention. Most were co-ops, with each counter serviced by an individual owner. He acknowledged that they were not all manned by Jews. But it made little difference. They were still Americans, were they not? Heathens, the lot of them. Enemies of Allah.

His hatred knew no bounds. Americans were the antithesis of his god: they were the devil incarnate.

Display windows now drew his attention. Jewelry set with diamonds; bracelets to earrings to necklaces. Extravagant in most cases; showy and ridiculous.

Yassin continued to walk. Soon, he noticed a young man approaching. He was talking on a cell phone. Another Hassidic Jew.

Instead of an elbow this time he aimed his shoulder. It caught the unsuspecting passerby full force in the chest. His cell phone went flying. "Hey," came the cry, the man in obvious pain.

This was music to Yassin's ears. He ignored his own pain that had suddenly flared: his old shrapnel injury. Instead, he fingered the knife in his pants pocket. One jab. An upward thrust into the area of the heart. It would be easy and so satisfying.

Self-discipline held him back. An agenda had been painstakingly devised. Release was just around the corner. He mustn't do anything foolish. These play-acts of his, on this street, were foolhardy enough. It was as far as he could allow himself to go.

He frowned. Restraint had been the story of his life. Just once he would like to act, to relieve his anger and frustration.

• • • • •

Nearing his destination, it dawned on Yassin how many women there were, either on the street, shopping, or behind the counters. He noticed once again that their heads and faces were sacrilegiously exposed.

He checked the address and stepped inside.

Counter after counter of glittering jewelry stood resplendent under shimmering lights. He heard a mélange of voices, some raised adamantly in the throes of a sales pitch, others talking quietly on cell phones. He detected English, Russian, Yiddish, and Hebrew.

"Can I help you?" someone asked.

"Let me show you something nice," offered another.

Ignoring the various sales pitches that followed him through the shop, Yassin finally reached the back, where he paused. It was paradoxical to have a contact located here. But they had become adept at living among their enemy. He knocked on a door that was partially hidden from sight.

Nothing happened.

He knocked again.

The man who appeared, Yasser Shafi, was in his late forties but looked older. Full mustache and beard: both speckled with gray. His hair was mussed as if disturbed from sleep. He did not offer a greeting. Instead, he turned and beckoned his visitor inside. Once the door closed, he fumbled his way through an embrace.

Yassin did not like what he was seeing. His host had a history of substance abuse. This was his second chance. But his eyes betrayed him. That, and the lethargic way he moved. This was not good, not good at all.

"It has been too long," Shafi said in Arabic.

Yassin ignored the comment.

The room opened up into a small, one-room apartment: kitchen in one corner, sofa and television in another. Photographs of imams or quotes from the Koran overpowered the walls. Each was five by seven or larger. All were held in place by thumbtacks.

Both men took seats on the sofa.

"Did you complete your task?" Yassin asked without wasting time.

Shafi nodded.

"How many people altogether?"

"Exactly one dozen. All naturalized Americans."

"Good. Good. And how about the split?"

"Eight men, four women."

"And what did you say to them?"

"What you told me to say. That they will be occupied for a number of months. Six at the most."

"And they accepted this?"

"Absolutely."

"You are sure?"

"Yes."

Yassin hesitated. The man couldn't be trusted. He had lied to him about breaking his drug habit. "Do you have the list for me?" he asked.

With some difficulty, Shafi lifted himself up. "I'll get your list in a moment, if you don't mind. I have to use the bathroom."

Yassin sat and waited. When his host returned his eyes were brighter, his nostrils enflamed. Sluggishly, he headed for the kitchen. He shuffled a few papers aside on the countertop. Then he removed a sheet and casually held it up. "This is the list of people I engaged," he said. "It includes their addresses and phone numbers."

Without hesitation, Yassin removed the knife from his pants pocket. He gripped the blade and flung it with all his strength. He intentionally missed his host's head by a mere inch or two. Embedded in the wall, the knife vibrated, making a pinging sound.

Stunned, Shafi's eyes widened in horror.

Yassin came to his feet, strolled to the wall, and pulled the knife free. "Next time I won't miss," he said. He snatched the sheet of paper from his host's hands.

Shafi seemed unable to speak.

"You told me you were done with your drug habit," Yassin lashed out.

"I *am* done with it."

"Liar!"

"No. It is the truth. I swear."

The man's weakness was troubling. Second chances were anathema to Yassin's nature; third chances were out of the question. But something held him back. For all intents and purposes, Shafi had performed his duty. He was lying about his drug use. But it didn't matter. Yassin would have him picked up in the morning and held in seclusion until their plans in America were concluded.

He left the man standing there, turned and walked out without saying goodbye.

CHAPTER 8

The first thing Blair did when he arrived at his office on Monday morning was call his ex-wife at Saks, where she still managed one of the cosmetic counters. When she came on the line, he asked if he could invite her and Sandra to dinner.

"Why?" she said, not in a nice way.

"Why not?"

"You mean, you have no reason? You just want to take us to dinner?"

"That's right."

"Blair?"

He held the receiver away from his ear. He didn't want to explain over the phone. Sandra's words still weighed heavily on his mind. He figured a meeting face to face would be the best way to clear the air.

"What is it that you really want, Blair?"

"I told you."

"Yeah. An innocent dinner, just the three of us. Well, why don't I bring Frank along? We can make it a foursome."

"I don't need the proctologist's company," he said, growing angry.

"He's not a proctologist!"

"Oh, yeah, I forgot. Anyway, can you make it or not?"

"I'll have to call you back. Give me a few days."

He wanted to tell her this decision hardly required one day, let alone a few, but she'd already disconnected.

• • • • •

That afternoon, Blair began reconfiguring some financial numbers on a scrap piece of paper. His entire future depended upon the success of *Cyber-tech*. Being reminded of that fact drove his nervous tension to the surface.

His cell phone went off. Caller I.D. revealed a familiar Montreal number.

"Hello, Mother dear," he said.

"Happy birthday, darling."

Blair paused. It hurt, hearing his mother slipping backwards again. "It's not my birthday, Mom."

"Yes, it is."

"No, it isn't."

"It *is*. I should know when you were born."

There was no point in arguing. His mother, only in her mid-sixties, had been suffering from Alzheimer's disease for the past three years. It was dreadful to hear her this way. There were still some lucid moments. But there were far too many others, like now, when she seemed completely lost.

He did everything he could to help out financially. His older sister was in the middle of a third divorce and could barely support herself. This left the onus on him to get his mother into a private-care facility.

People who didn't know better raved about the Canadian medical system, not understanding that socialized medicine came with a cost.

Taxes in Canada were exorbitant. The caliber of care was worsening annually. Trying to see a specialist often took months. And the system did not pay for private care. Thus it was Blair who had to cover this extra expense for his mother. And it wasn't cheap. Another good reason, he reflected now, why his business couldn't fail.

"You know something, Mom? You are right. You *should* know when I was born."

"Are you coming to visit me today?"

His mother knew he lived and worked in New York. She occasionally also knew the date he was born. From past experience, he understood that he should tread lightly. "I can't today, Mother dear. But I will soon."

"Why not today?" Her mood seemed to shift.

"For one thing, I'm working."

"Working? I thought you were retired."

He couldn't help but smile. "Not retired yet," he said.

"So when will I see you?"

"Soon, I promise." The last time he had visited her, less than a month ago, she hadn't recognized him.

"Today?"

"I can't today, Mother."

"Why, not? Why is it that I never see you?"

"You do see me."

"Not today."

"I'm busy."

"I want you to come."

"I can't."

"Your father came today. We spent a lovely time together."

His father had died from cancer five years ago. "Mother—"

"Please? I'd really like to see you."

This was getting more and more difficult. "I'll come see you soon. Okay?"

Silence.

"Mother?"

More silence.

Alarmed, Blair began shouting into the receiver: "Mom, would you talk to me, please?"

Finally, a stranger's voice came on the line. "I'm sorry, Mr. Mulligan. Your mother has fallen asleep."

"Is she okay?"

"Oh, she's fine. This is not uncommon. Happens on a regular basis lately."

"Could you do me a favor?"

"Of course, sir."

"Could you have someone send me an update on my mother's condition?"

"I'll see to it right away."

• • • • •

Blair had hardly shut his phone when a sense of urgency spurred him into action. His mother's situation made it clear that his life, *anyone's* life, could change in a heartbeat. He flipped open his cell once more and dialed the number.

"How are you?" he said when Mandy came on the line.

The sigh was audible. "You again. What now, Blair?"

"Have you made up your mind yet?"

"I said a few days, not a few hours."

"Yeah, I know. But I realized I couldn't wait."

No sigh this time. Nothing. "We can make it Wednesday night. Pick us up at six. And Blair—"

"What?"

"Don't be late. Okay?"

"Who? Me?"

"Yeah. I mean it, Blair. I'm not going to stick around like the last time."

"The last time I had dinner with you and Sandra? What was I, fifteen minutes late?"

"Try an hour and a half, darling."

"Well, something came up at the office."

"That's exactly what I mean. Don't let anything come up. Because we won't wait for you this time. *Capisce?*"

"Hey, that's my word."

"Too bad. I just borrowed it. Goodbye."

• • • • •

Leaving his office, his mind preoccupied not only by the conversation with his mother but also by the one with his ex-wife, Blair heard a honking horn. Believing it was for someone else, he continued walking. It wasn't until his name was called that he turned. But he couldn't make out who it was. Just a man in a Lincoln MKZ.

A hand beckoned him forward.

Warily, he approached.

"Get in," John Dalton instructed. "I'll give you a lift home."

Perhaps if his mind had not been engrossed he would have turned away. But he got in automatically, then silently cursed himself for having done so.

"Nice to see you again," the government agent said.

He didn't know which was worse, accepting a ride or facing the knowledge that the man had been waiting for him. "What are you doing, keeping tabs on me?" he asked.

The agent smiled. "You're valuable to us, Blair."

"I'm sure that I am."

Dalton was wearing an off-white shirt, open at the collar, and gray pants. But even his casual dress could not detract from his hardness, his too-cool demeanor.

"I appreciate the ride," Blair said, "but my answer is not going to change. I will not do anything to harm my relationship with one of my best friends."

"Even though this so-called friend is helping a terrorist group? We are not asking you to risk anything. It will be a matter of following some very simple instructions. You do what we ask while you are in Israel and that will be that. As a sign of our appreciation, we will deposit ten thousand dollars into your bank account. Treat it as found money. After all, I believe your savings are nearly non-existent at the moment."

Blair turned in his seat. Dalton was keeping his eyes on the road. But Blair sensed the smugness there, how pleased the agent was to have this knowledge about his personal financial situation. "You can leave me off here," he told him.

"Here? On 10th Avenue?"

"Yeah. Right here. Stop the car. I'd rather walk."

"Mr. Mulligan, be reasonable." Dalton kept driving.

Blair leaned his head back on the seat.

• • • • •

When the agent's hand nudged his shoulder, he jumped.

"We've arrived," Dalton said.

He peered out the window, recognized his building, and realized he must have dozed off.

Blair was about to open his door when he noticed the gun in the man's lap.

Dalton followed his glance, acting as if he'd forgotten. "Oh," he said, handing the gun to him, barrel first. "Would you mind putting this in the glove compartment for me?"

The heat rose from Blair's stomach to his neck. The threat may have been subtle, but it was a threat nonetheless. He opened the car door. "Put the damn gun in the glove compartment yourself, John," he said. And he walked away, leaving the door open.

"You have until tomorrow morning," came the warning behind him.

CHAPTER 9

It took less than fifteen hours for John Dalton to make numerous attempts to reach Blair—via e-mail, text messaging, and calls to his business and mobile numbers.

Blair sat in his office, shaking his head. Harassment was one thing, but this was ridiculous.

He recalled trying to find some mention of Dalton's agency, BIS, in the back issues of *Time*, without success. And he wondered now if the letters truly stood for what he had been told—Bureau of International Security—or if they, in fact, represented something entirely different.

Some years ago, stories of secret plots against America were the norm. President Bush had been accused of using these ominous threats to help his reelection campaign. By the time Barack Obama took office, most people were fed up and disillusioned.

So why should he believe John Dalton? Was America's well-being truly at risk? Who was BIS? And what was Dalton's role in all of this?

He fingered the man's business card, slowly shaking his head.

What if he's expecting this? Blair worried.

For what purpose?

I don't know.

You don't have to talk to him. Just see if he really works there. See if he comes to the phone.

I don't know...

Only way to find out.

Yeah, I guess so.

Dialing the number made his skin crawl.

"B-I-S." Female voice, businesslike.

Blair hesitated.

"Hello?"

"Yes, is John Dalton there, please?"

"One moment, sir."

He dangled the receiver in his hand.

When Dalton's voice came on the line, he disconnected.

Satisfied? he asked himself.

CHAPTER 10

On Wednesday night, Mandy guided Blair toward the den in her home by beckoning with her index finger as if she were a temptress. It was the first time since their divorce that she had allowed him past the entranceway. Blair found the house to be the same, yet different. Photographs on the walls had been replaced by abstract paintings. The dining room was stained in a light shade of taupe. The knickknacks were new. As was the jumbo papier-mâché Dora the Explorer positioned near the kitchen window.

Mandy's pink blouse was practically unbuttoned to her waist. She proffered a glass of champagne, almost forcing it into his hand.

"Where's Sandra?" he asked. He took a seat on the off-white leather couch.

"Why do you want to know?" came the coy reply as she sat down beside him.

"Mandy?"

"She's at a friend's house, sleeping over."

Blair put the untouched glass of champagne down on the coffee table and went to stand.

Playfully, Mandy pushed him back. She edged closer, slipped a hand to his thigh.

"We were supposed to have dinner," he said.

"So?"

"The *three* of us."

Mandy struck a pose, exaggerating her chest. "You mean, you'd prefer dinner over me?"

Blair laughed despite himself. "Who're you imitating? Lady Gaga?" He forcefully removed her hand from his leg and stood.

"Where you going?"

He was halfway to the door when he stopped and turned. "Sandra told me what you said. That I chose not to live with the two of you. That I hate you. A six-year-old kid, for God's sake. What's the matter with you, Mandy? Why would you tell her such a thing? You are the one who cheated on me. You are the one who asked me to move out. How dare you insinuate that it was my fault?"

Mandy came off the couch and approached him. "Is that what's got you so hot and bothered?" She went to put her arms around him.

He backed away. "I want you to stop feeding this crap to Sandra, Mandy. I mean it."

"Okay. I'll stop."

He waited.

"I will. I'll stop." She paused. "If you give us another chance."

He looked up in surprise. "Huh?"

"Let's try again. It doesn't have to be anything serious. Just a few dates to start with."

"A few dates?"

"That's right."

"I don't think so."

"Why not?"

"It wouldn't work."

"Yes, it would. You don't have anyone else in your life, do you?"

"What happened to your doctor friend? You dump him?"

"Not exactly."

The picture became clearer. "He dumped you, then? I guess you're never going to learn." With that, Blair turned for the door and opened it.

"What's that supposed to mean?" Mandy quickly asked.

"You figure it out," he said, stepping outside.

CHAPTER 11

The scene at Billie's on Saturday night was quite different from what Blair was used to. Gone were most of the married men and women, replaced instead by a number of couples, and the odd single out for a good time.

Dressed in his favorite charcoal brown suit and the mandatory accessory—his tie—this one a flowery design in beige from Italy, he took a seat at the bar.

Blair considered Billie's the most comfortable watering hole in town. Recessed spots in the ceiling, angled away from the floor, gave off a non-intrusive glow. The seats were more like captain's chairs. Each was upholstered, with swivel-ability and a contour that was appealing not only to the eye but to the oddest, or largest-shaped, butt. The music was eclectic, with an upbeat slant, varying from jazz to rock to pop, depending on the time of night. It seldom interfered with one's conversation and often worked as a pleasant backdrop.

Hearing his name now, Blair turned to the voice behind the bar. "What's up, Jimmy?"

"Same old, same old. The usual?"

Blair nodded.

"Thirsty?"

This was code for a double, so he nodded again. His drink, Johnnie Walker Black, was served in a highball glass filled with ice, just the way he liked. He thanked the bartender and took an easy sip. He looked at the time: not quite 7:15.

An attractive blonde was sitting by herself a few stools over. Next to her was a middle-aged couple in the heat of an argument.

It was unusual for Blair to come here on a weekend alone. But he was desperate to unwind. The last few days of the workweek had not been kind. It had begun with a phone call from John Broley, his distributor in Great Britain, a prematurely gray-haired man with a hard exterior but a good heart. When Broley advised that *Cyber-tech* had a serious competitor, Blair was flummoxed. *Cyber-tech* was a proprietary product. Jeremy said so and he believed him.

"Yes. I've been shown something rather similar," Broley continued. "Not as nicely packaged, mind you. Graphics not up to your standards, perhaps. But pretty damn close."

"Are you sure, John?"

"Absolutely positive."

Blair's head began to swim. He envisioned Broley's commitment of a hundred thousand pieces being reduced or canceled.

"Hello?"

"I'm here, John."

"Look, I didn't say I wouldn't remain loyal. But this other guy's price is lower than yours. You might want to look into it."

"Of course."

"Find out what's going on and get back to me. Will you do that?"

"I will."

He got off the phone and brushed his hand through his hair, tempted to pull out the strands one by one. Too often Blair stayed awake at night remembering his near-impoverished upbringing, how he used to pray for a way out, a way to earn a hundred dollars a week, naively believing that this would enable him to live comfortably. After having achieved success, he looked back upon his early aspirations with amusement. The fear remained that it could all be taken away, in a heartbeat, and he would be forced to start over again, from scratch.

He began repeating his personal adage: *If it were easy, everyone would do it.* But he hadn't survived this long by throwing in the towel. And he wasn't about to do so now.

• • • • •

Then, on Friday, his daughter called, practically in tears. When he asked what was wrong, she seemed reluctant to tell him.

"You can trust me," he reminded her.

"I know that," she said.

"You can tell me anything."

"I know, Daddy. You always say that."

"Well, then?"

She hesitated. "Mommy made me promise to keep this a secret. She'll be taking me out of school and moving us far, far away. I will never see you again." She started to cry.

Blair shook his head in frustration. A few days ago Mandy was talking about the two of them getting back together, trying to make a go of it again. *Was this revenge*, he wondered. *Because he had said no?*

"Daddy, can't you stop her? I don't want to leave you."

"I'll try very hard," he said.

"But what if she won't listen?"

"Then I'll come visit you, as often as possible."

"Will you?"

"I will."

"Even if we are a, uh, *bazillion* miles away?"

"Even then."

"Okay." Brightening. "I love you, Daddy."

"I love you, too, sweetheart."

CHAPTER 12

Blair looked down at his empty glass. He had tried to reach his ex-wife both at home and at work, all in vain. He was more successful connecting with Jeremy Samson in Israel, who had assured him that whoever was trying to knock them off would be stopped.

Meanwhile, for tonight at least, he wanted to forget about his problems. Mandy seemed to be purposely ignoring him. As for Jeremy, he had no choice but to trust him.

The bartender approached with his refill. Blair was just taking a sip when he felt a tap on his shoulder. The blonde was standing next to him, asking why he was ignoring her.

"I beg your pardon?" he said.

"I've been sitting here for over ten minutes."

Confused, Blair waited for the punch line.

"Well?"

"Well, what?"

"Aren't you going to apologize?"

He saluted her with his drink. "I'm sorry," he said.

"That's better." She thrust out her hand. "I'm Lisa. It's nice to finally meet you, Richard."

"And it's nice to meet you, too." He figured he could be Richard, if that's what she wanted.

"I loved your last e-mail," she said.

"As I did yours."

A suspicious look crossed her brow, but it didn't last. "That's what first attracted me to you," she admitted.

"What? The way I signed off?"

"No, silly. The romantic in you."

"Oh, that."

"The way you write. Your poetry."

"Jack and Jill went up the hill," he quoted.

She laughed.

"And speaking of which," Blair said, "you're not such a bad writer yourself."

"I'm not?" She seemed genuinely pleased with the compliment.

"Not at all. You have a certain style, an openness. How do the French say—a *joie de vivre*?"

"I do?"

Her mouth didn't exactly fall open with each word spoken, but it came close. And Blair now realized how much she resembled his ex-wife. There was the blond hair, of course. The shape of her dainty nose. Her full lips. Even her style of clothes. Red dress falling a few inches above the knee. Black belt pinching her waist. If there was a difference, it was in her eyes, the left being slightly crossed.

"Do you live around here?" he made the mistake of asking.

This time her brow remained creased. "You're not Richard, are you?"

He smiled. "Never was; never will be."

She backed away.

"But, I could be him," Blair quickly added. "If you want me to be."

She drank from her glass, some sort of pinkish-orange concoction that was likely a Fuzzy Navel. "I promised to meet Richard here," she said. "We've been corresponding for over a month. I kept refusing his request for a face-to-face. Until now."

"Don't sweat it. He'll show up. You know how men can be."

"No, I don't know." She looked at her watch. "Over twenty minutes late. And I thought he was different, somehow."

"I'm sure that he is. You just have to be patient."

"For how long?"

"How about an hour? If he doesn't show by then, you go off on your merry way and forget about him."

"Just like that?"

"Just like that."

She muttered something and went back to her drink.

Blair invited her to have a seat.

She hesitated, but not for long.

Jimmy the bartender performed to perfection, with refills flowing endlessly. Blair expected Lisa to object eventually. He began to notice other aspects of Mandy in her. From the way she drank, using all of her fingers to grip the glass. To the color of her nail polish, a pastel shade close to pink.

"Cheers," he said.

They clinked.

"To Richard."

"To Richard." She sort of laughed. "You know, you're exactly the way he described himself."

"I am?"

"Yes. Five foot eleven. A hundred and seventy pounds."

"That *is* close. What else?"

"Blue eyes, actually."

"And?"

"That's about all."

"Handsome?" he asked.

She smiled. "What's your name, by the way?"

"BM are my initials. You have to guess the rest."

"Bruce Matterhorn, like the mountain?"

"Nope."

"Billy Monte Carlo, like the country?"

"Uh-uh."

"I give up."

"Blair Mulligan, in person." He tipped an imaginary hat.

"Blair." She paused. "Is it really Blair?"

"I swear on my firstborn."

"You … you're married?"

He shrugged. "Was."

"For how long?"

"Too long. Can we change the subject?"

"What do you do?" she asked without skipping a beat.

"I play with toys."

"No, seriously, Blair."

"I'm serious. Ask James." He indicated the bartender standing close by.

"It's true enough, I'm afraid," Jimmy said.

"And what do you do?" Blair asked.

"Masseuse."

"Oh yeah? In a massage parlor?"

"Silly." She grinned. "I work for one of New York's top physiotherapists. Henry Fontaine. You ever hear of him?"

For the first time he noticed the definition in her arms and shoulders. "No," he said, "can't say that I have. Is he famous?"

"Very. His clients include members of the Mets, Yanks, and Rangers."

"No kidding?"

"Are you impressed?"

"Very." God, the drink was getting to him.

"Well— " they both said at once.

"Over an hour," Lisa said.

"Uh-oh. Time to go."

"Not necessarily," she said.

Blair brushed an imaginary hair away from her forehead. Then he touched her glass again. "Here's to Richard," he said for the second or third time.

"Uh-uh," she objected.

"Uh-uh?" he questioned.

"Here's to us."

CHAPTER 13

Brandt was Lisa's family name and she was an only child. She came from a working class family, born and bred in the Bronx. She was thirty, she said, but he found her demeanor to be that of someone older. Best of all, there was a genteelness about her, something soft and refined.

He told her about the toy industry, how he had started out with a distributor in Montreal, after first trying his hand at computer sales. "I found I had a knack for toys," he said with a self-effacing gesture. "Stayed with the distributor for five years before this opportunity presented itself here in New York. And the rest, as they say, is history."

"Are you good at what you do, Blair?"

"I made it to the Mean Apple, didn't I?"

Lisa concentrated on her drink.

It dawned on Blair that his mind was growing fuzzy. He took her hand in his.

"I like you," she said, before he could speak.

"I like you, too," he echoed her words.

She covered his hand with her own. "Can we go somewhere quieter?"

She was so bubbly. And nice. He couldn't remember being with a woman this nice. He wanted to give her a hug. "My place?" he suggested as he stood.

Seeing him wobble, Lisa put her arm around him.

How much did I actually drink? he wondered, no longer able to feel his feet.

• • • • •

He knew Lisa paid for the cab. But how they ended up inside his condo was a mystery to him. His building was one of the few in Manhattan without a doorman, so there was no one to lend assistance. Conversation was moot at this point. Leading him by the hand, it was nice to see her taking charge. Through the hallway, past the den and kitchen, into the master bedroom.

Lisa was not only in control, she seemed determined. His clothes came off, but not his underwear. He would have stopped had she tried to go that far.

Not that she tried.

Blair flopped down on the bed, belly first. Lisa said something about helping him feel better. It was all innocent enough, practically childlike. Until an iron-fisted set of knuckles began to knead the flesh on his shoulders.

"Ow!" he called out, quickly sobering.

"Your muscles are tight."

"They are?"

"Yes. I've never seen anything like it."

"You haven't?"

"Not really."

"Ow!"

"Don't be a baby."

The pain was bringing tears to his eyes.

"This will do you some good," she promised.

Blair wondered how an average-built woman could be this strong.

She might be a psychotic killer, he told himself. And she was in his apartment. And he was lying here, more or less vulnerable. "Lisa—" he tried to distract her.

He could swear she was humming to herself.

"Lisa?" he repeated.

"Yes, Blair?"

"Could you, uh, stop for a while? Just for a second or so? Let me catch my breath?"

"I will. Almost done..."

He groaned out loud; it was unpreventable.

"Feeling better?" she asked when she finally stopped.

"Oh, yeah," he muttered, the relief profound. "Much better."

"Perfect."

"And sober."

"Exactly my intention. Now, close your eyes."

He opened his eyes wide. If she were psychotic, this would be the perfect time to pull out a knife or gun.

"Blair?"

"Huh?"

"You're not listening to me."

He closed his eyes, praying for the best.

There was a rustle of clothing. Then the warmest body imaginable was lying next to his. Not quite naked, unfortunately. He could feel her bra and panties.

Blair went to kiss her.

She avoided his lips. "Sleep," she whispered.

He ignored her request and made a grab for her breast.

She pushed his hand away, gently.

Something stirred between his legs and it wasn't the blanket.

"Goodnight, Blair."

"But— "

"But, what?"

He sighed, feeling sorry for himself. "Nothing. Goodnight, Lisa."

In the morning, she was gone.

CHAPTER 14

Blair stayed in bed longer than usual on Sunday. His head was reminding him of how much he'd had to drink the night before. Then he felt the ache in his muscles. "Lisa?" he said aloud.

Did she truly exist? he wondered.

He tried sitting up, felt a wave of nausea, and immediately laid back down.

She was real; he knew she was. Just the thought of the massage she had administered. The fact that she had lain next to him. Her smile and slightly crossed eye.

Was it the left one or right?

He couldn't recall.

Did it matter? It was the first time since his divorce that he had felt something inside his gut. Call it chemistry. Call it what you will.

Call it too much booze, a voice in his head advised.

"No!"

The word popped out of him like a shot. True enough, he had had too much to drink. But long before that. When they had first met and she was calling him Richard, there was a connection there.

He would swear to it.

Suddenly, the urge to urinate overpowered his fear of being sick. He stumbled his way out of bed and into the bathroom. Then, holding on to the walls, he went in search of a note from Lisa, something that would indicate that she was indeed real.

From the hallway to the den to the kitchen.

There was no business card. No note. Nothing.

Disappointed, he returned to bed, crawled under the covers, and went to sleep.

• • • • •

It was past noon when his cell phone woke him. "About time," he said unkindly, struggling to sit up.

"And Merry Christmas to you, too," his ex-wife countered.

"Where have you been?"

"You going to lower your voice, or am I going to hang up?"

"Sorry," he said, not aware he had raised it. "Why'd it take you so long to get back to me?"

"I've been busy making plans."

"What sort of plans?"

"Wouldn't you like to know."

"You're traumatizing our daughter, Mandy."

"Traumatizing our daughter? What're you talking about?"

"What've you been telling her?"

"Who—Sandra?"

"No. Oprah Winfrey! Of course Sandra."

"Has she told you anything?"

"She hasn't said anything. But she's been acting strangely. I figured you must have something to do with it."

"Frank's been offered a job in California and asked us to move with him. I thought it would be a good change."

Change? Blair questioned in his mind. "What does that mean?" he asked. "A change from what?"

There was no hesitation. "From everything. From you."

"Me?" Blair practically shouted.

"Yes, you. And you're raising your voice again."

His head began to hurt. One minute his ex was trying to seduce him. The next she was following her boyfriend to the other side of the country. Where was the logic in that? "I thought you told me that you and Frank broke up?" he said.

"We did break up."

"And?"

"And now we're thinking of getting back together."

How apropos, Blair thought. His ex was more fickle than he had imagined. "Taking Sandra out of school and moving to California is not the best thing for her," he said. "Besides, the court granted me visiting rights. I won't let you do it."

"Oh, yeah? Let's see you try to stop me."

"Hey, I'm trying to be reasonable here. *Capisce?*"

"Sure you are. You can stop playing cutesy, buster. I will do what is best for me and *my* daughter. Whether you like it or not!"

Cutesy? he thought to himself, just as he heard the phone click.

CHAPTER 15

On Monday, being first to arrive at his office, Blair pressed the code to deactivate the alarm and immediately sensed something was wrong. He hit the light switch and froze.

In the forefront sat an average-sized desk with a partition rising four feet from the front edge to give the would-be receptionist some privacy. But it was superfluous. Ever since the downturn in the economy, there had been no receptionist. In her place sat a black telephone, along with a list of employee extension numbers.

The telephone cord had been ripped from the wall.

The Canon color copier standing nearby had all its trays pulled open. The various-sized sheets of paper they had once contained were strewn upon the floor. The file cabinet next to it had been tipped onto its side.

Blair paused.

The building had no security guard on weekends. One needed a key to get in. Upon his arrival this morning, he had noticed nothing out of the ordinary. No broken glass. No door under repair. Whoever had done this must have had a key. Not only for the door downstairs, but for the one up here as well. And the person would have had to have known the alarm code.

Blair made a mental note to contact the building supervisor. He'd be curious to know if any other companies had been vandalized. Although, he already suspected what the answer would be.

He stepped away from the reception area.

His secretary's desk was a relic. It weighed no less than seventy-five pounds. Often, they had joked that it would take a bulldozer to displace it. The desk had been slammed against the wall. Chunks of plaster lay scattered.

Blair made his way around the mess and into his own office. Nothing was left standing. Chair, file cabinet, computer: all toppled onto the floor. He stood, shaking his head. What got to him wasn't the damage so much as the violation of his personal space.

He left his office and headed down the hall. He entered the twenty-by-thirty boardroom. This was a place that not only was witness to important business deals being ratified, but also functioned as Blair's sanctuary. It was a room to which he came whenever he needed to be alone.

Lacking a television and phone, there were few distractions. Rectangular wood table. Ordinary, straight-backed chairs, two to a side, facing each other.

Blair took a seat at the table and purposely avoided the bookcase.

His secret passion was his collection of novels, some in limited edition, all in pristine shape. He had read most of them, a few more than once. He found them remarkable for their relevance even in today's irreverent world. From Cervantes's *Don Quijote* to Voltaire's *Candide*. Herman Melville's *Moby Dick* to James Joyce's *Ulysses*. Modern writers like Philip Roth and John Updike. Contemporary authors such as John Sandford, Joseph Wambaugh, and Carl Hiaasen.

After having graduated high school, Blair had been forced to forgo college and get a job to help support his parents. A few years later, he began taking night courses toward a Bachelor of Arts degree. His creative writing teacher, Linda Farquhar, whom he would never forget, had turned him on to the classics, and he was soon hooked.

Now, through the corner of his eye, he was able to catch sight of the torn jackets. He remained seated for an indeterminate amount of time. Minutes? An hour?

Finally, he stood and approached the bookcase.

Ernest Hemingway, he read along one partially dismembered spine. John Fitzgerald. His fingers reached out, handling the splintered pages delicately. And he gently touched each one as if he could will them back together and make them whole.

CHAPTER 16

The meeting place, a small deli off Broadway, was not of his choosing. And it troubled him that he was here at all. But he required no further proof of the extent to which John Dalton would go.

Both men were dressed in business attire: the agent's suit a severe shade of brown; Blair's navy blue.

The restaurant was half empty. And Blair could understand why. The dark tiled floor was badly in need of a scrub. The general atmosphere suggested sanitary codes were not exactly being obeyed.

Dalton had that same cold look in his eye, Blair noticed. The one that said, *Don't mess with me.*

Blair waited as the man selected a chicken salad sandwich and Coke. He didn't order anything for himself. Not that he wasn't hungry. He simply wasn't comfortable around Dalton; didn't like him, did not want to share a meal with him.

"So, how was your Monday morning?" the agent asked. "Anything exciting happen?"

Blair didn't want his look to kill, he wished he could just do it with his hands. "My Monday was fine," he said, playing along. "But boring," he quickly added. "How was yours?"

"Oh, the usual." A half-grin.

So much for an apology, Blair figured. "The usual, huh?" he said. "I'll bet."

"What does that mean?"

"Exactly what it implies, John. Don't you have something to tell me?"

"My, you're an edgy cuss, aren't you?"

Once more he observed the agent's slight accent, his choice of words.

"But I'm glad to see you've come to your senses," Dalton continued. "This trip won't take up much of your time."

"You keep saying that."

"It happens to be the truth."

Dalton's Coke and sandwich arrived, the fries piled high.

While he ate, the agent took an airline ticket from his briefcase. "First class transportation on El Al," he said. "Paid in full by Uncle Sam."

"Very generous of you."

"It *is*. We could have sent you coach."

"Oh, yeah? And I could have refused to go. What are the details, John?"

"Man, you always in this much of a hurry?"

Only when I'm talking to you, he didn't say.

Dalton finally started to explain: "Hillel Electronics use SDF as their prime manufacturing source for the mini DVDs that will work with *Cyber-tech*. However..."

"Huh?" Blair interrupted, surprised. "How do you know about *Cyber-tech*?"

"What do you mean, how do I know?"

"C'mon, John. Our gaming system has been kept under wraps. No one outside of a few select people are even aware of its existence. So how did you find out?"

"Oh … we have ways."

Blair detested the man's smugness.

The agent paused, but not for long. "We have known for some time that SDF is poisoned from within. Most of the profit they earn is diverted to an old Palestinian ally who's turned renegade. This is a man not only bent on the destruction of the Jewish State, but of the United States as well. He will stop at nothing. The recent bombing in Paris? That was him. The machine-gunning in the restaurant in London? The gunboat attack in Amsterdam? This person has much in the way of resources and nothing in the way of fear."

Dalton took a bite of his sandwich, chewed and swallowed, and wiped his lips with a napkin. "While we have known about SDF," he continued, "we have not been able to act against them. This is why we need you to convince your friend, Jeremy, that it would be in everyone's interest if he talked Hillel into switching production of the mini DVDs from SDF to a company called On Time Electronics. Losing an order this size will hurt SDF. If we stop their inflow of cash, we will have a far better chance of ending their operation."

Again, Blair had a problem accepting the agent's argument. "What if Jeremy is not convinced?" he asked.

Dalton gave a small shake of his head. "If he gives you a hard time, tell him your bank has done a thorough search and has come up with some questionable dealings. No matter what, you will not mention the truth to Jeremy. While he is aware of the SDF connection to terrorism, we do not want him to know that we know. This is very important, Blair. You will simply tell Jeremy that your bank insists on a change being made."

Blair hesitated, then stood from the table, leaving the airplane ticket behind.

"Hey, where're you going?"

Finally, a reaction out of him. "Back to my office," he said.

"You forgot the ticket."

"You can keep it."

"Blair—"

"No, I'm serious. Keep it. Or better still, try handing it over to the next patsy you find."

"You're not a patsy," the agent said, standing himself. "We desperately need your cooperation. By working with us this one time, you'll be helping America rid the world of a potential terrorist threat."

Blair recognized a disingenuous speech when he heard one. And it was troubling to know that the man still unnerved him. *Dare I call his bluff?* he wondered. "I'll tell you what," he said, going for it. "You pay for all the damages and I'll take this trip for you."

"What damages?"

He started walking away.

"Wait. Hold on a second."

He turned back.

"It's a deal."

"Huh?"

"We'll do as you ask."

Blair couldn't believe the agent's compliance, and still without uttering an apology. "I want everything replaced," he said. "The furniture and the books."

"Done."

"Just like that?"

"Just like that," Dalton said. "And don't forget the ten thousand dollars I said we would give you for your trouble."

"I don't want your money."

"Fine." He held up the airline ticket.

Blair snatched it out of his hand.

CHAPTER 17

He was at home watching television, dressed in sweatpants and a New York Mets T-shirt. When the doorbell sounded just after 8:00 PM, Blair strolled out of the den. He pressed the intercom and asked who it was.

"It's Lisa Brandt."

Surprised, he buzzed her in.

She came out of the elevator wearing a tight-fitting, cream-colored sweater and low-rise jeans. Blair smiled as she approached. He held the door open for her. She handed him a bottle of wine.

"What are you doing here?" he asked inanely.

"I felt bad about leaving the other morning without saying good-bye."

"You felt bad?"

"Uh-huh."

He invited her into the den. Black couch, an étagère, soft lighting.

"I'm starved," Lisa said. "Have you eaten yet?"

"Nope. Should I order something?"

"Pizza?"

"Pizza it is. Want something to drink first?"

"Yes, please."

"Fuzzy Navel?"

"You remembered."

In the kitchen, he ordered their pizza. Then he made her drink by following directions in a book he kept near the wine cooler. He filled his own glass with Scotch.

He carried their drinks into the den and put them down on the coffee table. It was an unusual pseudo-African design made of wood. The carving depicted a herd of elephants. When he turned to Lisa, he found he couldn't keep the grin off his face.

"What?" she said.

He shrugged. "Nothing."

"Tell me."

He placed her drink in front of her. "I'm just glad that you're here," he said.

She gazed at him, then touched his glass with her own. "I'm glad I'm here, too."

Blair stood, shut off the television and turned on his iPod. Beyonce's voice soon filled the room from his compact Bose speaker.

When the pizza arrived, he opened the bottle of Chianti Lisa had brought, and poured. As they ate, she pushed for more information about his failed marriage. "I mean, whose fault was it?" she asked.

"I can't discuss it," he said.

"Why not?" she challenged.

"Because. I don't know you well enough."

• • • • •

After their meal, they both helped clear the dishes. She rinsed. He placed them in the dishwasher. When they were done, she leaned in and kissed him. Soft lips—teasing.

"Tell me more about yourself," she demanded.

"I already told you everything you need to know," he said. "For now."

They kissed again. "Do you happen to have an extra toothbrush?" Lisa asked.

"In the bathroom," he said, pretending her question was one he expected.

By the time he came to bed, Lisa was already under the covers.

"I know just what you need," she announced playfully.

He cringed.

"What's wrong?" she asked.

He removed his pajama top to show her.

"Jesus," she swore. She touched each black and blue mark. "Did I do this?" she asked.

He nodded.

"Here." She patted the sheet. "Turn on your stomach."

Soon, light fingers were manipulating his shoulders and the back of his neck.

"Blair," she whispered.

"Yes?"

But he never heard the question. The sheer pleasure of her massage was overwhelming his senses. A drowsiness took over and his eyes began to close.

• • • • •

Blair's alarm went off at six. He quickly sat up and turned it off. He peeked at Lisa. She still seemed to be asleep. He got out of bed, trying to make as little noise as possible. He entered the bathroom and turned on the shower. Within a moment or two, the curtain parted and a naked Lisa came up beside him.

"Could you wash my back?" she asked coyly, handing him the soap.

He hesitated.

"Blair?"

"Mmm..."

"Please?"

"Lisa," he said, "couldn't we..."

"Couldn't we what?"

He wanted to say, "Couldn't we go back to bed." But he didn't want to insult her. Women commanded and he obeyed.

So he soaped her back, and her front. She had a slim waist, and toned arms and legs. And scars—one left of her navel, running up and down for about eight inches, another beneath her left armpit, a third on her right thigh. He wondered how she got them.

"Don't you like this?" Lisa was saying. She had taken the soap from him and was spending extra time on his engorged penis.

Blair found it ludicrous. His experience with his ex-wife, having sex in uncommon places, had been enough to last a lifetime. Yet, here he was, subservient again and unable to change a thing.

But he very much wanted to please her. He put his arms around Lisa, barely touched her lips with his own. She waited for him to do it again, then she kissed him; gently at first, then harder.

In one fluid motion, as if she were a contortionist, she wrapped a leg around his waist and guided him inside.

They soon hit upon a rhythm. But with each thrust, Lisa's head bounced off the wall. Blair feared for her well-being. He tried easing up.

"No! You mustn't!" she demanded.

It was thrust-ka-boom, thrust-ka-boom.

He was growing apprehensive.

"Yes!" she was soon calling out.

He imagined a compound fracture, possibly something worse.

"Yes, yes, yes!"

The police would be called, then an ambulance.

"Please, Blair!"

Despite his concern, he was losing control. Soon after Lisa climaxed, he came as well.

They held on to each other until they caught their breath.

"Not bad for a toy man," Lisa teased.

He studied the back of her head, was unable to find any sign of trauma.

They began to soap off.

She put a hand to his cheek. "I might be falling for you, Blair Mulligan," she said.

He pretended he hadn't heard, while inside he was tingling.

CHAPTER 18

Boarding the plane to Israel, Blair took his seat but kept his eyes glued to the front. He checked each male passenger as he embarked. He half expected John Dalton to show up, knowing the agent wanted to keep a close watch over him.

As the plane pulled away from the gate, he started to relax. The minute they reached cruising altitude, he ordered his favorite drink. Three glasses of Scotch later, he was beginning to mellow. He ate the meal—mixed salad with salmon and vegetables—then slept for a while. A movie starring George Clooney filled the remainder of the trip.

The airport in Tel Aviv was small yet functional. Customs clearance went smoothly, as usual. Blair stepped into the Arrivals Hall and scanned the crowd, disappointed not to see Jeremy. Still he waited, wanting to be sure, wanting to get this over with as quickly as possible.

Finally, he walked outside. The brilliant late afternoon sun caused him to blink his eyes. The pilot said it would be ninety degrees for their arrival. It felt like at least that, if not more. He removed his suit jacket and flipped it over his arm. For once he was pleased that he had forsaken his tie.

"Taxi?"

He turned to the voice.

The man was short with dark hair. He was wearing sunglasses. He could have been a Jew or an Arab. "Taxi?" he said again, apparently the only English word he knew.

Blair looked around but didn't see any other means of transportation.

"Come, come," the driver said, expanding his vocabulary and pointing. "Car over there." He took the suitcase from Blair's hand and led the way.

"David Intercontinental," Blair said once he was settled in the back seat of the beat up Volvo.

The driver turned and gave him a blank stare.

"My hotel." He spoke slowly. "Hotel … David … Intercontinental?"

The man nodded.

The hotel had a view of the Mediterranean, so when they turned onto Hayarkon Street, which ran parallel to the sea, Blair figured they were headed in the right direction. He took in the sights, admiring the expanse of white sand and beachfront. The boardwalk was crowded. Dozens of people were sunbathing.

The screech of the cabbie's cell phone brought him out of his reverie. The driver flipped on the phone and brought it to his ear. The higher his voice rose, the less attention he paid to the road. Soon, he was swerving back and forth across the center line.

Horns honked. Blair was reminded that it was illegal to use a cell phone here without a hands-free device. When they pulled up to his hotel without incident some twenty minutes later, he was relieved.

"Four hundred fifty *shekels*," the driver said.

Blair gaped at him with amazement. "I beg your pardon?"

The man's smile was gone, as was most of his accent. "You heard correctly," he said. He thrust out his hand. "Four fifty. Give, give…"

A quick calculation told him that the driver was asking for approximately one hundred and ten American dollars. "Four fifty?" Blair repeated. "For a trip that has never cost more than half that amount?"

The man's look soured. "Okay. Four hundred, then."

Blair was tired and out of patience. He counted three hundred *shekels* and handed the money to the driver. "This is all you get, bud. Take it or leave it."

Their eyes locked.

The man's hand went to a leather case that was concealed beneath his seat.

Blair tensed.

The driver pulled out a receipt and handed it to him.

Blair quickly took the receipt in hand and stepped out of the cab.

• • • • •

The hotel lobby was spacious, brightly lit, and crowded. A far cry from what it was like a number of years ago, when constant terrorist attacks badly impacted Israel's multi-billion-dollar tourist industry. There were still problems, just not as many.

"Welcome, *shalom*," the clerk at the check-in counter said.

Blair was impressed by her golden skin, bright green eyes. "Thank you," he said, handing her his credit card.

"Staying for three nights?" she asked.

"Yes, three nights," he confirmed.

"Welcome back, Mr. Mulligan. It is always a pleasure to see you. Will you be needing help with your bags?"

"No help needed," he said, indicating his small suitcase.

She handed him his computerized keycard. "Here you go, then," she said. "Fifteenth floor, as usual."

• • • • •

The room was spacious. Mahogany trim, with a king-size bed and mini-bar. A large desk sat off to one side. A leather swivel chair stood next to it.

It took him less than ten minutes to hang up his clothes and place his toiletries in the bathroom. He was disappointed not to see the message light blinking.

He picked up the phone and dialed Jeremy's cell, but got his voice-mail. He left a message and disconnected. He wondered if something had happened to his friend. Or if he was indeed preoccupied with a terrorist group and their nefarious plans.

He paused, knowing how ridiculous that seemed. There was no one man in Blair's life to whom he felt closer. It was impossible to believe Jeremy was anyone but who he said he was.

Without wasting another moment, Blair flipped off the lights and strolled out of his room.

• • • • •

It felt strange to be walking instead of driving with Jeremy in his car. Blair had never paid much attention to this part of Tel Aviv. Hayarkon was a long street that seemed to run forever. There were office buildings and hotels, for the most part. A number were only a few stories tall. He did not encounter many pedestrians. He spotted a few on the opposite side. And this lone male figure on his side, coming toward him now.

As the person approached, Blair kept his eyes focused. He realized he had no weapon he could use, that he was completely and utterly defenseless. *Is this what a suicide bomber looks like?* he asked himself.

As the person neared, he could see that he was not as old as he had first believed. A teenager, actually, concentrating on whatever was coming out of the stereo headset he was wearing.

They passed each other without incident. And the relief Blair felt was palpable.

He continued walking until a familiar sign on his right finally came into view: *Moira's Italian.* He climbed the short staircase and entered.

The restaurant was quaint. Tables were set for two or four, no booths. Each table was adorned with a plastic red and green tablecloth. The candle holder, a throwback to another era, was a Chianti bottle wrapped in basket-weave. The menu was basic Italian, with Mediterranean side dishes.

The owner was performing the duties of maitre d'. Short and robust, she had a nice way of greeting him. He asked for a table for two in case Jeremy showed up. This was his restaurant of choice. Jeremy knew to meet him here if they missed each other at the airport.

She led him to a table by the window facing the street. Before she could get away he ordered a half-bottle of Valpolicella. He looked around. There weren't that many diners.

The wine arrived, but he held off ordering dinner. It was 7:30. He would give Jeremy until eight o'clock.

The sound of laughter caught his ear. A group of children, girls aged five or six, were dining with two sets of parents at a table at the far end of the room. Each child had a Coke bottle in hand, and was shaking it and aiming the spray at the others. Their parents were either unconcerned, or oblivious to their behavior.

Blair found it common in this country: children were given far more freedom. With good reason, he supposed, considering what they lived with on a day-to-day basis.

"Pssst."

He turned to the voice.

"*Atta rotzeh et ha* Coke *sheli*?" A blond girl was beside his chair, pointing to her bottle and offering it to him.

"No thanks," Blair said.

Her smile widened. He could hear her friends giggling in the background.

"What's your name?" he asked.

She tried handing him the Coke bottle again.

He shook his head. "I don't want your Coke."

She remained in place.

Blair liked children. He admired their innocence and unconditional trust. Now, he took the cloth napkin in hand, flattened it on the table, then folded it into a reverse triangle. Holding both ends, he brought one toward the center and crisscrossed the other. Then he started to fold the napkin toward him until he it was curled into an elongated shape. He turned the pointed ends of the napkin inside out. He pulled on one end until it formed a tail and introduced his pretend mouse.

All this time the girl had been watching in silence. When he manipulated the mouse with his fingers so that it appeared to be moving, she jumped back, squealing with delight.

He continued his demonstration, repeating the tricks his father had taught him, the same ones he used on his daughter. Teasing the girl with them, waiting for her to try to touch the mouse before making it jump out of the way.

This went on for several minutes.

When the door opened, he expected to find Jeremy. Instead it was an elderly couple, gray-haired and overweight, wearing identification tags from a bus tour they'd been on. The maitre d' seated them far enough away so he was able to go on with his game without feeling obtrusive.

Blair wished he could get to know the girl's name. No matter how he posed the question, however, the answer remained elusive. Then something reflected in the plate glass window. It was a car on the street, trying to park next to the restaurant, even though parking was prohibited.

The girl's laugh distracted him for a moment. When Blair looked back, he caught sight of the driver as he got out of the car. And his heart leapt in his throat.

It was the same man who had driven him to his hotel from the airport. He was carrying something in his hand. A canister or bottle of some sort.

Blair didn't know why—it could have been a sixth sense—but something made him dive, folding his body over the little girl. He sent them both crashing to the hardwood floor, just as the windowpane exploded.

The sound was so loud it was painful. White heat followed, burning in its intensity.

There were screams, horrible screams.

Blair managed to maneuver both he and the girl under the table, just as the walls disintegrated. He was trying to see, trying to figure out a means of escape, when the very table protecting them blew apart.

A piece of debris collided with his back. Then another piece slammed into his head.

He lost consciousness.

CHAPTER 19

The mosque in Brooklyn was of a makeshift nature in a converted, small house. Ignoring his own discomfort, Yassin genuflected, lowering his forehead to the carpet until it touched.

Twenty minutes later, the service was over. Putting on his shoes, he caught sight of a boy aged eleven or twelve, huddling with the imam. It brought him up short. "Mohammed," he muttered beneath his breath. The resemblance to his dead son was uncanny. How could one boy look so much like another? Or was he imagining it? For the thousandth time?

Trembling, he turned away.

The earliest memory was painful: Yassin was born a year after his parents' unsanctioned marriage. His father had not only gone against custom by turning down the girl chosen for him, but had taken as his bride an outsider, a Christian from Norway, no less, a volunteer working for one of the many obscure charity organizations operating in Palestine.

After his birth, it did not take long for people to notice the lighter color of Yassin's skin as well as his other Scandinavian features. Growing older, he was heckled and harassed endlessly. His mother insisted he learn to speak English, and he spoke it well. This was a further black mark against him. To make matters worse, his siblings who were born two and four years later, a boy and a girl, were spared the same fate, having inherited their father's physiognomy.

Anger ruled his every waking moment. It festered, giving rise to near neurotic behavior. And it served as a catalyst, his impetus for making a name for himself among the militants who were so prevalent in Palestine.

Nine people lived in his small house in Jabalia Camp in Gaza: their immediate family of five, and four cousins whose parents had been killed in a raid a short time ago. This was the third house they had built in recent years. The first was destroyed by Israeli bulldozers when it was decided that the road needed widening. The second house was blown apart as revenge for the Qassam rockets that were fired into Israel by Hamas.

Attached to this third house was the restaurant Yassin's father ran. The smell of food infiltrated the walls, often making it difficult to fall asleep. All members of the family pitched in. The hours were long, but complaints about it fell on deaf ears.

When he wasn't attending school or working in the restaurant, Yassin spent his free time in training, learning how to prepare homemade bombs, learning the benefit of knives, rifles, and handguns, depending on the form of combat. He was not the tallest or heaviest among the volunteers, but few exhibited his stamina or determination.

Then came his twentieth birthday. There was no mistaking that the girl introduced by his family—Madras was her name—was intended to be his future wife. Hesitant at first, he was more than taken by her natural beauty. And something stirred inside, feelings that he never would have believed he was capable of having.

He and the girl began to see each other on a semi-regular basis. He found himself thinking about her more and more. It got to the point where he couldn't get her out of his head. He proposed a few months later, and they were married in a small ceremony with close relatives present.

As a wedding gift, his parents cleared out the den. This was the only spare room in the house. And it gave the young couple some privacy.

Yassin found himself changing, in subtle but meaningful ways. His life no longer seemed as hopeless or as bleak. He eased up on his after-hours training, and spent more time at home with his bride.

When Madras became pregnant two months later, panic set in. As someone who had lived with juvenile diabetes from a very young age, she had been warned about the risks of having a child. Yassin had pled with her to have an abortion. She refused. Their son, Mohammed, was born a month premature. His wife did not survive the Cesarean-section. Struggling to stay focused, Yassin became more moody and quarrelsome than he had been before. He started taking risks. When the Israelis began to clamp down, he once again volunteered for active duty with the terrorists. It was on a clandestine excursion into Tel Aviv that an incendiary device exploded close by. Shrapnel tore into his upper arm, the pain remaining with him to this day.

The memory of Madras kept him going. As did the boy, of course. More and more, Mohammed began to resemble his deceased wife. From his pear-shaped face to his near-sensuous eyebrows and lips.

Mohammed was studious in nature. But he possessed a rather frail physique. Yassin loved taking him for long walks, took pleasure in teaching him how to play soccer, found it surprising that the boy was quick and agile on his feet.

By the time Mohammed had reached his ninth birthday, it dawned on Yassin that his son was habitually quiet, introspective. He'd never known someone of his son's age so adept at memorizing and reciting multiple verses of the Koran by heart. It was no surprise, therefore, that the imam took a special interest. Yassin was honored that his son was being asked to go on weekend retreats with a few of the other boys.

Normally when Mohammed was away, Yassin would use the time

to catch up on his reading, to put his personal matters in order. But on one particular weekend in the summer, a date now ingrained in Yassin's heart, he found himself unable to concentrate. Time passed fitfully. A terrible apprehension filled his mind.

His relatives were on vacation, so the house was eerily quiet. By 10:00 PM that Sunday, hours after the time Mohammed should have returned, Yassin's patience ran out. He left the house and hurried to the mosque.

He began to bang on the door. No one responded. He walked the short distance to the imam's living quarters. He rang the bell but got no reply. Reluctantly, Yassin returned home.

Pacing his room, he prayed for hours, until it was six o'clock in the morning. He force-fed himself a coffee. Then he lifted the phone, was about to dial the imam's number, when he heard a knock on the door. He put the phone down and went to answer it.

The imam wore a solemn expression.

Yassin's heart sank.

The imam beckoned.

He did not remember closing the door, or even walking, for that matter. He followed the holy man, knowing but not wanting to know. They stopped on a deserted side street and the imam began to speak.

The Zionists were gaining ground. Their wall and their roadblocks were stopping the brave martyrs, the human bombs who sacrificed themselves, from crossing into Tel Aviv from Palestine. Only a strike into the deepest part of Israel would teach the infidels a lesson. To achieve this, they had concluded, they would have to use someone the Zionists would least suspect.

"Your son believed in the cause," the imam said. "He was one of the bravest boys it was my privilege to teach. He will go down in history as the one who made a difference. Twelve bodies recovered so far. I am certain they will find more..."

The imam's words traveled through Yassin's head as if through a sieve. He did not even know if he was hearing them correctly. Something about how proud he should be of Mohammed's sacrifice.

Yassin's stomach threatened to burst. In his mind's eye he was visualizing his son's frailness, overpowered by the weight of the bomb strapped to his chest. He could hear the explosion. He could see Mohammed's body parts disintegrating, flying through the air…

There was no way of knowing when the imam left his side. Or the exact time he returned home. All Yassin knew was that his life, for all intents and purposes, was over.

He stopped working. Stopped eating. Despite the efforts of family and friends, he remained morose. He felt like a phantom, floating through time and space.

No one had to tell him who was at fault. He did not have to be radicalized by fanatical clerics. The hatred he felt possessed him; he needed no other motivation.

When the imam suggested he take on a role in America, he jumped at the chance. He believed the imam when he said that the Israelis, with their American benefactors, had caused his son's death. If not for their oppression, the imam would not have had to use Mohammed as a human bomb. If not for the Jews, his boy would be alive today.

They would be made to pay, Yassin decided. His life would be devoted to nothing else.

CHAPTER 20

"Sandra!" Blair tried calling out. It seemed his vocal chords had gone mute. He twisted and turned, made every attempt to be heard.

It was hopeless.

He called his daughter's name again, believing it was she in the restaurant with him and not a stranger.

Then he went under...

• • • • •

Time passed with fuzzy irregularity. His thoughts were scrambled. Delirious, he became part of Sandra's plight.

Both of them were falling.

With a herculean effort, he called for help.

Then, a needle pricked his arm.

He tumbled backwards, flying through inner space.

He prayed for a safety net.

• • • • •

"Blair?"

He struggled to open his eyes. Light flooded in and they began to water.

"Welcome back, buddy."

He turned toward the voice.

Someone who resembled Jeremy Samson was leaning over his bed.

"Sandra?" Blair said in a whisper.

"What about her?" Samson replied.

"Did she make it?"

"Make what?"

"The restaurant…" He sat up too quickly and was overpowered by vertigo.

Seeing his discomfort, Jeremy helped ease him back down.

His eyelids drooped and he began to drift.

"Blair?"

Is this reality or a dream? he wondered. "Where am I?" he thought to ask.

"*Beit Cholim Shel Tikva.*" Jeremy pronounced the name like a native. "One of the best hospitals in Israel."

"Which is where, exactly?"

"Not far from your hotel. In central Tel Aviv."

"H … how did I get here?"

"Don't you remember?"

Sound stilled; he was gone again.

• • • • •

Darkness settled in his room. He tried moving onto his side. A fierce pain in his back took his breath away. Gasping, he lay still until it subsided. He went to scratch his scalp but touched a bandage instead.

Hesitantly, his hands traced a line from his neck to his arms. He touched his stomach and each thigh. Then his legs, one at a time.

All were intact.

He thanked God for small mercies.

• • • • •

Jeremy was there the following morning. "I'm sorry for not meeting you at the airport," he said. "There was another terrorist bombing. Near the factory, this time. They wanted to question me. To see if I'd noticed anything suspicious. I had no way of getting word to you. By the time I got through with the authorities, it was too late to meet you at the airport or at your hotel. I came right to the restaurant. I arrived just after the Molotov cocktail exploded."

"Molotov cocktail?"

"Yes."

"Jeremy—"

"I'm here, *boychick*."

"—what the hell happened to me?"

"You mean, you really don't remember? You're a hero, my friend."

"What?"

"Yeah. Don't look so surprised." Jeremy grinned.

"But I didn't do anything," Blair said, confused. He tried to think his way through it. He had been in his favorite Italian restaurant ... *my god, the girl!*

"How is she?" he quickly asked.

"If you mean the kid you saved, she's fine."

It was coming back. "And the others?"

Hesitation creased Jeremy's brow. "Ten dead altogether. But most of the kitchen staff, you, and the girl, got out okay. I don't know how you had the quickness of mind. You're far more athletic than I'd given you credit for."

Blair winced. "Yeah, I'm a real athlete."

"Hey, don't disparage yourself. You still work out at the gym a few times a week. It obviously paid off."

"Sure, it did." *All those people*, he was thinking. *The girl's parents and their friends. The girl's playmates.The elderly couple who had come in last. All dead.*

"What about the owner?" he asked. "That lady. I forget her name…"

"Moira Feldman? She survived as well. She is the one who spoke to the press about you. She saw what you did. Reporters are clamoring for a chance to interview you."

"Did she give them my name?"

"Uh-uh. She didn't know your name."

"Good. I hope she never finds out."

"Why do you say that? This is your chance for glory. A bona fide American hero. Don't you want to be famous?"

"Uh-uh. Seriously, Jeremy. I don't want you saying a word."

"Me?"

"Yes, you. If you value our friendship..."

• • • • •

The police interview took time. Finally, he was told he could leave the hospital. Truth be known, his headaches hadn't quite subsided to the degree he'd let on. But his purpose for coming to Israel weighed heavily on his mind. He disliked the position he was in. And he wanted to get this over with as quickly as possible.

Jeremy showed up, dressed in an open-necked white sport shirt and Bermuda shorts. His sock-less feet were adorned with brown leather sandals.

Blair reflected once more on his friend's youthful appearance, his red hair and freckles reminding him of a cartoon character whose name eluded him at the moment.

Jeremy handed him a small envelope with Hebrew writing on the front. "Your get-well gift," he said.

Blair opened the envelope and smiled. If he couldn't win the lottery back in the States, perhaps he could do so here.

"It's up to forty million *shekels*," Jeremy said.

He whistled at the amount, the equivalent of ten million American dollars.

Winded from the simple exercise of putting on his clothes, Blair slumped down on the edge of the bed.

"You sure you want to check out?" Jeremy asked. "That wasn't a love tap to your head, you know. An inch or two to the left or right and you would have been killed."

"Yeah. Thanks for reminding me. But I feel fine. Really, I do. I've got to get back to the States, Jeremy."

"That quick?"

"I'm afraid so."

Jeremy was quiet for a moment. "Stand up," he said.

"Huh?"

"Stand up."

When Blair stood, Jeremy put his hands on his shoulders and positioned him in front of the full-length mirror.

What Blair saw concerned him. Both eyes were swollen and bruised. A barely healed cut crisscrossed his cheek. He could spot some coagulated blood in his hair.

He turned to Jeremy. "No big deal," he said, lying. "I've seen worse."

CHAPTER 21

Once in the car, it took less than ten minutes for Blair to fall asleep. Jeremy shook him awake as soon as they reached his office. Blair couldn't quite get his bearings. This area of Ashod, in the central-eastern portion of Israel, catered to small and mid-size manufacturers. Despite having come here many times before, nothing looked familiar. "Where are we?" he asked.

Jeremy shot a curious glance his way. "What do you mean, where are we?"

He stepped out. The sky was blue and there was no breeze to speak of. "Just give me a minute," he said.

When Blair finally approached the building, Jeremy hurried ahead to hold the door for him. The manufacturing facility and warehouse stood on their left. On their right was the stairwell leading to the offices on the upper floor.

They climbed to the top. Blair took a seat in Jeremy's cramped quarters. The air-conditioning did not have the same functionality as back home. While cooler than the outside temperature, it was far from comfortable.

Files were strewn across the desk and piled on the floor.

"As neat as ever," Blair teased.

Jeremy sloughed off the comment. "Tell me, why the sudden urgency in seeing me?" he asked.

"I told you on the phone. I have a few concerns, not the least of which is the *Cyber-tech* knockoff."

"*Alleged* knockoff," Jeremy said. "The company who offered it is run by an ex-employee of ours. The *schmuck* stole a few of our secrets and thought he could get away with it. We're suing his ass. The bloody thing will be off the market before you know it. End of problem."

Blair steeled himself. "There is something else I've been made aware of," he said. "Concerning the manufacturer."

"Of the hardware?"

"Uh-uh. The software. From my recollection, I believe you said SDF would be producing most, if not all, of the mini DVDs?"

"That's correct. Hillel Electronics have been working with them for years."

"Yeah, but that doesn't necessarily mean SDF are the best."

A frown crossed Jeremy's brow. "What makes you say that?"

"Didn't you know? I'm a mind-reader." Blair coughed, hoping to hide his embarrassment. "I found out SDF are not the only ones in their field. As a matter of fact, I've heard, from reliable sources, that On Time Electronics is far better at what they do."

"OTE?" Jeremy practically leapt out of his chair.

Blair lowered his eyes.

"Do you even know who OTE is?"

"Of course," he said.

"How do you know? Tell me, please. I'm curious." Jeremy's voice had risen a few octaves.

"My bank told me about them." He plowed ahead. "They investigated SDF and came up with some unusual business transactions. I believe it was stock related, some incident of fraud or insider trading involving their top executives." To buy some time, he asked if he could have some water.

Jeremy stepped up to the small fridge in the corner of his office and removed a bottle. Tossing it to Blair, he went back to his desk. Then he reached for his phone and dialed. He spoke a few words in Hebrew, a language for which he'd shown a proficiency before, and disconnected. After he completed a second call, he stood and indicated for Blair to follow.

• • • • •

The offices and manufacturing plant for SDF were housed in a hundred-thousand-square-foot facility. This was large by Israeli standards. One needn't be observant to notice that the company was above average when it came to up-to-date workstations and state-of-the-art machinery.

The people Jeremy introduced, from a Mr. Rosen, to a Goldberg, to a Lichtenstein, all greeted Blair warmly.

Touring their premises, a feeling of dread began to build. These people did not appear at all to be what had been described to him. Terrorists? Criminals? It seemed utter nonsense.

Every facet of their operation was inspected, from the initial manufacturing process of the mini DVD and the descriptive sleeve it was housed in, to the assembly line where the DVD was inserted into its jewel case. He couldn't find fault with any of it.

Jeremy's grin was almost offensive. "Seen enough?" he asked.

• • • • •

Another drive. Shorter this time.

If SDF was the epitome of modernization, then OTE was the opposite. They weren't as decrepit as some of the sweatshops Blair had visited in parts of China, but On Time Electronics belied everything he expected to find. The executives, for one thing, from the president on down, were unfriendly and distracted. There was something slovenly about many of their workers and how they approached their tasks. The building itself, smaller then SDF by half, had no sense of organization. Much of the machinery was in disrepair. What there was of an assembly line did not have enough workers or supervision.

Blair now understood why Jeremy had seen the need for a "show and tell." Once they were back in his office, he figured he had to play his final card. "You know how difficult banks can be," he said. "Mine really didn't give me an option. Before I left New York, it was made plain that they don't want me dealing with SDF. And they control the purse strings. They can pull the plug whenever they like."

His bottle of water was three-quarters empty, and he was no longer thirsty, but he pretended that his thirst was unquenchable, draining the bottle and asking for another.

Jeremy stood, got the replacement, handed it over, and reclaimed his seat.

Blair took him back to the time he had started in business. He reminded Jeremy how his first bank nearly put him out of business. How it was the current bank that came to his rescue. "It all comes down to the relationship between the account manager and the client," he said. "I owe my guy the benefit of the doubt. You can see that, can't you?"

He didn't wait for an answer. Instead, he leaned forward and pretended to be serious. "Look, I didn't want to get into this, but I must tell you what I've learned, in confidence, about SDF. I have it on good authority that Mr. Lichenshmid is, in actual fact, a closet Nazi. His second in command, this Mr. Rosen, is a child molester. And Mr. Goldberg happens to screw around on his wife."

"Blair!" Jeremy stopped him, bursting into laughter. "First of all, it's Lichtenstein, not Lichenshmid. And the man is Jewish. He's been highly decorated by the Israeli Army. He's lived in this country for over thirty years. If he's a Nazi then I'm Joan of Arc."

"Joan, I didn't recognize you."

"Furthermore, both Goldberg and Rosen emigrated here from Poland years ago and have exemplary records."

"Still, you never know about people." Blair stopped abruptly. He realized he could only carry this nonsense so far. "Seriously," he said, "my bank has given me instructions and I'm hoping to comply."

Jeremy frown hinted of incredulity.

Feverish, embarrassed, no longer having the heart to continue, Blair wanted to go somewhere and hide.

"You could see the difference in the two companies we visited today," Jeremy said. "There is no comparison. SDF is professional, reliable, and well respected in the industry. OTE, on the other hand, is-notorious for screwing up their customers' orders, for putting out an inferior product."

"All rumors," Blair interjected.

"Not rumors." Jeremy said. "Fact. You can recognize the truth yourself. Bank or no bank, there is no way I can go along with you. I'm sorry. It just wouldn't make sense to do as you suggest." He paused. "I really don't think so, *boychick*."

CHAPTER 22

He arrived at the airport the following morning with his equilibrium still off-kilter. Waiting in line at the Business Class counter, he broke out in a cold sweat. If not for the pills the doctor in the hospital had prescribed, he probably wouldn't have had the strength to stand.

The clerk at the El Al desk was a bored young man who obviously didn't appreciate his job. He impatiently thrust out his hand for Blair's passport, then went about his business in a slow and deliberate manner.

By the time the formalities were completed Blair felt feverish. He proceeded to the El Al lounge on feet of lead.

The girl who welcomed him was far friendlier than the male clerk at the check-in counter. She seemed to recognize that Blair wasn't feeling well. She immediately stood up from her desk, guided him to an empty seat, and asked if she could pour him a coffee.

He gladly accepted the offer.

The lounge was unusually quiet. The girl served him the coffee. Blair took a few sips and his head cleared a little.

The restaurant bombing was still on his mind. It was too much of a coincidence to have the same man who drove him to his hotel from the airport involved. Blair believed that he himself was the target. But he didn't know the reason why.

A quick review of his life didn't reveal anything unusual. If anything, his reflections pointed to a rather mundane existence.

He hadn't cheated anyone, abused anyone, or purposely hurt anyone.

So what was it? What enemies had he made? Blair wondered. Who hated him enough to want to have him killed?

He just didn't get it.

• • • • •

When his flight landed in New York, Blair was still out of sorts. He was too weak to carry his small suitcase, so he solicited the help of a porter. The wait for a cab felt like an eternity.

He arrived at his condo after midnight. He did not bother to unpack. He dropped his bag on the floor in the hallway and walked into his bedroom. He was not up to washing his face or brushing his teeth. Instead, fully dressed, he collapsed on top of the bedspread.

CHAPTER 23

Eleven hours later he awoke feeling sluggish. Shaving and showering were onerous. He took a cab to his office. No sooner did he walk in than he was inundated with questions about the bruises on his face. "It's not as bad as it looks," he repeated too many times.

Then he paused and shook his head. The old furniture remained. The desks, chairs, and file cabinets now stood upright. Some work had been done to repair the damage to the walls. But it was not what had been promised.

Reluctantly, he approached the boardroom. The torn books, gathered off the floor and piled on the table, had not been replaced.

Blair walked back to his office and took a seat. He picked up a stack of messages that were held together by a paper clip. The majority were from John Dalton.

He leaned forward and shut his eyes. He desperately wanted his life to return to normal. The government agent had crossed the line more than once. He no longer wanted to deal with him.

• • • • •

Lunch was a quick bite at a burger joint down the street. To his dismay, upon his return to the office, he found John Dalton waiting for him, seated in the chair opposite his desk.

Blair's secretary whispered an apology as he walked past her.

He waved her worry away.

"How was Israel?" Dalton asked the minute he closed his office door.

Blair observed the agent for a moment. And he wondered if the man had even one redeeming feature. "Who invited you here, John?" he asked.

"I invited myself. We paid for your trip, remember? The least we'd expect is a concise report."

"Concise report?" Blair remained on his feet. "There is nothing at all to tell you."

"Oh? You can start with the bombing."

"What bombing?"

"Blair, Blair, Blair. Sit down, would you? I don't like you hovering above me. It makes me nervous."

The thought of something making Dalton nervous didn't compute. But Blair took his seat.

"Now, tell me about your meeting with Jeremy Samson."

Blair noticed that the bombing incident had already been forgotten about. "Where are the replacement books?" he asked.

"My budget's been cut. If you're patient, I'll find a way to make it up to you."

"Uh-uh. I want them now. Like you promised."

"I can't do it now. Didn't you hear what I just said?"

Blair paused. "Our meeting was uneventful," he said.

"And that's it?" The agent's voice took on a noticeable hardness. "No other details?"

Blair hesitated, then decided there was no harm in telling the truth.

"Jeremy took me on a tour of both factories," he said. "SDF was professional and outstanding, way above average. Your suggested replacement, On Time Electronics, paled in comparison. Shoddy workmanship and even shoddier workers. It was laughable. Jeremy refused my suggestion outright. And I can't say that I blame him."

"Didn't you try to convince him?"

A caustic remark came to mind, but Blair let it pass. "Of course, I tried. Used every argument I could think of. Even told him that my account manager at the bank was insisting on a change."

Dalton sneezed, was reaching a hand into his pants pocket for a tissue or handkerchief, when he winced in pain.

Blair could see his arm going into spasm. "Is something wrong?" he asked, expressing more sympathy than he intended.

Dalton's look darkened. "Nothing's wrong. But you'll have to go back there."

"I beg your pardon?"

"You'll have to visit Jeremy again."

Blair was incredulous. "I can't do that."

"It's necessary, I'm afraid."

"Necessary?" he said. And the anger he'd been suppressing finally came out. "John, I don't know who authorizes your operation, or makes you act the way you do. But I have to tell you, it really sucks."

"We are sanctioned by the Federal Government, my friend."

My friend? Now he was his friend, Blair thought. "Look, I hate to be rude, John. But I need you out of my life. I can't put it in simpler terms. I want you to stop bothering me."

Dalton stood and calmly said, "We need you to go back to Israel. Let me know once your travel arrangements have been made."

"I won't be going," Blair told him.

The man's hands tightened into fists. "You have forty-eight hours. If I haven't heard from you by then, I will not be responsible for the consequences."

CHAPTER 24

Two days after John Dalton's visit, Blair arrived at work and found himself deluged with messages from the government agent. He tried to convince himself that he wasn't bothered by them. But he was. And he wasn't alone. His secretary, Andrea Victor, came into his office and threw her hands in the air. "I can't take it anymore," she said. "Mr. Dalton won't leave me alone."

Blair asked her to have a seat.

Andrea had been with him since his arrival in New York. In her late thirties, the woman had a fragile appearance, ultra thin with brown hair and eyes, yet she was so efficient, he couldn't see himself doing without her.

"Tell me what he said to you," he requested.

"He threatened to have me arrested."

That caught his attention. "For doing what?" he asked.

"Obstructing justice."

"Because you wouldn't put his call through to me?"

"Yes. That's what he said."

Blair was amazed that the agent would go this far. He stood and came around his desk. He put his hand out and helped his secretary to her feet. "Andrea, I want you to take the rest of the day off," he said. "Go shopping. Go to a movie. Do anything. Only don't come back here until tomorrow."

• • • • •

That evening, when he arrived home, he found a dozen more voice messages from Dalton, all of which he ignored. He slept in fits and starts, expecting the man to come pounding on his door at any moment.

He thought of giving in. But there was nothing to give in to. Jeremy wasn't about to change his mind. Going back to Israel would be a waste of time.

CHAPTER 25

On Friday night, he was waiting outside his condo when Lisa arrived precisely as promised at 7:15. She had not only offered to treat him to dinner at Il Mulino, his favorite New York restaurant, but had insisted on doing the driving as well.

One look at her car, however, more than surprised him. The beige Chrysler was at least five years old. It was boxy and dull, and not at all the kind of vehicle he would have associated with her.

He opened the passenger door. "Nice bus," he said, and he went to take a seat.

"Don't get comfortable." She stopped him. "Our reservation isn't until nine o'clock. And there's nothing wrong with my car."

"Of course not. It's perfect for you." He stepped away and closed the door.

Surprisingly for Manhattan, she found a parking spot at the end of the block. She locked the car and started toward him.

Blair admired the low-cut, black leather dress she was wearing.

When she reached his side he held her at arm's length. Having a woman in his life was starting to make a difference. It revitalized him, somehow.

"You like?" she asked, blushing. And then she caught herself. "My God! Your face! What happened to you?"

"It's nothing," he said, turning to a side.

"Blair?"

"I was in a little accident," he said.

"Little?" She reached a hand out.

To divert her, he pointed in the approximate area. "Say, is that bra new?"

"Don't change the subject."

"Is it?"

"Why?"

"I don't know," he said. "You seem … uplifted."

"Smart-ass." She brushed past him. "C'mon," she said. "You can treat me to a drink in your apartment."

• • • • •

"I have a bottle of champagne in the fridge," Blair told her once they were settled on the couch. "Should I open it?"

She gave him a semi-serious look. "Duh…"

He went into the kitchen and removed the bottle. When the cork went flying, he let out an "*opa*," filled two flutes to the brim, and carried them, along with the bottle, into the den.

"*Skol*," he said, handing her one of the flutes and taking a seat beside her.

They clinked glasses and drank.

She asked again about the injuries he had suffered in Israel. He considered telling her, then changed his mind.

Her glass was half empty. When Blair went to fill it, she stopped him. "Want to get me drunk, mister?"

"Drunk and pliable."

"I'm serious. Champagne does funny things to me. Especially when I haven't eaten."

"Would you like a snack? Peanuts or chips?"

With glass still in hand, she leaned in and kissed him. "I'd like something more than a snack," she said.

Blair reached out to take the glass from her.

Misunderstanding, Lisa went to stop his hand's progression. This knocked her glass forward, its contents spilling on his tie.

He feigned hurt. "It's ruined," he said.

"Poor baby. I'll buy you another one."

He flung what was left in his own glass at her, catching her flush in the face.

Lisa wrestled him to the floor. He somehow maneuvered his way on top. She kicked and swung her arms until he lost his balance. Positions reversed, her legs suddenly scissored upwards, then in. They enveloped his chest and held tight. "Give up?" she asked.

He tried for a finesse move, caught her breast instead.

"Pervert!" she hissed.

He held her in a bear-hug.

In less than a minute, he felt this grinding motion. "Lisa," he protested.

She seemed oblivious. She was already undressing and motioning for him to do the same.

He thought about stopping. Only … her fingers had manipulated their way to his scrotum, and a wave of pleasure short-circuited his brain.

Blair couldn't remember making love this way before. One climax followed another. When they weren't on the floor, they were on the sofa. Often, it felt as if they were partially on both. The pauses grew longer; their satisfaction greater.

Then Lisa's hand grasped his injured back and he winced.

"What is it?" she asked.

He showed her the scar.

"My God," she said, "Is that from Israel, too?"

He nodded.

"I'll be more careful," she promised.

Soon, he was lost again.

At one o'clock in the morning, Blair asked if Il Mulino was still open.

Lisa said she doubted that they were.

He smiled.

• • • • •

When Blair awoke in the morning, Lisa was sitting up in bed, looking radiant. "How did we get here?" he asked.

She gave him a peck on the cheek and said she didn't know. "Is your back okay?"

He said his back was fine.

She took hold of his face in the palms of her hands. "I feel like I lost ten pounds," she said.

He laughed. "Me, too."

"I like losing ten pounds with you."

"Me, three."

She exaggerated the blinking of her lashes, which overemphasized her slightly crossed eye.

He asked her about it.

"Born this way," she said. She let go of his face and leaned her head against his shoulder. "I want you to always be honest with me, Blair. No secrets and no lies."

"Always is a long time," he said, trying to keep it light. But he sensed a hurt there, something in her past.

"I'm serious," she said.

"Okay, I promise. No lies between us."

She kissed him. "Tell me the truth about your injuries," she said. "What really happened in Israel?"

"I already told you."

"Yeah, but what you said was a load of crap."

"Lisa—"

"You promised. No lies."

"So I did."

"Well?"

"Starting tomorrow..."

CHAPTER 26

He and Lisa spent the weekend together. They went to a movie on Saturday afternoon, stayed home for dinner that night. They ate Sunday brunch at a nearby hotel. By the time Monday rolled around he was truly sorry to see her go.

He arrived at work before nine o'clock. He concentrated on his paperwork for most of the morning. After lunch he began to check in with his sales representatives across the country. He'd been neglecting them, so it felt good to get caught up. Not that there was much to glean from what they reported. Sales were soft. It had been that way for quite some time. Blair used encouraging words, while he himself was not encouraged at all.

On the subway ride home that afternoon, he decided to disembark one stop early to get a bit of fresh air.

The temperature was holding steady in the low sixties. The shops and restaurants he passed were familiar to him. There was nothing like the comfort of one's own neighborhood, he realized.

He turned the corner to his street and made out his building. By habit, he looked up. A light was on in his fifteenth-floor condo. But he always shut off the lights when he left for work. It was one of the things he was habitual about.

Blair's walk turned into a run.

• • • • •

The keys were already in hand. He unlocked the main door and rushed toward the elevator. He hit the button and then hit it again. It felt like it was taking forever.

Wait and see, a voice warned in his head. *You could have left the light on by mistake.*

Finally, the elevator arrived.

He stepped in.

A child holding her mother's hand said hello. He barely acknowledged her.

He hurried out on his floor.

The door to his apartment stood open.

Cautiously, he entered the foyer and paused. There were crushed CDs and DVDs strewn across the floor. He spotted liquor bottles, including his prized Scotch, lying on their sides. Their tops had been removed and the alcohol was leaving a river of stains.

Who would do this? he asked himself needlessly, the answer clear.

He walked into his bedroom and glass crunched underfoot. The television screen had a gaping hole in it. The spread and pillows on the bed were shredded, a pastiche of colors that didn't mesh.

Then something caught his eye.

Reluctantly, he approached the dresser and reached a hand out.

Be sure, he told himself.

He would know if this was his daughter's blouse. Mandy sewed her name into all her clothes.

He made himself look.

'SANDRA' popped out at him.

He paused.

The blouse had been deliberately torn. Tentatively, he brought it close. He shut his eyes for a moment, breathing in his daughter's familiar scent.

CHAPTER 27

Yassin knew to be careful. The other faction was observing his daily schedule, snooping into his operations, aiming to disrupt his plans. All for the sake of maintaining power. All to prove that only they should take the lead, should have the honor of striking America one more time.

He changed directions twice before leaving Manhattan. Taking the Bronx Expressway to I-95, he connected with I-295, then the Cross Island Parkway, and finally Northern Boulevard. Twenty minutes later, he pulled up to the address in Great Neck, Long Island.

This part of the work, attending to some of the lesser details, strained his patience. But after the meeting with his man in the Diamond District, he did not feel comfortable putting his trust in anyone else.

On Monday, he had spent time northeast of the city, in Westchester County. The properties he had visited would have been suitable, but the drive was problematic. Tuesday found him exploring various offers in Montauk. These were estate homes, large enough for his purpose, but not quite to his liking.

Now, he stepped out of the car and paused. The area was exclusive and quiet. He buttoned his suit jacket.

"Mr. Carson?" The real estate agent, a curvaceous, middle-aged brunette, greeted him by the name he had assumed for today's purpose.

He forced his smile.

"Right on time," she said, presenting her hand in greeting. "I'm Lynn Atkinson."

Yassin knew he was almost a half-hour late. But he let the comment pass. He gave her hand a cursory shake.

"How was the drive?" she asked.

He noticed her shorter-than-normal skirt, the tightness of her blouse. "The drive was wonderful," he said.

"Really? No traffic?"

"There is always traffic, as I'm sure you know. But it was lighter than usual today, for some reason."

"Good, good," she said too abruptly. "Shall we get started?" She turned.

Another infidel without manners, Yassin was thinking as he followed her into the house.

• • • • •

There was a monstrous chandelier hanging in the foyer. Much of the furniture ran from gaudy to bizarre. There was a black and white, ultramodern pattern on the dining room chairs. The oversized couch in the den was upholstered in bearskin. A brass sculpture of a female nude stood next to it. The walls were adorned with painted landscapes in freeform style.

After leading the way past the huge kitchen, the woman paused. "Butler's pantry," she said as if she were proud. "Every house should have one."

Yassin didn't know what she was talking about. He took in the alcove between the kitchen and main dining room. It was replete with a mini-bar, fridge, and storage cabinets. He concluded it was a waste of both money and space.

The tour continued. From library to family room to basement. Over twelve thousand-square-feet in all.

When they were done, the sales agent handed him a brochure. "Rent is reasonable," she said. "Only twenty-eight thousand a month, furnished. When may I expect your call?"

Not any time soon, Yassin wanted to tell her. "I'll be in touch next week," he said instead.

• • • • •

The drive back was tedious. He used every precaution to confirm he wasn't being followed. It was late afternoon by the time he arrived at his destination in downtown Manhattan.

He pulled up to the curb and turned off the motor.

Another car, a blue Lexus, was parked close by. A short man with an aquiline nose and large, black-rimmed glasses slowly hobbled toward him. His left leg was deformed. "Mr. Carson?"

Disliking the agent at first sight, he held his silence.

"You are Mr. Carson, are you not?" the man asked.

"I am."

"Stanley Vineberg." No offer to shake hands. "You're late."

He silently railed against this American. And it upset him that he could not act, to cut this Jew with the knife he was already fingering in his pocket.

Inside the house, on his tour, Yassin could see that it was gloomy but spacious. There were enough rooms to lodge a small army. The walls were sufficiently thick to deflect noise. Now, as he descended from basement to subbasement, he knew he had found what he wanted.

"How much?" he asked once they returned to the main floor.

"As I mentioned to you on the phone," the real estate agent said, "the owner does not want to be bothered with any request for modifications. You take it the way it is. Furnished. Minimum twelve-month lease. Twenty-six thousand a month."

Yassin held his temper. It wasn't the money so much as the principal. That, and this despicable person he was dealing with. "I'm afraid twenty a month is as far as I can go," he said.

"Twenty-five?"

"Twenty."

"Twenty-two-five. I don't believe the owner will go lower than that."

Yassin paused. He was tempted to place his hands around the agent's throat. To choke the life out of him. "Twenty is all I can offer," he said.

Mr. Vineberg rocked on his feet as if lost in contemplation. "You strike a hard bargain, Mr. Carson."

"Ah, well," he said, using a phrase he'd only recently learned, "you win some, you lose some."

CHAPTER 28

In the kitchen, Blair looked down upon the mess the intruder had made. He kicked aside the boxes of cereal and canned goods that had been thrown to the floor. Then he took a seat at the table, picked up the phone, and dialed.

When Mandy answered, he asked to speak to his daughter.

"Blair," she said, "I was just going to call you. I was hoping you could come over tomorrow evening for a chat."

"Where's Sandra?" he asked.

"She's playing in her room. Did you hear what I just said?"

"I heard you, Mandy. Go get Sandra, please. I need to talk to her."

"Blair—"

He exploded: "Go get her, goddammit!"

The line went dead.

He held onto the receiver. He knew he shouldn't have shouted. Losing control wasn't going to help. He redialed but got a busy signal. He waited five minutes before dialing the number again.

"Hello?"

"Sandra?" He almost choked with relief.

"Yes, Daddy. Mommy says you wanted to talk to me."

"I did—I mean, I do. How are you?"

No reply.

"Is everything okay at school?"

He waited.

"Darling?"

"I'm here, Daddy. But why does your voice sound funny?"

"It does?" Leave it to a child to pick out the nuances. "Does this sound better, Pumpkin Head?"

She giggled.

"Sandra," he said, "your mother wants me to come over tomorrow night. Maybe you and I can go out for an ice cream. Would that be okay with you?"

"I like ice cream. But not for dinner."

"No, no. After dinner, darling. It'll be your dessert."

"Okay. Can I have pis...um…piss… You know, the green-colored one."

"Pistachio?"

"Yes. *Pis-tach-o*."

"Pistachio it will be," he said.

"Hold on, Daddy. Mommy wants to talk to you."

He thought of stopping her, but it was already too late.

"Blair, I need to see you."

"So you said. What's this about?"

"We'll discuss it tomorrow night."

"Keep Sandra home from school."

"*What?*"

"I need you to do this for me. Keep her home from school. Not just tomorrow, but for the rest of the week."

"Have you lost your mind? Why would you ask such a thing?"

Dalton had warned he would play hardball. And Blair had seen evidence of that tonight. How much further the agent would go was anyone's guess. "I realize how this must sound to you," he said, making up the spiel as he went along. "But my business has gotten a little weird recently. Threats have been made."

"Against you?"

God, this was hard. "Against me, you, our daughter. That's why I want to use caution."

"What kind of threats are we talking about?"

"Does it matter?"

"Yes, it matters! I will not take my daughter out of school because you have personally been threatened. We have absolutely nothing to do with your business. Now, are you coming over tomorrow night or not?"

"Mandy, please," he tried to reason with her.

"Yes or no?"

He didn't know what other argument he could use. He was flying on a hunch. And that hunch could be wrong. "Okay," he finally said. "What time did you have in mind?"

"Around six o'clock."

He remembered promising his daughter dessert. Now he could spend even more time with her. "Maybe I'll buy Sandra dinner afterwards," he said.

"Fine. That won't be a problem."

"And what about school?"

"What about it?"

"Can you keep her home, at least for tomorrow?"

"Goodbye, Blair."

CHAPTER 29

Early the next morning Blair was at the gym. The cardio portion of his routine was out of the way. He was just starting the first of two sets of weight and conditioning training.

He took a seat at the cable rowing machine and automatically checked the current setting. One hundred and ten pounds. Almost double his capacity. He quickly glanced around, trying to pick out the colossus that had used the machine last.

He readjusted the weight to sixty pounds and began his twenty reps.

The break-in at his apartment had definitely set him off. Blair wished there were a magic elixir, a potion he could swallow to raise his height from five ten, to increase his weight from a hundred and sixty-seven pounds.

He observed the others in the gym. He caught sight of spandex and tank tops, the posers already in place, seldom spotting a mirror they didn't like. Most were hulks craving reaffirmation that their bodies hadn't sagged in the last five seconds or so.

Blair wondered what it would be like to have time to pamper himself, to not have commitments, to not have a care in the world.

He went to use the knee-flexor machine. Once more he had to change the weight. He lowered it from seventy-five to forty pounds. Halfway through, he felt a twinge in his back. Another reminder that he wasn't completely healed from the ordeal he'd been through in Israel.

What a wimp, he thought, as he went from triceps press-down to vertical bench press, readjusting one weight after the other, all the while disparaging himself.

• • • • •

Jeremy Samson called him via Skype before ten in the morning and told him they had a bit of a problem with the competitive product. "It concerns our lawsuit," he said, just as the video feed came into focus.

Blair took in the computer screen. His own face popped up in the top left-hand corner. "What kind of a problem?" he asked.

"We served our papers last week. To our surprise, we got served in return. Looks like it's not going to be as quick a process as I first believed."

"So what does this mean for our launch?"

"Nothing. It means nothing, *boychick*. That's why I'm talking to you. In case you hear more rumors. The guy isn't going to go quietly. Fine. Our lawyer assures us we'll still win in the end. Meanwhile, carry on like normal. Okay? Remain confident."

"Yeah, sure," Blair said, not feeling confident at all.

• • • • •

Just before four o'clock it was time to leave for Long Island. He had brought his car into work that morning. He walked toward the outdoor lot on 39th Street where he had a monthly arrangement.

The attendant, a young Hispanic man who always seemed to have a smile on his face, handed over his keys and went to move the double- and triple-parked cars that were in the way.

Blair figured two hours would suffice to make it to Queens. But the moment he got on the FDR he could see he'd be cutting it close. The bottleneck appeared to run forever. One of the benefits of living in a metropolis like New York, he grimly reminded himself.

He turned on the radio but kept the volume low. He occupied his time by wondering why Mandy wanted to see him. Most likely it concerned her moving to Los Angeles. Just as Sandra had warned.

Horns began to honk. It was the New Yorker's way of letting off steam. There wasn't anything specific upon which he could blame the slow traffic. It was stop-and-go most of the way.

Still, he made it with ten minutes to spare. He turned the corner on to his old street. This was the part of Flushing that had never appealed to him. He pulled into the driveway of the modest house. Then he shut the engine and got out of his car.

The door flew open before he could knock.

Mandy was standing there, trembling. Behind her he could see her boyfriend, Frank. His arm was draped around her shoulder.

"Sandra's missing," Mandy said. "She never came home from school." Her voice was shrill.

Blair waited for the punch line, waited for his ex-wife to tell him this was a joke. But nothing more was forthcoming. He turned, moved headlong toward his car.

"Where are you going?" Mandy called after him.

It took an effort to stop and look back. "I told you to keep her home from school!" he hollered at her. "Christ, Mandy! Why didn't you listen to me? One day! That's all I was asking! Would that have been such a bother?"

"Hey, don't turn this on me, mister! You said the threats were related to your business!"

"And that they could involve you and Sandra!"

"How?"

"I don't know how. There was nothing specific."

"Exactly! And you expected me to follow your suggestion on a … whim?"

"Mandy, we're wasting time. I'm going to her school."

"I've already been there. That's the first thing I did when she didn't show up."

"Did you call the police?"

"No, we were waiting for you."

His hand was just going to the car door. He let it drop. "Waiting for me? Why, for heaven's sake?"

"The school authorities suggested it. They wanted to first do a thorough search themselves. I figured by the time you got here, we'd know the results."

"But they haven't called?"

"No. Not yet."

"How long ago was this?"

"Um, almost an hour ago."

A full hour? For a moment, Blair wanted to throttle her. The school authorities were trying to protect their asses. And she had let them do it. "I'm going to the school anyway," he said.

He got in the car and started it.

His cell phone went off.

"We have your daughter," John Dalton said.

CHAPTER 30

He couldn't remember shutting off the engine. But he must have done so. The air conditioning had stopped working and it was now sweltering inside his car. He turned the motor back on.

"Blair?" He heard his name being called.

"You bastard!" he swore. "Who the hell are you, John?"

"You know who I am."

"No, I mean, really."

"What are you talking about?"

"There isn't a government agency in the world that would kidnap a six-year-old child!"

"Blair, we didn't kidnap her. We, uh, borrowed her for a while. To convince you to listen to reason."

"I want the name of your superior, your supervisor, whoever it is that you report to!"

"I'll be glad to give you his name, after your mission has been completed."

"No! I want it now!"

"You won't get it now, Blair."

He bit down on his lip. "How do I know my daughter is all right?"

"I guess you'll have to trust me."

"Trust you? That'll be the day! I want to talk to her, John."

"I can't let you do that."

"You sonofabitch! I will not cooperate!"

"Blair—" The agent's voice became conciliatory. "—has anyone ever counseled you about your temper?"

He was livid and petrified, both. "Let me see her, John." He tried another tack. "Please?"

"You'll see her when we want you to see her."

"What am I supposed to tell my wife?"

"You mean, your *ex*-wife, don't you? Make up something. But whatever you do, don't tell her the truth. Just get out of the car now and go talk to her."

Blair jerked his head around. The bastard was watching him. "Where are you, John?"

"Closer than you think. Now, go talk to Mandy. And keep her boyfriend out of this."

Again, he tried to find him. He lowered himself in his seat, looked in front, in back, both sides.

"Make up a good story," the agent instructed. "Talk to your ex, then call me back. Do you still have the card I gave you? It's got my mobile number on it."

"No, I don't have your card."

Dalton recited the number. Then he uttered his warning again: "Don't divulge the truth to your ex-wife, Blair. Or to anyone else, for that matter. Unless you want to endanger Sandra's life."

The phone went dead.

CHAPTER 31

He remained in his car.

Reason was telling him that Dalton's agency was run by the U.S. government. They wouldn't harm his daughter. But experience dictated that the agent himself was completely untrustworthy and capable of doing anything.

Blair didn't know what he should say. Mandy wasn't stupid. She would pick out any lies he tried to tell in a heartbeat. His only course, he decided, would be to walk the thin line between fact and fiction.

He stepped out of his car. The clouds were darkening, the breeze picking up.

"What's wrong?" Mandy asked as he approached. "You look like you've seen a ghost."

"Can I talk to you?"

She indicated her boyfriend. "You can talk in front of Frank."

"No. I mean in private, Mandy."

She hesitated. Then she followed him back along the driveway until they reached the curb. "What is it?" she asked angrily.

"I just spoke to a friend of mine," he said, without a clue where the story was coming from. "The guy's a cop. Sandra's okay. But she has to stay under his protection. The police are concerned that Sandra could be used as bait, to draw me out. But you mustn't discuss this with anyone. Especially not with Frank."

"Why not?"

"Because it could compromise our daughter's safety. I'm just following orders here, Mandy."

"How long will they have to keep her?"

"I don't know. Until the threat against me is nullified. Maybe a week or two at the most."

"A *week or two?*"

"Maybe less," he quickly said. His lies were becoming second nature to him.

"Can I see her, then?"

"Uh-uh. It would be too dangerous."

"But, I'm her *mother*! What's the name of this police friend of yours? I want to talk to him."

"Mandy, don't make this worse. You don't want to put Sandra's life in jeopardy, do you?"

"I have a right to see my own daughter!"

"You can't. Just be cool for now. Okay? I'll try to find out more."

It began to drizzle. Still, Mandy seemed hesitant to seek shelter. "Why do I have the feeling I'm being manipulated?" she asked.

"It's raining," Blair said, hoping for a reprieve.

"I don't care about the damn rain! I want to know what you're not telling me!"

Blair wished this charade could end. "I've told you everything I know. You've got to trust me."

"I'll give you one week," she said. "Not a day longer."

"What are you talking about? I already mentioned how long this could take."

"One week, Blair," she said. And she walked away.

• • • • •

He waited for her to reach the house. He watched her lips to see if she was already relating their discussion to her boyfriend.

It was impossible to tell.

He got in his car and slowly backed out of the driveway.

A few blocks later, still in a residential area, he pulled over to the curb. He needed to think. But the confined space felt restrictive. He opened the door and stepped onto the sidewalk.

A car came to a quick stop behind him. Before he could move, the driver rushed out and confronted him. "Mr. Mulligan," he said, "John Dalton would like to have that meeting with you now."

Blair waited.

The man moved in and put an arm on his shoulder.

He shook it loose.

Unfortunately, the one man became three, each massive, incongruously wearing a suit and tie.

"Mr. Mulligan," the same man repeated. He tried to guide him toward the car.

At first, Blair didn't resist. But then something snapped. His daughter had been taken hostage. These were obviously the men responsible. His brain shut down and a feral instinct took over. He fought even though he wasn't a fighter. And he wanted to give as much as he got. Even as his nose was flattened, making it difficult to breathe. Even as a tooth rattled in his mouth, causing him to spit blood.

He continued to flail away, until a punch connected with the side of his head.

Images began to blur … and he descended into darkness.

CHAPTER 32

Blair was on his hands and knees, throwing up in the toilet of a darkened bathroom.

Gradually, the nausea eased.

He wiped his lips with the back of his hand.

Other than the incident in Israel, he had only been knocked out once before, when a neighborhood friend, Tommy Curry, had taken a shovel to the back of his head. He'd been all of seven years old at the time.

Now, he leaned back on his haunches and tried to get his bearings. He searched for something in the dark to act as a focal point. He reached a hand out until it made contact with the wall.

He was just coming out of the bathroom when someone opened the door to the window-less room. The light was so strong, he had to shut his eyes for a moment.

"Mr. Mulligan?" a female voice inquired.

He imagined someone young.

"Rena Castaway," she introduced herself.

He opened his eyes.

Castaway was not only young, but attractive. A brunette. In her mid-twenties, he guessed.

She motioned; he followed. Along a dingy corridor, past three locked doors, behind which he could hear muted voices.

"Are you hungry?" she asked, a slight accent in her voice.

He figured he was in the basement of a house or townhouse. "Hungry?" he repeated.

"Yes. It's almost dinnertime. Perhaps I can fix you something to eat?"

"No," he said. The thought of food made him ill. "But I could use some water." It came out like "*wadder*."

"Fair enough," she said.

They came to a kitchen and Castaway led the way inside. There was a stove, refrigerator, double sink, and a dozen or so cupboards. The windows were covered by black curtains.

She lit a candle and placed it on the wrought-iron monstrosity of a table. "Have a seat," she said.

The metal chair screeched as he moved it back on the tiled floor.

"Are you all right?"

He sat in the chair, his hands doing a lousy job of supporting his chin. "I'm fine," he said, as a fresh wave of dizziness swept over him.

"Take this," she instructed. She placed two pills and a glass of water in front of him.

He sat, staring at them, wondering if she was trying to poison him.

"They're aspirins," Castaway said as if she could read his mind.

He forced his head up. "Can I ask you a question?"

"Of course."

"How long have I been here?"

"A little over two days."

"And what happened to my nose?" It sounded like "*node*."

"Your nose suffered a bit of damage. But it's not broken. You also have a chipped tooth, plus the odd cut. Nothing serious. We had a doctor examine you."

That accent of hers; he couldn't place it. "Where's John Dalton?" he asked.

"He's tied up."

"Such a busy man…"

"What's that?"

"Do you work with Mr. Dalton?"

"Yes, of course. We all work together."

"Like one big, happy family?"

"I'm sorry. I really can't make out what you are saying."

"I could use a coffee," Blair requested.

"Take the pills, Mr. Mulligan," Castaway said. "They'll help you." She placed the kettle on the stove. She stood by it as if her presence could bring the water to a boil sooner.

Finally, she poured the coffee and carried it to him. She leaned in close. Her ample bosom brushed against his shoulder. "Here you go," she said. "You take it black, don't you?"

His stomach roiled from the aroma, then settled. He took a tentative sip. *How does she know I take it black?* he wondered. *And was that breast-brush an accident or intentional?*

Neither spoke until he finished the coffee. Then he asked if he could see his daughter.

"She isn't here," Castaway said.

"Oh? Where is she, then?"

"I'm not at liberty to say." She turned.

He became aware of how short her skirt was, falling five or six inches above the knee.

"Wait here a moment," she said. "I'll be right back."

• • • • •

After she left, he slowly came to his feet. He began to probe into the cupboards and drawers. There were no secret documents, nothing incriminating he could use against John Dalton.

He reclaimed his seat. His head began to throb. A quick nap would be nice, he was thinking, just as Castaway returned.

"Here," she said, handing him an envelope.

Opening it, he found an airline ticket to Tel Aviv. He placed it on the table.

An awkward moment passed between them.

Castaway came to his side. She touched his shoulder in a provocative way. Then she told him that he must hold on to the ticket.

He began to wonder what would happen next. If her sweater would come off in a slow tease.

"You and I must reach an understanding," she said.

He purposely played dumb. "What do you mean?"

"Your return trip to Israel."

"I'll let you know," he said. "Now, if you don't mind, I'd like to get out of here."

Castaway's face sagged. "You can't leave yet."

"I want my daughter back."

"You *will* get her back, after this is over."

"No. I want her back now, before I consider helping you."

"Blair, I explained that this isn't possible."

He noticed the change to a first-name basis. "Too bad, then," he said as he stood.

"Listen to reason. *Please?*"

"I've listened to enough reason," he said.

• • • • •

Still unsteady on his feet, Blair entered the corridor. He headed in the direction opposite to the one they'd taken earlier.

"You'll need a key to get out," Castaway advised.

That stopped him.

"But I can't let you go yet," she said.

He held his ground, told her he was leaving whether she liked it or not.

She looked daggers his way. Then, like a chameleon, she quickly changed back to her more pleasant persona. "Have a seat in the kitchen. I'll see about your release."

"I'll wait here." He indicated the empty hallway.

"But there's nowhere to sit."

"I like standing."

Her sigh was close to a groan.

When she returned some ten minutes later, there was a burly character with her, all neck and shoulders. "We'll have to blindfold you," he said.

Blair didn't comment. He didn't want to lose his nerve or to have them gain theirs. The blindfold went on and he was led up a flight of stairs. Along a hallway and finally outside. The blindfold loosened a little and he was able to catch a partial glimpse of the exterior of the house. Unusual brown brick. Black-framed windows with shutters. And an address ending with the digits 7-5-6.

They guided him into the backseat of a car.

The ride was quick; less than five minutes. No one spoke. They came to a stop and he was asked to get out. "Do not remove the blindfold for sixty seconds," Castaway warned.

He counted to ten before ripping it off.

• • • • •

Blair observed his surroundings.

He was close to the East River. He caught the name of the street he was on as well as the one on the opposite corner.

He began to walk, keeping his eyes peeled for a cab. It was late afternoon. The sun was barely visible in the clouds. Before he could go a hundred paces, he heard his name being called.

"Don't turn around," John Dalton said.

He turned.

The agent's appearance surprised him. Gone was his suit and tie, replaced by blue jeans and sweater. His always-perfect hair was disheveled. And his dark eyes, usually cold and penetrating, now seemed to have softened somewhat.

"Blair," Dalton said, "I need you to pretend you don't know me."

He refused to cooperate.

"This is serious."

"So is kidnapping my daughter."

"We didn't kidnap her."

"I want an explanation, John."

"All right. You'll get one. But I need you to keep moving. Both our lives are at stake."

He didn't believe him. But he brought his eyes forward and began to walk.

"They are getting close," the agent said, keeping a few paces behind. "Should anything happen to me, you are to work with Rena Castaway. She has your best interest— "

Suddenly, gunfire rang out.

"Run!" Dalton shouted.

Blair's pulse spiked. He had no idea where the shots were coming from. He was just scouring the rooftops, when a bullet whizzed past.

Dalton groaned, stumbled, and went down.

Blair bent over him.

"Save yourself," the agent breathed.

The gunfire was getting closer.

He didn't want to leave Dalton alone. He searched the man's waist and found his gun. He'd never handled a weapon in his life. Blair's hands were of average size. But the gun felt awkward when he palmed it.

There were two shooters that he could see. And they were gaining ground. He took aim above their heads and pulled the trigger. The impact blew him back on his butt.

"You mustn't let them catch you," Dalton barely whispered.

Blair rolled onto his side, uncertain what to do next.

The sight of the two men retreating made up his mind for him. That, as well as the car just coming into view, the same one that had transported him a few minutes ago. He could make out Rena Castaway, seated in the front passenger seat.

He dropped the gun.

Then he rose to his feet, turned, and ran.

CHAPTER 33

He unlocked the door to his condo, hurried into the kitchen, and removed a highball glass. He barely had it in his hand when the glass fell and shattered on the floor.

Blair stood for a moment, shaking his head.

He cleaned up as many of the broken pieces he could find, then reached into the cupboard for another glass. He filled it with ice, poured the Scotch and, holding on with both hands, dragged himself into the den. He took a seat on the sofa, gulped the liquor, then began to replay the shooting of John Dalton. There was a surreal feel to it. He knew it had happened and that he was involved, but it was almost as if it had happened to someone else.

He quickly finished his drink, leaned back on the sofa, and closed his eyes. He was half asleep when the doorbell rang. He heard the ringing but willed it to go away. Only when it persisted did he force himself to his feet. He approached the intercom and pressed the buzzer.

It didn't take long for Rena Castaway to reach his door. She seemed overcome with emotion. He barely had time to greet her when she fell into his arms. "Thank God you're unharmed," she said.

"Rena—" He tried to pull away.

"Shh," she muttered, holding on for dear life.

He wormed out of her embrace. "How is John?" he asked.

"John?"

"Yes. How is he?"

"...dead."

"*Dead?*" Blair rocked back on his heels.

"Yes," she said. "That's why I was so worried about you." She began to cry.

Blair didn't know how to react. John Dalton was not someone he could ever like. But to be killed this way, gunned down on the street. It shook him more than he would have thought possible.

"May I come in?" Castaway asked.

He'd forgotten they were still standing in the entranceway. "Sorry," he said. He waved her in and closed the door behind her. "Would you like something to drink?"

"No, thank you."

He retrieved his glass in the den. Then he led the way into the kitchen, where he invited Castaway to have a seat.

He sat down opposite her at the table.

"Please take this," she said, very businesslike.

He opened the envelope and found a card with her direct line listed. And the same airline ticket she had offered him before.

"Your flight leaves at the end of the week," Castaway explained. "You will ask a personal favor of Jeremy Samson. We just need him to slice off the mini DVDs to OTE."

Blair shook his head in exasperation. "It won't work," he said. "Don't you get it? Jeremy turned me down."

"Tell him your bank insists upon it."

"I've already tried that."

"We need you to catch the El Al flight," Castaway said, ignoring his comments. "These people suspect we are close. If they are desperate enough to shoot down one of our agents, there is no telling what else they might do. Let Jeremy know that your bank will cancel your company's line of credit unless he comes through for you."

He no longer had the will to resist. But the thought dawned on him that he could use this opportunity as leverage. "I will agree, but on one condition," he said. "I want my daughter to make the trip with me. You can drop her off here, before my flight, or at the airport. I don't care which. But I will not go without her."

"That can't happen."

"Why not?"

"Because—" She paused.

"Look," he said, "either Sandra comes with me to Israel or I don't go. It's as simple as that."

Castaway began to pace the room, the minutes passing in awkward silence.

"Well?" he finally pushed.

"All right," she said. "We'll have your daughter at the airport."

• • • • •

The phone rang a few minutes after she had left. He picked it up in the bedroom.

"I've been trying to reach you," his ex-wife said in an obviously irate frame of mind. "Why haven't you answered my calls?"

He couldn't tell her the truth. "I was traveling," he said.

"Traveling? While your daughter is being held? Some father you turned out to be."

"Mandy—"

"You have twenty-four hours. If I don't have Sandra back by then, I will hit you with the biggest, goddamn lawsuit you've ever seen in your life! For child endangerment, if nothing else! *Capisce?*"

He couldn't blame her for being upset. "Just hold on for a while longer," he pleaded.

"I will," Mandy said defiantly. "For twenty-four hours."

• • • • •

Blair went to the bathroom, where he made the mistake of peeking in the mirror. His eyes were blackened, his nose swollen. A welt on his cheek left the surrounding skin discolored.

After washing his hands, he headed into the den. He picked up his BlackBerry and dialed Lisa's number.

"I'm free tonight," she told him once he got her on the line.

"I can't tonight," he said.

"Oh? Why not?"

"Too much work to do."

"At home?"

"Uh-huh. I have to go back to Israel. Something urgent came up. But I won't be gone long. And then you'll be able to see me as often as you'd like." *Once the damage to my face has cleared up*, he neglected to say.

"Promise?"

"Yes, ma'am," he said.

• • • • •

Blair turned on the TV. He flipped the channel to CNN. He was curious to see if John Dalton's murder made the news. After watching for several minutes, he switched to the other networks: NBC, CBS, ABC. There was no late breaking story. Nothing out of the ordinary.

A vision of his daughter popped into his head. He wanted to send her a telepathic message. He wanted to let her know that her daddy was thinking about her, that very soon they would be reunited.

He hoped and prayed…

CHAPTER 34

"Blair, it's about Mom," his sister, Cynthia, was saying on the phone. "I don't mean to alarm you, but she's taken a turn for the worse."

He steadied himself. "How much worse?"

"She's not going to die, if that's what you're asking. But her lucid moments are becoming far less frequent."

"Shit!"

"Sorry. I shouldn't have bothered you. I just thought you'd like to know."

"It's no bother at all. I'm glad that you called." He paused.

All day long he'd been racking his brain for someone he could turn to for advice. His ex-wife was adversarial. Jeremy Samson was his best friend. But he, more than anyone else, was involved in this situation, whether he realized it or not. Andrew Sciascia, his lawyer and another friend, was a good guy, though Blair didn't believe they were sufficiently close. So that left only one prospect. Why not turn to his sister? If he went to Montreal he could visit his mother, then spend time with Cynthia. He would confide in her. She would have a different perspective on things.

"Blair?" she was saying now.

"I'm here."

"What are you thinking?"

Go for it, he told himself. "Look, how would you feel about my driving up there? If I leave early tomorrow morning, I can be at your place by mid-to-late afternoon."

"*Really?* That would be wonderful."

"Okay," he said. "If there's any delay, I'll call you. Oh— " He caught himself. "One more thing. Make dinner arrangements at Gibby's for us."

"Gibby's? Isn't that a little extravagant?"

"No problem. You deserve it. See you tomorrow, Cyn."

• • • • •

He was on the road the next morning before six.

Some three and a half hours later, he was driving through the Adirondacks. The clouds had darkened and a light hail was beginning to fall, making the condition of the road precarious.

He questioned his decision to drive instead of fly. But he had lost faith in air travel, the hassle it had become.

A Daughtry song came on the radio. It was the second week of May but many of the farms Blair passed still evidenced a light blanketing of snow.

He was getting closer to Canada.

• • • • •

When his sister opened the door to her apartment, a bachelor pad in the Montreal suburb of Notre Dame de Grace, Blair was taken aback by her weight. The moment they embraced, however, he realized how much he missed her. And that was all that mattered.

She held him at arm's length. "My God, what happened to you, Blair? Your face…"

"It's nothing."

"Nothing? Not only your face. It looks like you lost twenty pounds. Tell me your secret. I could use a little weight loss myself … as you can see." She did a pirouette. "But never mind. With the crappy weather just about gone, I'll start jogging again. It's the damn winter that does this to me. Too friggin' cold to do anything."

They gave each other another hug.

His sister liked to talk and for once Blair found it therapeutic. He became lost in such mundane topics as their cousins and their kids, everything that had happened to them in the past six months or so. These were not thumbnail sketches, by any means.

Then Cynthia mentioned the man she was dating, a fireman. She wasn't in love, she said. But her relationship with the guy was the next best thing.

Blair observed that even with her added weight, his sister was still attractive. Over five feet, five inches tall, blonde hair cut short. Smooth, wrinkle-free skin. Her face was only marred by the Mulligan curse, the start of a double chin.

"Where's your bag?" Cynthia asked. "I thought you were staying over?"

He moved into the foyer. And his heart sank. "It's in the car," he said. "I'll get it later."

Disposophobia was the clinical term for her condition, an obsessive-compulsive disorder that caused her to hoard newspapers and magazines, shoes, clothing, and everything in between. But to Blair, "hoard" wasn't sufficiently descriptive.

Cynthia's apartment was designed in an open style. But its concept was defeated by the columns of unwanted goods. They were piled almost to the ceiling. Along the walls in the foyer. In the kitchen. Throughout the hallway.

She caught his expression. "Don't say it," she said.

"I thought you had it under control," he admonished.

"Blair..."

He didn't want to criticize. But it hurt him to see that Cynthia wasn't getting any better.

• • • • •

"Do you want to wash up before we head out?" his sister asked a few minutes later. "You must be exhausted from the drive. Can I get you a drink?"

He gave her arm a squeeze. "It's so good to see you," he said.

She placed her hands on his shoulders. "Good to see you, too. But you are troubled, my brother. I can see it in your eyes. Blair, we don't have to go out. I made a reservation at Gibby's, like you requested, but I can cancel it."

"No, no, Gibby's is fine," he said, "but let's leave now, so we can spend some time with Mom."

Cynthia nodded. "Okay. My car or yours?"

On the rare occasions he had allowed his sister to drive, he'd felt in need of a tranquilizer. "We'll take mine," he said.

• • • • •

Blair knew that Montreal was an easy city in which to get around. Especially in May. If this were mid-summer, road construction on most major routes would likely have been slowing traffic to a crawl.

From N.D.G., he took Cote des Neiges. They entered the downtown core some ten minutes later. A few turns and they were parked at the special-care facility that housed their mother.

Cynthia led the way inside the converted three-story office building. There was a strong antiseptic smell in the air. Nurses and doctors were speaking in hushed tones. The reception area was painted an austere shade of gray.

"Est'ce que je peux vous aider?" a woman in her mid-sixties, wearing a form-fitting off-white dress, called to them from the lone desk. "Ah, Cynthia," she caught herself. *"Je m'excuse. Je ne vous ai pas vu."* She indicted toward Blair. *"Et c'est ton frère, j'imagine?"*

"Oui," Cynthia said. Then she switched to English. "Blair, meet Monique. Monique, Blair."

He approached the desk and shook the woman's hand. This was not the same receptionist he'd met the last time he had visited. *"C'est un plaisir,"* he said, enjoying the use of what little French he still remembered.

"The pleasure is all mine," Monique said in perfect English.

Her smile was infectious. And it dawned on Blair how charming most French Canadian women were, no matter their age or status in life.

"I guess you've come to visit your mother," Monique said. "Let me call someone who will bring you to her." She reached for the phone.

• • • • •

The wait took longer than expected. Finally, a male orderly dressed in hospital green led the way to their mother's private room. The unit was of average size, approximately twelve by fourteen.

The apparition Blair spotted on the bed frightened him. Much of the woman he remembered was gone. She'd been replaced by a stick figure. Skin and bones, and not much else.

"Ian?" his mother said when she saw him.

Blair moved closer to the bed. "No. It's me, Mother. Your son. Not your husband."

The woman raised a scarecrow arm. Then she yanked the bottom denture from her mouth and cackled. "I don't have a son." She pointed at Cynthia. "And whose bitch are you?"

Stunned, Blair felt his mouth go dry. In all the time he had lived at home, he had never known his mother to use foul language.

In commiseration, his sister placed her hand on his arm. "Mom," she said in a gentle voice. "Blair's driven in from New York to see you."

"Who?"

"Blair."

Their mother began to cry. Galloping tears streamed from her eyes.

Blair recalled their last telephone conversation. She had appeared to be losing it then. But this was worse.

Cynthia bent over the bed. She used a Kleenex to wipe her mother's eyes. "Now, now, Mom. You should be happy. Not sad."

As quickly as they had begun, the tears ceased. "Blair?" the woman questioned.

"Yes, it's me," he said, brightening.

"How is New York?"

He wanted to humor her. To keep her going on the straight and narrow. "New York is wonderful, Mother dear. Congested as usual. Do you remember the time you visited?"

A near-beatific look crossed the woman's face. "I remember," she said. Then her eyes closed, opened again. "Ian?" she said.

"No. It's Bla—" He caught Cynthia's head shake and stopped in mid-sentence. There was no point in correcting her.

His mother nodded off.

"She looks terrible," Blair said.

"She has her good days and her bad."

"Worse than this?" he was afraid to ask.

Cynthia shrugged. "No. Not worse."

He used what little comfort that knowledge brought him to silence his other concerns.

• • • • •

"Remember when you were a kid," Cynthia broke into his thoughts a short time later. "And Tommy Curry bopped you in the head with that shovel? The doctor suggested Mother keep a twenty-four hour vigil. Instead, she took it upon herself to monitor your breathing non-stop for five full days. She wouldn't let you out of her sight. Morning, noon, and night. Dad got really pissed at her."

"He did?"

"Who could blame him? She stopped making his meals. Sharing his bed. All because poor Blair was hurting."

"I wish I could remember."

"You were only seven."

A noise came from the bed that startled them both. Their mother was talking in her sleep. But the voice was like that of someone possessed. It kept rising in pitch.

They looked at each other. Neither said a word. Then Cynthia broke into a laugh.

"What?" Blair said.

"I was thinking of the time I brought my first date home to meet Mom. We were only going to the movies. But she gave that boy the third degree. He was to be careful where he took me. He was not to leave me alone. And he was to naturally get me back at a decent hour. I never heard from him again."

Blair caught his sister's laughter turning to tears.

"Dammit," Cynthia said. "Why couldn't she grow old with dignity?"

CHAPTER 35

Back in the car, Blair asked his sister if she was hungry.

She shook her head. "Uh-uh. What time is it?"

"Umm—six of six. When's our reservation for?"

"Seven. Do you want me to change it?"

"No, no. Seven is fine. Let's take a drive first."

"Okay. A drive would be nice."

Blair knew exactly where he wanted to go. As a young man, when dating, he would often end up atop Mount Royal, the mountain that separated the downtown core from the rest of the city.

More a hill than a mountain, Mount Royal would be subject to ridicule for its compact size were it not for the impressive view the "lookout" afforded of the south-eastern extremity of the island. In the distance, one could see the St. Lawrence River and part of the town of Longueuil beyond it.

There were no other cars when they arrived. And Blair could see why. The signs, written only in French, warned about a sinkhole. The road and much of the protective barrier of trees and shrubbery had been torn away.

Despite the warning, however, and not to be deterred, he pulled in and parked.

In front of them, void of vegetation, they could see the drop. It was long and precipitous. Nothing but rocks and tree stumps trailing most of the way down.

Blair shut the motor and set the emergency brake. Then he leaned back. "Okay, bring me up to date," he said. He was hoping they could divert themselves from the subject of their mother for at least the time being.

"About what?" Cynthia asked.

"I want to know more about this fireman you're dating. His name, age, social status, the works."

"His name is Francois. French Canadian and lovely."

"Oh yeah? Like Marcel?"

She laughed. "Wasn't he a beaut?"

Blair recalled that Marcel, a hairdresser, was unusually thin, practically bald, and had the annoying habit of squinting whenever he spoke. "What did you ever see in him?" he asked.

"I don't know. But he was great in bed."

"Cyn!" he said in mock horror.

"Blair—" She grew serious. "—what do you do to relax?"

"Relax? I don't understand the concept."

"I was afraid you'd say that." She turned toward him. "Do you still golf?"

"Not often enough."

"But you love the game."

"Yeah, I do."

"Did you know I've taken it up?"

That startled him. "You?"

"Yes. Why are you surprised?"

"I don't know," he said. "I thought you once told me the game was stupid."

"It *is* stupid."

"So?"

"I find it's a great way to meet men. That's how I met Francois, as a matter of fact."

He laughed.

She reached out and squeezed his hand. "I really hate seeing you this way."

"Which way is that?"

"C'mon, Blair," she said. "You can't kid a kidder." Her favorite expression.

"Cyn…" he began to say, intending to move the subject away from himself, when he felt something hard collide with the back of his car.

• • • • •

His sister screamed.

Blair quickly looked in his rearview mirror. All he could see was the front end of a truck. A blob of blue.

The truck was pushing them forward.

He hit the brakes.

Nothing happened.

Then he remembered they were power assisted. He started the car and tried again.

Even with the emergency brake still engaged, they were being forced closer to the edge.

Cynthia's eyes widened. "Blair?"

"Hold on," he said.

It would be impossible to survive a drop of such depth, he knew. He quickly released the emergency brake, shifted into reverse, and floored it.

The tires spun crazily on the asphalt. He heard a screeching sound.

His car began to rock from the pressure.

The smell of burning rubber wafted into the air. But the Beemer was no match for the blue truck behind them.

Blair shoved the gear into park and slammed his foot on the brakes, trying to swallow his fear but not succeeding.

Think, an inner voice demanded.

"Cyn," he said, speaking quietly. "I need you to do something for me."

"W...what?" She was obviously going into shock.

"You must remain calm, Cynthia."

"We won't make it, Blair. I know we won't!"

"Listen to me," he said with more conviction than he felt. "We *will* make it. I promise." He tried to estimate the time they had left. He knew it was close. "Put your hand on the door handle," he instructed.

His sister didn't budge.

"Cyn?"

She turned to face him. "I don't want to die, Blair."

"You won't die."

"I will!" she shrieked.

"Cynthia, we're going to jump out of the car. It's our only chance."

"Jump?"

"Yes. I need you to follow my directions. Please, Cyn. You'll be all right. Now—take hold of the door handle."

She semi-positioned her hand. But it hovered.

"At the count of three," he said. "Grab the handle, push the door open, then roll out."

There was no response. His sister had gone mute.

"Cynthia? We have to do this. At the count of three. One..."

• • • • •

Gunfire rang out.

"Get down!" Blair hollered.

His sister crouched low.

After the incident with John Dalton, Blair had no doubt of the sound he was hearing. But were the shots aimed at them?

He bent as low as possible on the seat, waited for the bullets to strike, waited for the car's windows to shatter.

Miraculously, he sensed the pressure from behind relenting. Slowly, he raised himself up and glanced in his rearview mirror. The blue truck was flying into reverse.

He counted to ten in his head. "It's safe, Cyn," he said.

"I … don't know."

"Trust me. You can get out of the car. But be careful."

Blair stepped out himself and hurried around to the passenger side. Cynthia came into his arms with such force it knocked them both to the ground.

More gunfire, this time from afar.

He could feel his sister trembling. "We're okay," he said, wanting to reassure her. "We'll be okay."

The blue truck was barreling up the road. It was being pursued by a beige box of a car that looked vaguely familiar. He waited until both vehicles disappeared. "Can you stand?" he asked, turning back to Cynthia.

Her nod was not enthusiastic.

He helped her to her feet. "C'mon," he said, "let's see about the damage."

The trunk of the Beemer was slightly bent. There were a number of blue paint marks staining the bumper. "I thought it would be worse," he said, not wanting to traumatize his sister any further.

Blair guided Cynthia back into the car. He closed her door, came around to the driver's side. "Ready for Gibby's?" he asked, forcing a measure of normality in his voice.

Cynthia glanced his way. "Aren't you going to call the police?"

"The police?" he questioned a bit too emphatically.

His sister regarded him as if he had two heads. "Oh, my God!" she said. "What in the world have you gotten yourself into?"

CHAPTER 36

As he drove he monitored traffic, fearful that they might be followed, that the people in the blue truck—he now believed it to be a Ford Explorer—were not done with them yet.

They were on the way back to Cynthia's apartment. His sister had made it clear that she couldn't possibly think of going to a restaurant. And he had agreed. But he traveled a circuitous route. When they arrived, he found the identical parking spot he had occupied before, which he took to be a good omen.

He grabbed his overnight bag and followed Cynthia out of the car and into her building. They rode the elevator in silence, and exited on the eighth floor.

Cynthia opened the door to her apartment. She hit the lights, then dimmed them. "Scotch?" she asked. She was already leading the way into the living room.

She pushed a stack of old newspapers and other waste aside. The small bar had been set up next to the credenza. She struggled to get the door open. "Here," she said, handing him a bottle of Chivas. "You pour."

Blair filled two glasses with ice. Then he tipped the bottle until their glasses were full. He handed her one and quickly took his first sip.

Reality hit them both at the same time.

Cynthia came into his arms.

They stood in place as if dazed.

There has to be an explanation, Blair was thinking.

"I made such an ass of myself," his sister said as she finally eased away.

"No, you didn't."

"I *did!* I panicked. I lost control."

"You were fine."

"I wasn't fine. It's just … I was so afraid."

"You were afraid? Let me tell you something, sis. I was never so close to puking in my life."

"Serious?" she said.

"Of course, I'm serious. So don't talk to me about being scared. Now, come. Let's get comfortable. And bring that bottle of Chivas with you."

• • • • •

With the stacks of refuse filling the apartment, Blair realized it had the appearance of being half its size. The living room also served as the den. Traditional furniture without anything too extravagant. Shades of burgundy, for the most part.

There was a Murphy bed for guests. They sat down on it.

A few minutes went by before Blair understood why the car that had come to their rescue looked familiar. A beige Chrysler. Lisa's car? But how did that make sense?

"What are you thinking?" Cynthia asked.

"I was thinking of how paranoid I'm becoming. A friend of mine in

New York drives the same kind of car that saved our butts today."

"Who is he?"

"She. He is a she. Someone I met recently. We've been dating."

She shot up. "You've been dating? A woman?" She smiled. "So Mandy's hold over you isn't what everyone believes?"

"Cyn, I just met her. Give it a chance."

"Oh, I will, baby brother. I will."

• • • • •

"Hungry now?" Blair asked. It was 9:00 PM and they still hadn't eaten.

His sister shook her head. "Not a bit. You?"

"Uh-uh. Let's just drink."

She wagged a cautionary finger. "Not good for you."

"I know," he said as he sipped.

"You'll wake up with a hangover."

"I know that, too."

"But you don't care?"

"I don't." He picked up the bottle. "May I pour you some?"

"Oh, what the hell." She proffered her glass.

They both laughed. But it was fleeting.

Cynthia grew serious. She asked what was going on.

"What do you mean?" he said, playing dumb.

"Blair, what have you gotten yourself into?"

"Me?"

"Yes, you."

He lifted his glass to his lips and drained the Scotch. He had come here today to confide in his sister. But this was now impossible. Trouble followed him wherever he went. There was no way he could involve her.

Cynthia poured them each another shot. "I want the truth," she said.

What the hell is the truth? he asked himself. *Do I even know? With all the crap that's been happening? Here in Montreal? In New York? In Israel?*

"Blair?"

His sister deserved an explanation. But he couldn't give her one. The less she knew, the less *anyone* knew, the better. "I think I'll hit the sack," he said. "Got a big drive ahead of me tomorrow."

Cynthia's look was one of concern. "I want you to know something," she said. "I'll be here for you. Whenever you need me. But if not me, then seek the help of a friend. Don't keep this locked up inside, Blair. Whatever it is. You'll compromise your health if you do. And I don't want to see that happen. Please. Will you promise me?"

He finally put his glass down. "I promise," he lied.

CHAPTER 37

Too many questions kept him awake. Why was John Dalton gunned down? What was Jeremy Samson's role in all of this? Who were the people in the blue truck?

The crawl out of bed the next morning was not a pretty sight. Shaving, he opened a cut on his chin. It didn't appear deep but he couldn't stem the flow of blood.

"Here you go," Cynthia said, once he coaxed himself to the breakfast table. She proffered a plate of bacon and eggs. "Coffee?" she asked, a little too cheerful for his liking.

He noticed four aspirins. They were standing like white Centurions, next to a tall glass of water. He forced them down slowly. His sister had been right. Drinking too much Scotch, especially on an empty stomach, was not beneficial to one's health.

Cynthia waited for him to finish eating. Then she handed him a Xerox copy of a Loto-Québec subscription for the entire year.

"For me?" he asked.

She nodded.

He stood and gave her a hug. "This is so nice of you. Thanks." He remained on his feet. "Before I go," he said, "I need you to do something for me."

"Anything."

"I want you to get help for your problem."

"I can't afford it. Psychological consultation isn't covered by the RAMQ."

Blair knew she was referring to the *Régie de l'Assurance Maladie du Québec*, the government body that handled the administration of the healthcare program in the Province of Quebec. "Screw the RAMQ," he said. "I'll pay for it."

"You can't!" His sister was adamant. "You're already paying for Mom. And you're not exactly rolling in dough."

"It doesn't matter."

"It matters to *me*."

"Cyn, let's not argue. You promised you would seek help."

"I will. On my own."

"You can't afford it on your own."

"So I'll wait."

"That's just it. You can't wait. Please, Cynthia."

Her frown turned into an oblique smile. "I'll tell you what," she said. "You tell me what's really going on in your life, why you arrived here in town with your face all beaten up, why someone in a blue truck tried to push us into oblivion yesterday, and I'll do as you ask."

He paused, tempted to come clean, but knowing he could not.

CHAPTER 38

By the time Blair reached his condo in New York, he was worn out from the drive. He had no sooner unpacked than he began to repack for the next day's trip to Israel. He did not plan on staying long so he chose as little as possible. As for Sandra, he would purchase clothes for her as soon as they arrived in Tel Aviv.

He opened the top drawer of his bedroom dresser and found his daughter's passport. Another stroke of luck, he figured. He had insisted they apply when Sandra had turned three. The passport arrived just before the breakup of his marriage. As far as he knew, Mandy wasn't even aware that he still had it in his possession.

• • • • •

Blair was in bed early but didn't get to sleep much before two-thirty in the morning. The alarm may have gone off but he missed it. When he finally awoke, he had to rush. The cab got him to Kennedy Airport with an hour to spare. He thought that was pretty good under the circumstances.

The clerk at El Al, a middle-aged woman with red hair, was not pleased, however. And the look she gave him was none too friendly.

Blair was disappointed to not see his daughter. Yes, they were holding Sandra's seat, the clerk advised, but they would not hold on to it much longer. "Our regulations call for each passenger to be here no later than two hours before departure," she admonished, pointing to the list of rules on display. "You have ten more minutes before we lock out all pre-assigned seats."

He turned away, tension creeping into his neck and shoulders. At the window he noticed streams of people disembarking from cabs and private cars.

There was no sign of his daughter.

His flight was called and passengers began lining up.

"Blair?"

He turned.

Rena Castaway, looking as fetching as a model out of *Vogue*, approached.

"Wh...where's Sandra?" he asked.

"Get on the plane," she said. "Your daughter will not be joining you."

It took a nanosecond for everything to connect. She had played him, just as John Dalton would have done.

He dropped his attaché case. He took hold of her arm and twisted it behind her back. "You gave me your word!" he said.

She leaned in close, turned halfway, suddenly broke clear. "Don't make a fuss," she said, surprising him with her physical prowess.

"Where's my daughter?" he asked again, heart beginning to pound.

"You have nothing to worry about," came the evasive reply. "You take this trip and complete your assignment. Sandra will be waiting for you upon your return."

He couldn't believe that this was happening.

"Blair—"

He felt the con, could almost taste it. But what choice did he have? If he refused to go, the inevitable would only be delayed. He took hold of her arm again, wishing he had it in him to hurt her. "If anything happens to my daughter," he said, "I don't care how insignificant, I'll come after you. I swear I will!"

Something flared in Castaway's eyes. It was defiance and something else; something cold and impenetrable.

Before Blair could say anything more, she yanked her arm free, turned, and walked away.

CHAPTER 39

His flight was delayed. At first they kept all passengers onboard. Then they were allowed to deplane. After two more tries, many became incensed. Blair, on the other hand, was so distracted, it all washed over him.

He tried to rationalize BIS's position. John Dalton's murder had obviously rattled the agency. If they were desperate enough to hold on to Sandra, they were capable of doing much worse. He had to put an end to it.

After they became airborne, Blair remained deep in thought. For one of the few times in his life, Johnnie Walker had no appeal to him. Neither did the meal that was offered.

He dozed for a while, tried reading a book. The irony of his situation didn't leave him. He was flying to see one of the few people he liked. A man who, he'd been told, was a secret terrorist. He had no other argument he could use. Yet if he couldn't get Jeremy to change his mind, he had no idea what he would do next.

• • • • •

Even though it was late, Jeremy insisted on dinner at his golf course.

Yam Ve'chal, only open a few months, was already the hottest ticket in town. Privately owned, the initiation fee alone cost well over a hundred thousand American dollars.

On their way, Blair's neck became sore from twisting it so often, looking for anything untoward. And he realized that his paranoia was getting worse.

It was dusk by the time they entered the property. But there was still enough light for Blair to marvel at the landscape. Here he was, in a supposed arid land, yet the grass was a brilliant green, the ponds crystal clear. Manmade, of course. Which proved once again what money could buy.

As they neared the clubhouse, Jeremy turned in his seat. "This is so nice of you to help me celebrate, by the way."

"Huh?" Blair said. "Celebrate what?"

"*Cyber-tech*. We've stopped the competitor in its tracks. Our lawyer is putting the finishing touches to the agreement."

Blair wished he could care more than he did.

• • • • •

They parked. But instead of going directly to the dining room, Jeremy insisted on relaxing first.

The bar was a throwback to another era. Clubby, it had a smoky atmosphere without the smoke. Dark brown, leather chairs. Blow-up photographs on the walls of famous golfers, from Ben Hogan to Jack Nicklaus to Rory McIlroy.

There were three other patrons. They took a seat as far away from them as they could get. Jeremy was about to say something, when his attention was drawn to the TV. The announcer was describing another car-bombing in Times Square. There were no deaths, apparently, but over a hundred injuries.

Jeremy's demeanor changed. "Bloody terrorists!" he said. "You ever notice how much attention they get? It's as if the media love them. You watch—this story from New York is all we're going to hear about for the next several days.

"One feeds off the other. The press believes it is their obligation to keep us informed. They know the average guy on the street has a morbid curiosity that has to be constantly fed.

"The terrorists crave publicity. But if no one was told anything, if there was a world wide news blackout, for instance, do you think this crap would happen in the first place?"

Blair frowned. "And how would you possibly manage that?"

"Ah-ha. Collusion by governments around the world. Call it state censorship. Call it anything you like. The proliferation of social media has resulted in too much power. There are no checks and balances. No control. Take away the voice of these madmen and what do they have? No one to publicize their deeds or their dogma."

Blair studied his friend for a minute. What he said was spoken with a passion that could not be faked or misconstrued. Could he really have a secret agenda? One involving the very terrorism he was railing about?

"How many years have I known you?" Jeremy asked out of the blue.

"Umm." Blair thought for a moment. "Seven? Eight?"

"Nine years this September. Yet in all that time, all you and I ever talk about is business. Not much else. Oh, sorry, and women. That, too."

"On your part, maybe. Not mine."

"It doesn't matter whose part. I talk, you listen."

"So?"

"Isn't it refreshing to discuss something meaningful for a change?"

"Excuse me," the waitress interrupted. She was a nubile, peroxide blonde. Blair was ignored as she leaned forward, cleavage exposed. She asked Jeremy what he wanted to drink. He asked for a Coke. As if an afterthought, she turned to Blair and took his order.

Jeremy laughed as soon as she was gone. “It’s my charm,” he said. And he gave the back of Blair’s head a playful tap.

CHAPTER 40

The following morning, they were seated in the coffee shop of Blair's hotel. Jeremy was wearing mustard-colored shorts and a yellow, short-sleeved shirt. Blair, in his suit and tie, felt not only overdressed but conspicuous.

Their night had ended early. Jeremy wouldn't stop talking about his idea of censoring the news media. When he wasn't lamenting the reach of fanatics in the Middle East, he was expressing his disgust with the way the war on terror was being fought. Blair decided that broaching the one topic on his own mind would best be reserved for today.

The hotel was busy but they were able to snare one of the last available tables in the coffee shop, where the buffet spread was extensive. From tuna and salmon to smoked fish; herring, hummus, and couscous. Plus a variety of breakfast meats, as well as dairy products.

Blair was too nervous to eat. He chose a single slice of rye toast and coffee.

Jeremy, on the other hand, heaped more onto his plate than the plate seemed able to hold. Eggs and sausages, pancakes and bacon. He'd even added hash brown potatoes and a grilled tomato. "Good thing I'm not hungry," he said.

Blair leaned back and kept his thoughts to himself. Jeremy began to discuss *Cyber-tech's* potential now that their rival had been eliminated.

Once his friend completed his meal, Blair steadied himself. But before he could speak, Jeremy said, with a grin, "Still have that huge bug up your ass?"

"What bug is that?" Blair asked, playing dumb.

"You mean, I have to spell it out for you?"

"Jeremy…"

"I'm listening. What bullshit story are you ready to tell now?"

"It's not bullshit."

"Oh, no? What is it, then? Didn't you come back here for the same bloody reason as before?"

Blair could see the disappointment in his friend's eyes. "I'm here to ask for a favor," he said.

"Sure you are. And why is that?"

"I explained on my last trip. My bank—"

"Fuck your bank! They can't tell you how to run your business!"

Blair's spirits sunk. "I have to make this happen," he said quietly.

Jeremy remained mute.

Before losing his nerve, Blair removed a check from his shirt pocket. It was for seven thousand dollars. All the money he had in his saving's account. He handed it to him.

Jeremy's look went from disbelief to anger.

"Call it an investment," Blair quickly explained. "To be used at your discretion."

"Do you want dessert?" Jeremy asked.

Blair shook his head.

"Some fruit, perhaps?"

He waited.

"They have great kiwi here. Or maybe some watermelon?"

Blair prepped himself, knowing he had no other card to play.

Jeremy handed the check back. "I can't accept this," he said. "And you should be ashamed for even offering it."

Embarrassed, Blair held his tongue, but he soon started to feel awkward. Finally, he thought to ask his friend why he left the city of his birth, Los Angeles, to start a new life in Israel.

Jeremy regarded him with a bemused look in his eye, but he held his tongue.

"What?" Blair said. "It's something we never discussed."

"So, after all these years, you're suddenly curious?"

"That's right." Blair's smile was forced.

Reluctantly, it seemed, Jeremy began to explain about his past, how his father had split when he was still a boy. "It was just me and my mother," he continued, "left to fend for ourselves. My mom was a breast cancer survivor. She slaved away as a bookkeeper, putting in well over sixty hours a week. We weren't exactly rich, but we never lacked for anything. She made sure I had what I needed to get through college.

"After I graduated, I ended up working at a number of sales jobs in the toy industry, eventually becoming a Costco specialist. Which was fortuitous, as you know, what with Costco being one of the few major accounts still headquartered on the West Coast.

"After a few years, I was able to build up a decent nest egg and I decided to do something meaningful for my mother. She'd been working so hard, never taking time off, never taking a vacation.

"Week after week I tried handing her brochures on some of the most exotic places in the world, from Hawaii to New Zealand, to Bali in Indonesia. She kept turning them aside.

"But I persisted. I told her people got sick, had nervous breakdowns, even died from too much work, and I wasn't going to let this happen to her. She didn't say yes overnight, but eventually I got her to understand how much this meant to me.

"Almost another month went by. And I guess she grew tired of my pestering her, because she finally agreed. Her choice was a cruise to the Middle East."

"To Israel?" Blair interrupted.

"It was part of the itinerary," Jeremy said. "Anyway, by the time she was packed and ready to go, she was acting like a kid, and I knew I had done the right thing.

"I started to receive emails almost from the first moment her ship left Frankfurt, Germany. I got to know about every port she stopped at, every city and country she visited.

"Then days went by without a word. One minute I was inundated with information, the next there was nothing. I figured she must be in one of those blackout zones that happen when you travel, especially by sea.

"It was at the end of day five when she got in touch by phone. Apparently, my mother wasn't feeling well so she had visited the ship's doctor who, in turn, had insisted she see a specialist in Tel Aviv.

"The news couldn't have been worse. My mom's cancer was back. This time, it had metastasized from her breast to her lungs. She needed immediate treatment.

"My mother wanted to have it done there. I didn't like that idea, told her it would be best to get a second opinion from her oncologist in LA. She wouldn't listen. So I immediately dropped everything and flew to Israel, met with the doctor, did not like the prognostication. I stayed for almost three weeks before returning home.

"Two trips later I knew what had to be done. My mom had sacrificed so much for me as a child; I couldn't allow her to fight this battle alone. I wrapped up my affairs and left America for the last time."

Blair sat at rigid attention. This was not the kind of story he expected.

"The first thing I did after arriving in Tel Aviv was move into my mother's flat, just on the outskirts of town. She had picked the apartment in haste and there wasn't much to recommend it, but it suited her purpose.

"In just a short period of time my mom lost a ton of weight. As a matter of fact, her health in general seemed to deteriorate before my eyes. You have no idea what it's like to care for someone and see this bloody disease eat away at them, to consume them.

"We talked for hours at a time, my mother reminiscing about her childhood in Hungary, where she was born. It was a great relief to immigrate to the United States, she told me, but it still did not quite feel like home to her. Israel was where she always felt she belonged, where she wanted to be buried, where, before she died, she wanted to rediscover her Jewish roots."

Blair's ears perked. *Jewish* roots?

"For the next few months," Jeremy went on, "I helped her do just that, arranging meetings with history buffs and scholars, volunteers for the most part, all well-versed in fact and fiction. My mother took it all in with a zeal I never knew she possessed, right up until the final weeks of her life, when she was bedridden and barely conscious.

"After my mom's passing, I realized I wanted to stay in Israel. Truth is, the moment I first set foot here, I became enthralled with the people.

"Not only did I want to stay, I decided I wanted to make a difference. And I did. In ways that would surprise you. In ways you couldn't imagine.

"End of story."

CHAPTER 41

Blair now understood it was decision time. His intention in coming back to Israel was to cajole or bribe Jeremy into agreeing to switch the DVD production. The truth about his daughter was never to be revealed. But what Jeremy just said changed everything.

He stood and excused himself, saying he had to use the washroom.

At the sink, he splashed cold water on his face. Then he dried off with a paper towel.

Jeremy was not who Rena Castaway, and John Dalton before her, said he was, but the complete opposite. Not a terrorist at all. Not a gentile in a Jewish land, as he himself believed, but someone actually Jewish.

Did this mean he could trust him, however? Bring him into his confidence? Ask him to help find a solution? What if, even though it was a large "if," the story Jeremy had just related was a lie? An elaborate and contrived one, but a lie nevertheless?

He knew he wanted to believe him. No one could be that good an actor.

Or could they be?

When al-Qaeda attacked North America, years of planning had gone into it. The destruction of the World Trade Center didn't succeed because these people were stupid.

And why would Jeremy bring up his background today? After all these years? What did he mean about making a difference in ways Blair couldn't imagine? What was that all about?

Was Jeremy a friend? Blair asked himself now. The person he said he was? And more importantly, could he be trusted? Unconditionally?

• • • • •

He returned to the table still undecided. Before he could say anything, Jeremy accused him of hiding something from him. "You're not yourself," he said. "Haven't been for quite some time. You don't have to confide in me, if you don't want to. Although, I thought we were friends. Close friends, as a matter of fact."

"We *are*," Blair quickly jumped in. He didn't know where Jeremy was going with this.

"Not by the way you're acting."

"How am I acting?"

"Keeping secrets from me."

Blair felt his pulse rise. "What secrets?"

"Mr. Innocent."

"I'm not trying to be."

"No. Of course, you're not."

"Jeremy—"

"Do you think, for one minute, that I didn't notice the marks on your face? The lack of sleep in your eyes? But it's okay." He shrugged. "If you don't have enough faith to confide in me, I'll have to live with it. Just tell me what your plans are. I mean, for right now. You going home? Or is there something else on your mind?"

Blair realized that this was it. The moment to come clean. But Sandra's fate was in the balance and he couldn't take a chance. "I'm going home," he said. "Or, I will be, after you agree to what I want."

Jeremy's expression softened. "Go get your things and check out," he said. "I'll drive you to the airport."

Blair didn't budge.

"Did you hear me?"

"I can't leave yet, Jeremy."

"I understand what you're saying. Go pack. We'll talk in the car."

• • • • •

The first thing Blair did was ask the concierge to see if El Al had a seat available on the next flight to New York. Once he received confirmation, he took the elevator to his room to gather his things. He knew that if he didn't get Jeremy to bend, he could always check back in.

On the drive to the airport, Jeremy was especially talkative. He mentioned a vacation he was planning in Australia and New Zealand. How he heard so much about both countries. How there was so much to see and do. "Apparently, they have some of the best golf courses in the world," he said.

Blair finally told him that he could go on talking forever, if he wanted to, but he would not be diverted.

"Diverted from what?" Jeremy asked.

"You know what."

Jeremy slapped his hand on the steering wheel. "Goddammit! Why is this so important?"

"I've already told you why. So if you're not willing to bend, I need you to take me back to the hotel."

"And you'll do what? Stay in Israel until you drive me crazy?"

Blair held his tongue as they arrived at the terminal building.

Jeremy parked in the allotted area and shut the motor. He pulled out his wallet. "Here," he said, handing over a crumpled piece of paper.

Blair went to unfold it.

Jeremy stopped him. "Put it away," he instructed. "Somewhere safe. It's a New York phone number. I don't know what mess you've gotten yourself into. But if your situation should worsen, and you can't reach me in time, you are to call that number."

Blair was jolted. What situation was he talking about? Did he somehow know the truth?

"Goodbye, Blair. Have a good flight."

"Wait a minute."

"I'm listening."

"Jeremy, I'm calling in a personal favor. *Yes*—based on our friendship. I'm sorry to have to put it this way. But it's all I have left. Please…"

"Don't beg."

"I *am* begging."

Jeremy glanced at him, then looked away. And he sighed. "If this goddamn production means so much to you, you can have it. The first one hundred thousand pieces will go to OTE. But that will be it, Blair. I mean it. I'm doing this against my better judgment. And I never want to hear you mention this subject again."

The relief Blair felt almost brought him to tears.

"And whenever you're ready to share your secret with me," Jeremy continued, "I'll be waiting."

"There's no secret," he said, his throat constricting.

"Not another word, *boychick*. Just get your ass out of my car…"

CHAPTER 42

The return flight from Israel passed quickly. Blair even found the airline staff to be accommodating, including the crotchety women who posed as stewardesses.

"God bless you, everyone," he wanted to proclaim.

The delay in getting his luggage in New York was a mere inconvenience. As was the long lineup for a cab.

Nothing bothered him.

Finally at home, Blair undressed and changed into pajamas. It was too late to call anyone—well past midnight—but he very much wanted to call everyone he knew.

He approached the window in his bedroom. The view revealed a portion of the Hudson River.

He used the remote to turn on his iPod. He caught the refrain of a Norah Jones song and he began to hum along.

Life was good, he decided.

• • • • •

He woke at seven. He had slept through the night for the first time in weeks. He showered and shaved. He was ready to leave for work, when his doorbell buzzed.

Castaway appeared as stunning as ever. Sexy, of course, in a black skirt and rose cardigan.

"Well, well," Blair said. "Look what the cat dragged in."

She seemed unsure of herself.

"Would you like a drink?" he asked. "I've spiked it with arsenic."

"Arsenic?"

It dawned on him again that English was not her native language. "Where are you from, Rena?" he said. "Germany?"

She blushed ever so slightly. But it quickly dissolved.

Her training coming into play? Blair wondered.

"What makes you say that?" she asked.

"Every once in a while I detect an accent."

"You do?"

"Yeah."

"But I am a native American."

"Sure you are," Blair said. "Iroquois or Sioux?"

"I beg your pardon?"

"Which tribe?"

She was stuck for an answer.

"Hold on a minute, Rena," he said. "I have something for you."

Hurrying into his bedroom, he dug into one of the bureau drawers and removed the statuette he had placed there long ago. It was something he had won at a golf tournament. It was tall enough and sufficiently abstract to resemble the Oscar.

He stepped back into the foyer and handed it to her. "Here," he said.

"W...what is it?" She reluctantly took it in hand.

"Your Best Actress award. You deserve it."

"Blair, what are you talking about?" As she spoke, she moved closer to him.

"About that drink," he said. "Do you want one or not?"

"With arsenic?" she asked.

Maybe she wasn't as dense as he thought, Blair surmised. "No," he said. "No arsenic. You want a beer? Some wine?"

"This early in the morning?"

"Hey, as the song says, it's five o'clock somewhere."

"No, thank you."

"Oh yeah, I forgot. You're working."

"Don't make it sound like that," she said. Then she deftly changed subjects. "What happened in Israel, Blair?"

He counter-questioned: "When can I have my daughter back, Rena?"

"After you tell me what happened."

"Uh-uh. It's not going to work that way. Not this time. You and your agency have put me through enough."

Castaway hesitated. She removed her cell phone from her purse and told him she needed privacy.

He pointed to the bathroom.

"It would not be wise to listen in to my conversation," she said. "Understood?"

"Of course," he replied.

The minute she entered the bathroom, he crept forward and put his ear to the locked door.

The water taps had been turned on full. He couldn't make out what she was saying. He moved back into the hallway and waited.

When Castaway came out, she seemed calmer. "I have to explain something," she said. "As a precaution after John was murdered we moved your daughter out of state. We'll need some time to bring her back."

"How much time?"

"An extra day. You meet me tomorrow, say around the noon-hour. I'll have Sandra with me then."

“Where?” he quickly asked. “Where will we meet?”

She headed for the door and placed her hand on the knob. “You pick the spot.”

He tried to think of somewhere public. “On Broadway,” he said. “In front of the Toys ‘R’ Us store.”

“Fine,” she said. And she opened the door. “We’ll be there at noon.”

CHAPTER 43

Blair gathered his attaché case and walked out of his apartment. He was whistling to himself. A few minutes ago, Lisa had called to say she wanted to cook for him tonight. She was planning on something Italian. And she had hinted that dessert would be of a personal and exotic nature.

Downstairs, the first thing he did was stop and purchase eight lottery tickets, eight being a number the Chinese associated with good fortune and wealth.

He was feeling lucky. Lucky and relieved. He didn't mind the subway ride. Despite the crowd, he was somehow unaffected by the noise and peculiar odors.

At his office, he invited his secretary to come in and have a seat. Andrea was wearing a tight lime-green dress that made her look even thinner than she was. Before leaving for Israel, Blair had given her a number of assignments, the most important of which was a meeting with Marianne Lattanzi at Target.

The retailer was the last piece of the puzzle he needed to have resolved. He already had Walmart and Toys 'R' Us on board. Target would round out the accounts he was hoping to have participate in *Cyber-tech's* initial launch.

Marianne Lattanzi went against the Target mold. Middle-aged and Italian rather than a twenty-something Wasp, her down-to-earth nature appealed to Blair and the two had stayed in touch over the years

Now, Andrea's voice warmed as she related her encounter with the Target buyer. "At first, she was disappointed you weren't there," she said. "But I won her over."

"Used your charm, did you?"

"I didn't have to. I did as you suggested. Just laid the sample in front of her and told her to try it."

"And?"

"She flipped. She said it was the best thing she'd seen in a long while. She asked how many pieces she could have, how soon."

"And you said?"

"What you told me to say. September launch. No advance release. Take it or leave it."

"In those words?"

She laughed. "Not exactly. I'm paraphrasing. I know how to talk to buyers. You taught me well."

"Good girl. Were you nervous?"

"Scared to death, if you want to know the truth."

Blair told her he was proud of her. "You did a great job, Andrea," he said.

CHAPTER 44

He remained at work until three o'clock. He was pleased about seeing Lisa tonight. And he was more than excited about being reunited with his daughter tomorrow. With the extra time on his hands, he decided to walk home. He stopped on his way to pick up a bottle of Moët & Chandon. Then he found a flower shop where he selected a single, long-stemmed rose.

Alone in his condo, Blair found it wonderful to have positive thoughts for a change. He sensed, with some certainty, that the bad mojo in his life was over.

He had faced adversity and survived.

Hallelujah!

The word popped into his head and stayed there. A sound of joy, melodically repeating itself: Hallelujah, hallelujah…

• • • • •

By six o'clock, unfortunately, a pessimistic refrain began to creep into his subconscious. He tried his best to ignore it. He spent extra time setting the dining room table. He hid the flower he had purchased for Lisa in a place she would never bother to look. Then he sprayed the kitchen and den with air freshener.

But his thoughts persisted. His conversation with Castaway earlier in the day replayed itself in his mind. It wasn't like her to acquiesce so easily. She was the one to ask him to pick the place where they could meet tomorrow. And she had selected a time without hesitation.

What did it mean? Blair wondered.

He wanted tomorrow to go off without a hitch.

Now, it worried him.

• • • • •

Lisa arrived just after seven o'clock. Her white blouse was partially unbuttoned. Her dark-brown miniskirt bordered on risqué. When she asked about the bruises under his eyes, he told her she was seeing something that didn't exist.

"I don't think so," she said. "You remember our pact about honesty, don't you, Blair?"

He shrugged self-consciously. "If you're seeing anything, it's from the same injury of a while ago."

"Oh, yeah? You mean the injury you never told me about?" She smiled. "What am I going to do with you?" She took him in her arms. Kissed him.

Blair led her into the den and said he would be right back. He took the champagne out of the fridge. He carried it into the den along with two glasses, popped the cork, and poured.

"What are we celebrating?" she asked.

He offered no reply. Instead, he moved to the television set. He reached behind it for the single rose he had hidden there earlier. Then he turned toward her.

"For me?" Lisa gushed.

He clicked her glass. "All for you," he said. He was wishing he could relax. But he was unable to banish the demons in his head.

• • • • •

While Lisa prepared dinner, Blair opened and poured the wine. It was a Chianti Classico Riserva.

The meal consisted of breaded veal. There were two kinds of pasta—a tortellini in oil and garlic and fettuccini in a tomato sauce. It was all preceded by a Caesar salad.

"Where did you learn how to cook like this?" Blair couldn't help asking.

"My mommy taught me well," Lisa said.

"My God. It's a wonder you're not three hundred pounds."

"I don't eat like this every night. Only on special occasions."

"Like now?"

"Exactly."

He forked another mouthful. His appetite was gone and he knew he would have to fake it.

"A penny for your thoughts," Lisa said.

He chewed, swallowed, took her hand in his. "I'm just glad that I met you," he admitted.

"Why thank you, sir. I'm glad I met you, too."

• • • • •

Blair asked if Lisa would like a coffee. She said no. He asked if he could tempt her with something sweet. She turned him down flat, reminding him of her promise of an "exotic" dessert. Standing from the table, she invited him to do the same. He began to clear the dishes. She stopped him.

There was no time to hang up his clothes or brush his teeth. In the bedroom, she playfully pushed until he tumbled onto the bed. She tugged at his shoes and socks. Then at his shirt, pants, and underwear.

When he tried to protest, she ignored him. Her eyes locked into his as she slowly undressed. She was being playful about it. She removed her garments deliberately. And she threw each piece into the air. Her blouse, then her skirt. Her pantyhose, and finally her bra.

"Come here." He reached for her.

She pushed his hands away.

Meticulously, she pulled the spread to one side, then smoothed out the sheet.

He made another attempt to take hold of her.

She wouldn't allow it.

Blair folded his arms behind his head and closed his eyes. The first thing he felt was the most delicate touch of her fingers. She began to massage his toes, one by one, followed by the soles of his feet.

Waves of pleasure soared through his body.

This was a different Lisa now. She kneaded his flesh with an extreme gentleness. From his ankles to his calves. The front and back of his knees. It felt as if a thousand butterflies were fluttering their wings.

Blair's experience may not have been extensive. But he believed he was possibly above average in his desire to please. Experiencing what he was going through now was so vastly different for him. And he wished there was something he could do in return. Something to show he cared. But the worry on his mind interfered with Lisa's ministrations, and he remained embarrassingly soft.

Lisa obviously noticed but didn't say anything. Instead, she stopped what she was doing. She pulled the covers over both their bodies and slipped into his arms.

Blair began to apologize.

She shushed him.

Just before daybreak, Lisa stirred awake as did Blair. She asked what was wrong.

"Just your imagination," he said, grateful for the darkened room.

Blair wanted to confide in her. He wanted to tell her about his daughter. But reason prevailed. As did caution. There would be time to explain it all later, he decided. Once Sandra was released.

"Go back to sleep," he told her. "I have never felt better in my life."

CHAPTER 45

He stood on the corner of 44th and Broadway, next to the entrance to the Toys 'R' Us store. Blair remembered the first time he had come here and how impressed he had been. He wished every toy store could match this one in size and atmosphere. A fantasyland for the ages.

The noon-hour came and went.

It was a strain, searching out people in the crowd. Every time he spotted Castaway or his daughter, he'd get a closer look and realize his mistake. There were simply too many blond girls. And too many Castaway look-alikes.

He paced in front of the store.

At 12:30 he asked himself if he had gotten the time wrong. Then he wondered if he had misunderstood where they were to meet.

He gaped at his watch every few minutes.

By one o'clock, his mind began to contemplate various scenarios, not one of which was encouraging.

• • • • •

Blair arrived home at three o'clock. He tossed his BlackBerry onto the kitchen counter and took hold of the house phone.

There were no messages.

He dragged himself into the den. He was thinking of checking the news on television, to see if there was a major traffic problem somewhere in town. He took the clicker in hand. The doorbell rang. And this overbearing weight lifted from his shoulders.

Dope, he teased himself. *Worrying for nothing*.

He called his hello through the intercom. Then he hit the buzzer.

A few minutes later, a knock came on the door.

The apprehension he was feeling vanished. This would be Castaway, he knew, bringing his daughter back to him. As promised.

He didn't move along the corridor, he glided. He paused to compose himself, to allow his silly grin to dissipate. He placed a hand on the doorknob and turned.

There were two of them. Each was wearing a blue, nylon jacket. The word *POLICE* was stenciled across their chests in bold, white lettering. The taller of the two introduced himself as William Campbell, NYPD. "Blair Mulligan?" he asked.

"Yes?" he tentatively acknowledged.

The cop handed him a document. "We have a warrant to search the premises," he said.

The hair on the back of Blair's neck bristled. "What's this about?"

The shorter of the two policemen pointed to the document. "Read it," he said.

He started to. But he was so disappointed in not seeing Sandra, he couldn't make any sense of it. "Why don't you summarize for me?"

The cop looked at him askance. "Your ex-wife claims you have conspired to keep your daughter away from her against her wishes. We are here to seek out clues to your daughter's whereabouts. You're lucky we're not arresting you."

All Blair could do was step aside.

The policemen split up. One began to rummage through the kitchen cupboards and drawers. The other started his search in the hall closet. After an hour, Blair approached the taller of the two and asked if he could help him find what he was looking for.

"Afraid not," the cop said.

Blair was just turning away when he remembered Sandra's torn blouse, the one he had found on his bed when his apartment had been ransacked. Instead of leaving it lying around, he had locked it in the trunk of his car. If he hadn't done so, his arrest would no longer be pending but imminent. *Thank God for small favors*, he thought.

When the policeman's search of the kitchen was completed, Blair took a seat at the table. He picked up the phone and dialed Castaway's office number.

After the seventh ring he grew apprehensive. Why wasn't voicemail picking up?

He strolled through his apartment.

"You guys get paid by the hour?" he finally asked the shorter cop.

He was waved off.

"Well, how much longer are you going to be?" he asked.

"As long as it takes," he was told.

CHAPTER 46

At his office the following morning, he let Rena Castaway's line ring for over a minute before disconnecting. Rationalizing, he told himself voicemail wasn't picking up because it had been turned off or was full. He would give it another hour before trying again. In the meantime, he considered calling his ex-wife, to vent his anger at what she had done, getting the police to search his condo.

He picked up the phone and began to dial.

Something stopped him. He put the phone down. To occupy his time, he tried doing a comparison of sales numbers from last year to this. It was hopeless.

Just after ten o'clock, he punched in Castaway's number and let it ring a dozen times.

No answer.

She was probably called back to Washington, he concluded. As an employee of the federal government, Castaway would be asked to travel on a moment's notice. But why was her voicemail turned off? And why didn't she show up yesterday, as promised?

• • • • •

Blair left his office at one o'clock and went out for a bagel and coffee. When he returned a half-hour later, he immediately tried Castaway's number. After two rings, a mechanical voice said: "The number you have dialed is out of service."

He stared at the receiver, figuring he must have dialed wrong. He hung up and dialed again.

"The number…"

It can't be, he told himself.

Blair peered at the phone as if it could unravel the secret.

He had two other numbers for Castaway, just as he had for her predecessor, John Dalton. One was for her general office, the other her cell. Both were local New York numbers.

He tried the general office number first; he received the same recorded message about the line being out of service. He dialed Castaway's cell. No answer.

Quickly, he punched in directory assistance.

"For what city, please?"

"Washington, D.C." He spoke slowly. "B … I … S."

"We are sorry, there is no such company listed."

"There has to be!" he yelled into the receiver.

He was cut off, as if the mechanical voice knew he was hollering at it.

He reached for his attaché case. He found his Day-Timer, and began to rummage through it. Page after page of names and numbers, all drawing a blank. Quickly, he began scrolling through the contact list on his BlackBerry.

What the hell am I looking for? he asked himself.

He didn't know. Some name to tweak a memory? If he couldn't reach Castaway, how in God's name would he be able to obtain Sandra's release?

• • • • •

At soon as he arrived home that night, Blair picked up the phone in the kitchen and tried Castaway's cell.

There was no answer.

He tried her direct office number; once again he received the same annoying recording about the line being out of service.

He took a seat at the table and began to go through his mail. There were bills mostly. But one was a letter from a law firm in Queens.

Speed-reading, the gist of it became clear. Apparently, he had five days in which to return Sandra to her mother. Otherwise, he would face the consequences of legal action being commenced against him.

• • • • •

On Sunday, he retrieved his car and headed out to the suburbs. His intention was to keep himself occupied by doing store-checks, to see what new toys were on the shelves. Unfortunately, no matter where he went, he could hardly concentrate.

On Monday at his office, every time his phone rang he expected it to be Castaway, calling to give him an explanation, to tell him everything was fine.

It wasn't until late afternoon that he questioned the unthinkable: if terrorists were responsible for the death of John Dalton, could they not have eliminated Castaway as well?

Blair stood from his desk and went home.

• • • • •

He poured a stiff Scotch.

Sandra was out there somewhere and he was going to find her.

But how?

He needed help, and he needed it now. The time for procrastination was over.

He tried Castaway's cell. This time it rang twice and then went into limbo, meaning it too was no longer in service.

Blair thought of Jeremy. He placed the call to Israel. The connection was poor and he could hardly hear Jeremy's secretary. She said something about his friend having gone on a business trip to Europe.

About to drain his drink, he paused. Thinking of Jeremy reminded him of something else. Hurrying, he rummaged through the top kitchen drawer. Jeremy's words came back to him: how he was to call this New York number if his situation should become worse. He found the piece of paper and unfolded it.

Blair picked up the phone and dialed.

A mechanical voice answered, male and robotic: "After the tone, please speak your name and phone number clearly. Your call will be returned."

He did as he was told. But he was tempted to hold on to the receiver, as if this act by itself could bring help that much sooner.

• • • • •

No one called back.

Every half-hour or so, Blair would peek at his watch and cringe.

A little after 9:00 PM, someone rang from the downstairs lobby.

A voice in his head told him it would be Rena Castaway. Without hesitation, he buzzed the caller in, then opened the door and waited in the hallway, his heart pounding.

Lisa came out of the elevator and walked toward him without a smile or "hello."

He was about to tell her that this was not a good time, that he wished she would have called first.

She told him that she got his message.

He looked at her strangely. "What message?"

"Your phone message."

"What are you talking about?" he said, his frustration beginning to show.

"Blair—" She tugged on his arm, guiding him inside the apartment. "Come take a seat for a minute."

CHAPTER 47

Yassin was in the same makeshift mosque in Brooklyn. He leaned forward on his haunches, closed his eyes, and let his mind wander. He was surrounded by a dozen or so worshippers, yet felt quite alone.

His plan was in place. There had been a few bumps along the way. But his people knew their roles and were handling them well. This operation was complicated. It had started off as expected and he was certain it would follow its course to a positive conclusion.

The chant of familiar prayers reached his ears. Yassin had studied the Koran from a young age. It amazed him how its verses had been misinterpreted by non-believers. Not that it mattered. As a messenger of Allah, he would see that the world finally understood.

The service came to an end.

Yassin slowly rose and moved to the back of the room. It did not take long to make eye contact. He indicated with his head.

The other man acknowledged him.

• • • • •

They met a few blocks from the mosque.

A white Lincoln pulled to a stop. Yassin opened the door and waited for the other man to get in. Instructions were given to the driver in Arabic.

Like ports in other large cities around the world, New York's had a pulse all its own. Numerous warehouses lined their route. It was noon and traffic was heavy.

They pulled into the parking area of a two-story building. The sign out front read, *G.H.McSwain and Sons, Importers. Est. 1915.*

Yassin knew that the business was no longer owned by the McSwain family. Years ago it had been sold to Saudi interests through an intermediary. Now it was registered to a numbered company whose head office was located in the Cayman Islands. It was one of thousands of such U.S. businesses controlled by the Saudis, totaling billions of dollars.

This thought brought a smile to Yassin's lips. They would not only win the physical war, but the financial one as well. Americans remained either stupid or oblivious. Perhaps both.

He was first out of the car. He pretended to stretch but was actually observing his surroundings. Once he confirmed that there was nothing out of the ordinary, he followed his compatriot into the building and closed the door behind them.

A jovial, pot-bellied man in his fifties, whom he had never met, greeted him as if he were a long, lost friend. "Come, come," he said, guiding him further inside. They were joined by two of the man's subordinates.

They headed along a brightly lit corridor and passed a large showroom. Yassin noticed modern glassware and stemware. There were vases of various sizes. Serving bowls and plates. Decorative pieces. And statues in brass, gold, and silver. His host made mention of there being something to satisfy anyone's taste.

They continued up a staircase and passed a series of offices. The man paused in front of a bold-lettered sign marked ***Danger! Keep out!*** He inserted a key into the lock. The door opened and they stepped inside.

Yassin was confronted by a showroom that was a fair bit larger than the one below. There were risers on tables and recessed lighting brightly illuminating the wares.

His host laughed at Yassin's expression. "Nothing can beat our selection or price," he boasted. "Come, let me show you our most recent arrival." They moved to a corner of the room where he pointed out an odd-looking, cast-iron chair. It was straight-backed with unusual wide arms. "This just came to us from Germany," he announced proudly. "You know the Germans. They don't miss a trick." He touched a remote switch. There was a crackling sound. And a blue electric charge lit up the base of the seat.

"It won't kill you," the man explained, "but it will give you third-degree burns and a sizeable shock."

Yassin smiled at the thought.

"But there is more," his host continued. "Much more. Come, come…"

There was an updated version of a ball and chain. An odd-sized pair of pliers. Various cat o' nine tails, brass knuckles, knives, pistols, semiautomatics, and an assortment of machetes.

"Ibrihim," the man called to one of his employees. "Come here for a moment."

The boy stepped forward rather sheepishly. In his early twenties, rake-thin with a shy demeanor. His right hand was hardly brushed with the blade of one of the machetes. A narrow line of blood immediately appeared. The boy did not flinch. Instead, he licked the blood away.

"Nothing as sharp as these in the world," came another boastful statement. "Perfect for beheadings, if you are so inclined."

Before Yassin could pose his question, his host explained how thousands of containers arrived at U.S. ports on a daily basis, how no country, let alone one as ill-prepared as the United States, could manage to inspect each and every one. "Besides," his host said, "I am a legitimate importer of giftware, am I not?" He laughed. "But you tell me what you would like. We can have everything delivered to any address you choose in the continental United States. Freight prepaid."

Yassin excused himself and gestured to his companion. They headed off to compile their list. He doubted he would have need for most of what had been shown to him. But some of it was worthwhile.

It did not take long. "Don't give out our address," he warned when they were done. "Make arrangements to pick everything up. Use Yusef, if you have to. And the other one. Ahmed."

He returned to his host. In order not to lose face, he began to haggle over price. It went back and forth. Once they had an agreement, they shook hands as if they liked each other and made their goodbyes.

Yassin walked out. He was more anxious than ever to get his mission started. He figured it would be a matter of a day or two, possibly one more week at the most. Then his dupe would take the final bait and the trap would be sprung.

Inshallah…

CHAPTER 48

"You called a private number that few people in New York know exists," Lisa said once they were seated.

Blair's mouth fell open. "Jeremy's contact?"

"One and the same."

"You?"

"Me. I'm sorry, Blair. I was going to tell you."

"You?" he repeated. Stunned, he got back on his feet. "No lies between us," he said. He pointed a finger at her. "You made me promise—remember? What the hell was that all about?"

His mind flashed back in time. "Billie's wasn't a coincidence," he said. "Being stood up by whatever the hell his name was supposed to be—Robert? Richard?—was all a load of crap. Wasn't it? Jeremy probably asked you to keep an eye on me. So not only do you throw your eye my way, but your body. You feigned an interest, acting as if we were what?" He snapped his fingers. "Simpatico? Yet all the while it was your bloody job!" His voice rose. "So what does that make you? Not only a liar but a whore?"

"Blair," Lisa said, "Please sit down. I'll explain..."

Despite his anger, he couldn't deny his attraction. Even now. It served to make everything he was feeling worse. "I've heard enough explanations," he said.

"You haven't."

"Get out, Lisa." He indicated the door.

"I'm not leaving. I can't leave until I tell you the truth." She came to her feet, and tried to approach.

He moved into the corridor.

"I didn't mean for it to happen," she said. She remained by the couch, her voice a whisper. "I was given instructions to get close to you. To get you to like me. To get you to confide in me."

"Was Jeremy behind this or not?" Blair couldn't help interrupting.

The pause was abbreviated. "Yes, Jeremy was behind it. He was worried about you. He suspected something was going on."

"How intuitive."

"He knows you like a book, Blair. At first, the plan was for me to call you. I was to tell you that I had just arrived from Israel. But Jeremy knew you would never ask me out. So … I followed you for a while. Got to know your habits. Got to see which bars and restaurants you preferred. That night we met you talked to me for hours. Remember? And for the only time in my professional career," she hesitated, "I became attracted to one of my assignments."

Blair's jaw dropped. "Is that how you think of me?" His voice flared. "As one of your *assignments*?"

"At first, I did. And I tried everything in my power to turn this from being personal back to business. The internal warning signs were everywhere. But it was already too late. Attraction isn't something…" She sucked in her breath. "Attraction isn't something you can regiment. It was totally unprofessional of me. I know that now. But my resolve wilted. I fell for you, Blair." She paused. "And now I want to help. I can see how angry you are. And I can't say that I blame you. But Mossad has invaluable resour…"

"*Mossad?*"

"Didn't Jeremy tell you? We both happen to work for a division of Mossad. I thought you knew."

Jeremy's personal story came back to him. About how he moved to Israel. How he made a contribution in unimaginable ways. "So you being a masseuse is all bullshit," he stated flatly.

Lisa tried to make light of it. "I *am* a therapeutic masseuse," she said. "That's my cover. And I'm good at it."

"And Jeremy's cover is what—toys? With Mossad's blessing?"

"They prefer it. The toy industry necessitates the need for travel. Jeremy is responsible for more than one part of the world."

"I'll bet he is," Blair said. "What about Montreal?" he asked. "That was you, wasn't it?"

Lisa blushed. "Good thing I was there, wouldn't you say? You could have been killed."

"Did you find whoever was in the blue truck?"

"No. I tried to, but I lost them in the downtown core." She paused. "Take advantage of my offer, Blair. I will keep it strictly business, if that's what you want. Only, please, don't shut me out."

What he really wanted was to take her in his arms, to say all was forgiven.

"Blair—"

"I want you out of here," he said, his pride controlling his brain.

Lisa took her purse in hand and moved past him. "Don't decide anything right away," she said. "Sleep on it. Okay? I'll call you in the morning."

"Don't call me in the morning," he said, opening the door.

"When, then?"

"Never! I don't want you to call me again!"

She walked out.

He watched her go, regretting every step that she took.

CHAPTER 49

Headed for the den, he changed his mind and walked into the kitchen. He stood there, commiserating with himself. "Bitch" was the choice epithet that flashed in his head, and he wished he had used it in Lisa's presence.

He was reaching for the bottle of Scotch when his hand stopped in midair. His daughter's face suddenly flashed in front of his eyes, and shame washed over him. How dare he be concerned about his personal feelings?

He left the bottle where it was and took a seat at the table.

Once again he wondered who BIS was, and if it even existed. To verify that it was legitimate, he remembered placing a call to the New York number John Dalton had given him. When Dalton answered, he had assumed he was on the up and up, and that no further proof was required.

Now, he began to pace the apartment. His mind searched for answers, but they were elusive.

Darkness fell and he was beside himself with worry. If BIS wasn't a government agency, then his daughter was in worse trouble than he had first imagined.

• • • • •

Awake for most of the night, Blair's mind flipped back to all that he'd been through. The first time he met Rena Castaway was important. Though he couldn't figure out why.

He continued to toss and turn. He sought answers from a higher being. He offered to forsake every material thing he could think of. From the Scotch he enjoyed, to his cherished BMW. But his concessions not only seemed trite but ridiculous, and his cheeks burned with embarrassment.

Finally, he closed his eyes and washed everything from his mind.

Castaway came back to him.

He moved himself into a sitting position. He leaned forward and rested his elbows on his raised knees.

Something to do with his meeting her, he realized. They spoke for a while. Then he was blindfolded and led outside…

The answer became clear.

His blindfold had come loose. And he had caught the last three numbers in the address plaque above the door. 756. This was the house where he had been held. The same house where Sandra was being held now. He could bet on it.

• • • • •

Just before dawn, Blair went from bed to bathroom, from condo to parking lot. Every second thought that processed through his mind contained the word, "please."

Traffic was light at that early hour.

He passed the TriBeCa area and a few of the restaurants he frequented from time to time. He followed West Broadway to Chambers, then headed south on Church Street. He continued his progress past the New York Stock Exchange, and doubled back along Nassau. A few blocks over, he found a parking lot.

He left his car with the attendant and began to walk. He craned his neck from one side of the street to the next. Nothing was familiar. Just an endless combination of numbers, none of which fit.

It was a warm day. Sweat glued his shirt to his back. The hours passed from morning to afternoon, then to early evening. By the time darkness fell he knew there was no point in continuing. He would have to return tomorrow and begin his search over again.

CHAPTER 50

He awoke the next morning anxious to get going. Dressed in a short-sleeved, blue sport shirt and pair of jeans, he covered block after block. The only time he paused was to mark down the names of the streets he passed in a notepad he'd brought along for this purpose. He had learned his lesson yesterday, when on at least two occasions he had visited the same street twice.

Even if he found the house, even if Sandra *was* being held there, he realized that getting her out safely would take an awful lot of luck. Acting impulsively, without a plan, was foolhardy at best.

But was there a choice?

He covered a number of residential areas. They were quiet for the most part, until just before noon, when a preponderance of fast-food delivery vehicles made their appearance.

His mind repeated the digits of the partial address like a mantra: 7-5-6, 7-5-6, as if he could will the house to come forward by divine intervention.

• • • • •

He skipped dinner, and once again found it difficult to fall asleep. When he got out of bed in the morning, he was famished. Or so he believed at first. Halfway through his breakfast of bacon and eggs, he began to feel stuffed. He pushed the plate aside.

On the road once more, doubt slid into his subconscious. So many factors were stacked against him, not the least of which was the size of Manhattan's downtown core. But he recalled being driven from the house where he was being held to an area close to the East River. He remembered the name of the street where he had been dropped off and the one crossing it, and that the drive had taken approximately five minutes. Last evening he had consulted a map and soon concluded that his search should not be this daunting.

Now Blair decided to use another tack. Instead of parking, he drove the area where he felt the address was most likely to be. All the while he timed himself, stretching it to ten minutes in each direction.

Nighttime approached and he was no further ahead.

• • • • •

On day three his luck changed. He couldn't say exactly why he took the route he did. But he turned a corner and there it was. The street caught his eye immediately. It was one of the few in Lower Manhattan with a handful of refitted brownstones. They had been combined into townhomes of formidable size. Each had a one-car garage, a true luxury.

Blair counted down to 1756.

He recognized it at once. Brown-bricked, with black-framed windows and shutters. The house seemed empty. There were no lights on and none of the shades were drawn.

He slowly drove down the street. He made a U-turn, crossed to the other side, and parked. Now he had an unimpeded view.

When he noticed the garage door going up a few hours later, he wasn't so much taken aback as relieved. A Lincoln MKZ pulled out of the driveway. It was being driven by a man of about thirty years of age. He activated a remote switch. The door started to go down and he drove away.

Blair waited.

In less than a half-hour the man returned.

Blair counted the time it took for the garage door to go up. Fifteen seconds. Then he timed it on the way down. Just over ten seconds. Not very good. But the next time it was activated, he would take a chance by throwing himself beneath the door before it started its descent.

He remained in place, his mind willing someone else to come out and run an errand.

Night fell, but it was not to be.

CHAPTER 51

The following morning, dressed in the same shirt and pair of jeans, Blair was at the address before six o'clock. At home he had practiced sliding under the couch from a standing start in the hallway. It was a poor substitute for a garage door, but better than nothing.

Now, he sat in his car, trying not to think of the risk involved. Whatever Rena Castaway's intentions, he was ready to confront her. No matter the danger, he had to get inside the house and hopefully find his daughter.

The hours dragged by. Mail was delivered. Close to eleven o'clock a woman came out of one of the townhomes next to where he was parked. She glanced at him briefly, then continued on her way. Blair knew that if he was still in position when she returned, she would become suspicious.

He waited until noon. He stepped out of his car, locked it, and proceeded toward the house. When he was almost parallel to it, the garage door began to rise. Quickly, he hid behind one of the few trees lining the property.

The driver put the car in gear and drove away. To Blair's astonishment, the garage door remained in the upright position. He speed-walked toward the garage, entered, and maneuvered his way into a corner. The light—obviously on a timer—dimmed, then shut.

Blair tried the handle of the door leading into the house. It was unlocked. He couldn't believe his luck. He stepped inside and closed the door behind him.

He took small steps. The main floor wasn't all that familiar to him. He spotted a cluster of furniture in the living room. A couch and two loveseats. Continuing, he paused at the stairs leading to the basement.

Hearing nothing, he began his descent.

The long corridor was what he recalled most. That, and the number of rooms.

The first door he opened led to an empty space. The next exposed a drab cubicle. There was a cot and a bathroom. He was certain this was where he had been held.

He closed the door and moved forward. He arrived at the huge kitchen, with its two-tub sink and old-fashioned appliances. His heart skipped a beat. One or two of the cigarette butts in the ashtray were smoldering. Steam was rising from one of the coffee mugs. A sound came to him from below. He looked down as if he could see through the tiled floor to the subbasement.

He moved out of the kitchen. He headed along the corridor and tried each room as he went. There were few with windows, most with beds. He had to swallow the temptation to call his daughter's name.

The corridor widened.

There were only two rooms remaining, both on his right. He tried the door nearest him. It was the first one that was locked. Blair recalled his home in Queens, after he and Mandy had first moved in. Somehow the latch to the master bathroom had engaged after he had closed the door. Using a knife, he had jiggled the blade for a few seconds and the lock gave. Now, nervously, he pulled out the pocketknife he had brought along for just such an occasion, and set the blade in motion.

It did not take long. Wiping perspiration from his brow, he moved into the room … and gasped.

Sandra was lying on her side. She was dressed only in underpants. He could see the bedsores on her body. They ran along her arms, back, and legs. He moved closer and whispered her name. He was ready to clamp a hand over her mouth if she cried out.

She remained asleep.

Blair stood for a moment, ramrod stiff. It seemed like months, not weeks, since he had last seen her. What had they done to his baby girl?

Sandra's eyes flickered open, then widened in fear.

"It's daddy," he said.

Her body shook, even after he took her in his arms.

She had lost weight. All he could feel was skin and bones. She was void of color. Her hair was matted and damp. Blair felt a surge of anger so powerful he had to literally bite his lip to keep control.

"Daddy?" she questioned, her voice a whisper.

"Yes," he said. He swallowed hard. "It's me, darling."

"Daddy?" It was as if she couldn't believe what she was seeing.

He took her clothes in hand that were lying in the chair next to the bed and tried to get her to put them on.

She was lethargic.

He dressed her, then lifted her up.

Sandra's parched lips told him she was most likely dehydrated. He moved into the kitchen and opened the fridge. He removed a bottle of water and twisted off the top.

"Drink slowly," he advised as she took the bottle in hand.

She began to guzzle, then coughed.

"Slowly," he reminded her.

Blair made out voices from below; they were on the move. He quickly bent to one knee and placed his hands on his daughter's shoulders. "I need you to listen to me," he said. "Very, very carefully. Do you think you can walk on your own?"

She nodded without hesitation, which encouraged him.

"Good," he said. "But if something should happen to me and I tell you to run, you must do so at once. The minute I say run. Do you understand me, Sandra?"

"Y...yes," she said, not sounding quite as sure.

He hugged her. "You will be fine, darling. You are going to go out through the garage. The door will be open. Once you reach the sidewalk, you are to run in either direction. Run for as long as you can. Okay?"

"But where will you be, Daddy?"

He forced the calm in his voice. "I will be with you. I am only telling you this in case something happens to me. The people in this house are bad, Sandra. We must get you away from them. No matter what mommy and daddy have told you in the past about talking to strangers, you are now going to make an exception. The first person you see on the street, no matter who it is: a man, a woman, even someone your own age. You are to ask them to call the number you know to use in an emergency. Do you remember what that is?"

She recited 9-1-1.

"Good." Blair straightened, then he took his daughter's hand. "Just pretend you are Alice in Wonderland," he said. "This is quite an adventure you have been on. But it will all be over soon. Okay, Alice?"

She gave the slightest hint of a smile.

As soon as they came out of the kitchen, Blair heard footsteps. He led the way along the corridor. A man's voice called out in a foreign language. Blair lifted his daughter in his arms and began to run.

They mounted the staircase.

The sound from behind told Blair they'd be cutting it close. He neared the door leading to the garage. He lunged for the handle and turned.

Nothing happened.

Blair set his daughter down. He examined the door. He couldn't find anything impeding it. He tried the handle again; it gave. He guided Sandra forward. "Run!" he instructed. And he gave her a push.

CHAPTER 52

Before Blair could turn, a hand flew over his shoulder and reached for the door. He fought to keep it closed. A fist slammed into the back of his head. He shot his elbow out blindly but caught nothing but air.

A glancing blow connected with his chin. Fists began to pummel his chest. He refused to give up his position.

Another pair of hands went for the door.

He turned his fingers into claws and raked them along the hands until they let go.

Someone grabbed him from behind.

He feigned to his left, then quickly shot to his right. The hold on him loosened. There wasn't a lot of room. His intention was to back up and draw them with him. He no sooner completed his move when he realized his mistake. Three of the men followed him. The fourth had the door open and was heading through it.

Blair knew he only had one chance. He dove at the man, aiming for his ankles. But he missed. His chin hit the floor and he felt a jolt in the back of his neck. As soon as he caught his breath, he reached for the penknife in his pocket and pulled it out. Before he could flick the blade open, however, one of his attackers knocked the knife to the floor.

He tried to retrieve it.

A punch to his kidneys crippled him.

Another punch, practically in the identical spot.

He keeled over … and was lost.

• • • • •

Sandra?

The thought of his daughter jolted him back.

He was seated in a strange-looking metal chair with wide arms. A hard leather strap bound his ankles in place. Another was tightly enclosed around his hips. A third went over his arms.

Blood dripped from his nose. His head was pounding. There wasn't a part of his body that didn't ache.

For a moment he felt disoriented. He closed his eyes; then opened them. *Did Sandra make it?* he wondered.

He took in the room, noticing how average it seemed.

Feeling sick, he slowly leaned back.

His daughter must have made it, he was thinking.

• • • • •

He was left alone for over an hour.

The lights had been dimmed. But he could make out a rectangular conference table with chairs lining both sides. There was a phone and a laptop computer with a wide-screen monitor. The wall directly opposite had a window cut out of its center running approximately six feet diagonally. He wondered if it was one-way glass, if he was being observed.

The wait got to him.

He wanted to know, *had* to know, about Sandra.

• • • • •

The door opened and Rena Castaway, dressed conservatively in a brown dress that fell below her knees, approached. Her eyes narrowed with what could have been hatred. And Blair acknowledged that her role in all this was far more odious than he'd first imagined.

"You enjoying yourself?" he said, angry with her, angrier with himself.

Castaway looked away, ignoring him.

But he couldn't let go. "You must be feeling awfully proud. Aren't you?"

"Shut up!" she hissed. "Your time to speak will come." She turned on her heels.

From his position in the chair, Blair had to strain to follow her movements.

Castaway opened the door and nodded toward someone.

Blair struggled to see, but the leather straps dug into his flesh.

A man wearing a *djellaba* walked in. There was an attachment to his white robe, not unlike a *hijab* that some women wore, partially concealing his face.

Blair's heart leapt in his throat.

"Mr. Mulligan," the man said, his voice accented but familiar.

Not a delusion but the truth, Blair was thinking.

The man removed the covering from his face.

It couldn't be.

But it was: John Dalton, alive and well.

CHAPTER 53

It didn't seem possible.

Dalton was dead. Blair had seen him murdered with his own eyes. So how could he be standing here? And why was he wearing an Arab robe?

Blair felt as if he'd been sucker-punched.

He replayed the scene in his head: Bullets flying. Dalton going down and urging him to run. Not one sign of blood. In his anxiety he hadn't grasped it at the time. But he was certain of it now. There was no blood.

"Al-Qaeda has a particular hatred for infidels like you," Dalton said.

Al-Qaeda? The name chilled Blair. "John, what kind of game are you playing?" he asked.

"My name is not John. You will address me by my proper name—Khalid Yassin."

"Fine, John. Whatever you say."

Dalton's eyes narrowed. "Not John," he said with menace in his voice. "Do I have to threaten you?"

"I don't think so," Blair said. "You've done enough of that to last me a lifetime."

Dalton/Yassin shrugged. "We're not done with you yet, Mr. Mulligan. Far from it. We have been waiting for you, knowing it was only a matter of time. Why else did we loosen your blindfold when you were released from our custody a short time ago? Did you actually believe we would make that sort of mistake? The blindfold was made to come loose so you would notice the address and be able to find your way back. Same with the garage being left open today. And the unlocked door leading into the house. It was all choreographed for your benefit." Amusement filled his eyes. "You took our bait. And I thank you for that." He paused.

"I hope you weren't too attached to your car, by the way. We've permanently disposed of it. But let me bring you up to date. I wasn't getting anywhere with you, so I figured Rena would have a better chance. I admit the plot to get me out of the way was a bit melodramatic. But it worked, apparently. You are so predictable. You and your fellow Americans. You made it easy for us."

Realizing how true the sentiment was, Blair flinched.

"So you go back to Israel like a good little boy," Dalton/Yassin continued. "And this time you are successful. You convince Jeremy Samson to cooperate, to get the DVD production moved to OTE. You return to New York and Rena says she is making arrangements to get your daughter back. What you don't know, however, is that she is stalling. She had to give us time to put our last-minute preparations in place.

"Meanwhile, I should tell you that some of the things that happened to you were not of our doing."

"What things?" Blair asked bitterly.

"Oh, nothing important. The bombing in the restaurant in Tel Aviv? The truck incident in Montreal? These were all instigated by a rival faction, aiming to get you out of the way and disrupt our plans. Lucky for me, they didn't succeed. Otherwise, I would have had to start over again."

"Lucky for you?" Blair said, disbelieving the man's indifference, how easy it was to dismiss the attempts on his life.

• • • • •

Dalton/Yassin now motioned with his hand.

The light in the adjoining room came on, giving Blair a clear view through the window. It was not one-way glass, after all.

Two bearded men wearing *kaffiyehs* sat at a table awaiting instructions.

Dalton/Yassin stepped up to the computer and turned it on. "You will soon understand the importance of your role," he said. He pointed toward the window. "The equipment in that room is identical to that which you will find in the office we will provide for you. You will have access to a computer and all the amenities you are used to." His lips parted in a half-smile.

"You are a one-man show," Dalton/Yassin said. "Our research told us everything we needed to know. Your habits, your customs, the way you run your business, and your personal life. We couldn't have found a better candidate. Out of the three potential men we considered, you came out on top."

"I'm flattered," Blair muttered.

"What's that?"

"Nothing, John. Carry on, please."

The slap on the table reverberated across the room. "Not John! My name is Khalid Yassin. Say it!"

"I hear you. I don't have to say it. Now, where were we?"

Dalton/Yassin gestured to the men seated in the other room. One of them typed something on their computer.

Blair noticed the monitor in the room in which he sat coming to life. Soon, he caught his name scrolling across it after a ten-second delay.

"Give me a phrase or a sentence," Dalton/Yassin requested.

Kiss my ass, was the one he wanted to use. And he almost said it out loud. "The little brown cow," he offered instead.

Once again, one of the men in the opposite room typed and the words appeared on the screen in front of Blair.

"Everything you do," Dalton/Yassin continued, "no matter the time of day or night, will be observed. Trying to trick us won't work. The built-in delay allows us to stop any information you might try to disseminate before it is released.

"We know that you are involved in every aspect of your business. For instance, the standing orders you have at your distribution center, where nothing of value can be shipped without you being present. This most importantly suits our purpose."

Blair paused, absorbed what he'd just been told, and involuntarily shook his head.

Killgallon Logistics was the company he used to handle his warehousing and shipping needs. He and the owner, Larry Killgallon, a broad-shouldered man in his mid-fifties, liked each other, socialized together, and had grown fond of one another.

A year ago, a shipment scheduled for Walmart had ended up going to Toys 'R' Us. The product was stickered with the Walmart code and was priced at two dollars less than their competitor. It didn't take long for the Toys 'R' Us buyer to become aware of this price discrepancy. And even though he had paid the same cost as Walmart, he held Blair's company accountable. This resulted in a price concession of over thirty thousand dollars. In addition, because the promised ship date to Walmart was missed, he was hit with a five-thousand-dollar fine.

Blair immediately instituted a new policy. By paying a premium to Killgallon Logistics, they agreed to have a person on staff dedicated solely to his company's needs. This was someone who would check the veracity of each shipment before it went out.

Despite this precaution, however, another incident occurred that was far worse. It involved a major release of a new, television-advertised product. An action-figure line licensed by the latest trading-card craze originating in Japan. The top three retailers, Target, Toys 'R' Us and Walmart, had each clamored for an advance release. But Blair had refused. Unfortunately, when it came time to ship the product, the person in charge at Killgallon Logistics missed most of the Bills of Lading and only shipped Target. By the time the error was caught, Target ended up with the advantage all three had requested in the first place. The grief Blair got from Toys 'R' Us and Walmart was severe. No explanation could mollify either one.

The person at Killgallon Logistics was fired. From that day forward, the only way a major release could go out was by Blair supervising the shipment in person. An inconvenience, but one that he felt was necessary.

Now, Blair very much regretted ever having put the policy in place. And he realized he was about to find out how much this policy was going to cost him.

• • • • •

The door opened. The two men he'd seen in the other room entered. They were guiding a small table on wheels in front of them. Something was hidden beneath a nylon covering, which was not unlike an oversized, opaque scarf.

Dalton/Yassin made a show of removing the covering and a sample of *Cyber-tech* was revealed. It had been split apart, its guts exposed. There were few wires. The motherboard contained mostly snap-in modules.

An alarm clanged inside Blair's head.

"I said before that you were the best of our three candidates," Dalton/Yassin said. "You see, no one else had access to what we truly needed." He pointed to the broken-apart sample on the table. "Here, let me show you something,"

He picked up the sample of *Cyber-tech* and brought it closer. "This is called a capacitor. It is used to divert the electric charge from what was originally intended. In today's world of miniaturization, you have transistors that are infinitely smaller and more versatile. All we had to do was insert a capacitor, then convert the starter to a trigger mechanism so that this innocuous-looking substance over here can be ignited."

Blair could see nothing but a minuscule, colorless blob that resembled a swatch of hardened glue.

"NC3," Dalton/Yasin said with pride. "The latest, most versatile form of *plastique* available today. Thanks to your generosity, *Cyber-tech* comes with its own batteries. All the customer has to do is pull out this flexible tab like so." He demonstrated. "And the contacts are no longer protected. Just turn on the switch, and voila…"

Sparks flew, and a strange sound was emitted, "*phht*," like a flame igniting.

Dalton/Yassin laughed. "Imagine if the wiring was in place now?" he said. "You and I would be visiting with Allah as I speak. But here comes the best part. Thanks to your ingenious marketing plan, the total production of one hundred thousand pieces will have a specific lay-down date on the evening of September 7th." He paused. "Why do all good things happen to you Americans in the month of September, I wonder? Anyway, precisely at midnight, Walmart, Target, and Toys 'R' Us will keep their doors open to allow their foolish customers to be the first in line to purchase this latest technological device.

"Imagine the headline: '*Cyber-tech*, now coming to you with enough *plastique* to blow you to smithereens.'"

His laugh rose in pitch, sounding eerie, almost demented.

"You see what I'm getting at, my friend? One hundred thousand homes filled with children. Nieces and nephews. Grandchildren."

Envisioning exactly what was being described, Blair began to feel sick.

"To be honest with you," Dalton/Yassin said, "there is the possibility that not all one hundred thousand pieces will sell out the first night. And even if they did, it is highly unlikely that everyone will turn them on as soon as they reach their homes. After all, some will be purchased as gifts.

But worst-case scenario, say only twenty-five thousand units are activated. This will result in a minimum of twenty-five thousand people, or more likely double that amount, being killed." He smiled. "And your company will become famous. Can you not see the irony, Blair Mulligan?"

CHAPTER 54

The truth of his own gullibility shamed him. The number of potential victims sent him into shock. Twenty-five thousand fatalities. Even more.

Blair wondered how Khalid Yassin could reach this point, how anyone could be this devious, so utterly demented.

The man had done an excellent job in conning him, twisting the truth in such a way that it was all made believable.

Blair knew he couldn't turn back the clock. He had played perfectly into Yassin's hands. And for that there was no forgiveness.

• • • • •

He sat in the chair, his mind reeling. He didn't want to hear any more of his questions answered.

He watched now as the men removed the table. Then Khalid Yassin turned back to him. "Let me explain the balance of my plans," he said.

Blair had found his accent faint but perceptible the first time they had met. Yet most of the time, Yassin spoke English like an American. "Were you educated in the States, John?" he asked.

The Arab's face twitched with anger. "You know my name," he said. "Why do you persist in insulting me?"

"Sorry. It was a slip of the tongue. Tell me where you went to school."

"You are not in a position to be asking questions."

"Oh? Why is that? Don't you want me to understand you? So that I can better cooperate? Obey your every command?"

Khalid Yassin's smile was more a smirk. "Obey you will," he said. "Whether you like it or not."

Blair's temper ramped up a notch. "What makes you so sure?"

"Who is strapped in this chair? Me or you?"

"Does it matter?"

"Of course, it matters. Have you lost your mind?"

"No, but you've definitely lost yours!"

In one leap, Yassin was in his face, tightly squeezing his shoulders. "Show some respect! Infidel!"

"And if I don't?"

"You don't want to go there."

"Oh, yes, I do, I want to go there very badly. Because there is nothing more you can get me to do. *Capisce?* Any chance of my cooperating further is kaput! *Fini!*"

The man leaned even closer. "Don't push your luck," he warned, spittle running from his mouth.

And Blair's control was gone. "I *am* pushing it, you bastard!"

The Arab moved back, pulled a remote switch from beneath his robe, and pressed it.

Suddenly, a blue light streaked across the front of Blair's chair. He noticed it before the pain, before an excruciating force attacked his lower extremities. His body convulsed. Once, twice, a third time. And he lost consciousness.

• • • • •

When he came to, the severity of the assault had been such that it took an effort to move.

"No more of your insolence," Yassin was saying. "Do we understand each other?"

He didn't reply.

"I will not ask again."

He nodded.

"What's that? I can't hear you."

"Yes," he said quietly. "We understand each other."

"Yes, what?"

"Yes, Khalid."

"Khalid Yassin."

"Khalid Yassin," Blair repeated, disgusted with himself.

His attention was drawn through the window to the adjoining room. One of Yassin's men came into view. He was pulling someone behind him.

Reality hit Blair with such power, he wanted to scream. He had failed. At the one thing that mattered the most.

Sandra was hardly able to walk.

The second man appeared, holding something metallic-looking in his hand.

Yassin pointed to the computer monitor.

A picture filled the screen, a close-up of Sandra's face. Blair noticed how pale his daughter was. She seemed worn out. And frightened.

The camera panned the room. It zoomed in on the object in the second man's hand. An instrument was exposed that resembled a dentist's pliers.

A knot formed in Blair's stomach and started to burn. He turned in Yassin's direction. "What are you doing?" he asked.

There was no reply.

"Khalid," he pleaded.

"You need to be taught a lesson."

"She's only a child," Blair said, feeling faint.

The picture on the monitor changed. It flipped from Sandra's face to her hand. It was now being held by one of the men in what seemed a viselike grip.

"Three weeks before *Cyber-tech* is to be released to the public," Yassin said in a blasé tone of voice, "you will be driven to your distribution center. There you will give the okay to ship the product to the retailers' various warehouses across America. If you do not follow our instructions, your daughter will be made to suffer." He paused. "Let me show you what I mean."

Blair's heart fluttered. "No, John," he began to say, then quickly caught himself: "I'm sorry. I mean Khalid. Mr. Khalid Yassin. Please. Whatever it is you want me to do, I will do. I understand you perfectly well now. Only don't hurt my daughter. She means you no harm. Please…"

An unknown force drew Blair's attention to the computer monitor. The more he watched, the more his eyes felt physically assaulted.

The pliers were not pliers at all, at least not in the conventional sense. The tip of the bottom arm was ultra narrow. It was flattened and seemed as sharp as a razor. The man inserted this part beneath the nail on Sandra's pinky finger of her left hand.

Blair was surprised that it fit, her nail being so tiny.

The upper arm of the pliers had a serrated edge. The man brought it down until it closed on the nail. And he gave the instrument a vicious pull.

Blair's mouth flew open in shock. He saw the nail being yanked free, then blood squirting, Sandra's blood, as her holler filled the room.

The bile rose in Blair's throat and he knew it wouldn't stop there.

"This is the least painful part," Yassin said as if he were describing an everyday occurrence. "If you disobey us, if you become incapacitated before the ship date, if you cause any delay in our plans whatsoever, your daughter will be torn apart, limb by limb, leaving nothing left for you to bury. Do you understand what I'm saying?"

Dizzy, the bile not only rose to Blair's mouth, it came spewing out.

PART TWO

JUNE • AUGUST

CHAPTER 55

When Sandra was born, Blair was out of town visiting Walmart. He never would have made the trip had his wife not assured him that the baby wasn't due for another week at the earliest.

By the time he arrived at the hospital in Queens, Sandra was a day and a half old. He hurried to the obstetrics ward on the sixth floor. He gave his name to the nurse and explained who he was there to see.

The woman was Puerto Rican, in her late thirties, attractive in an understated way. But slow to smile. Her finger traced names along a foolscap sheet of paper. Then she apologized and asked him to wait a moment.

Blair didn't think anything of it. The nurse was most likely following protocol. He took a seat.

The wait turned into twenty minutes.

"Mr. Mulligan?"

He jumped at the sound of his name. He came face to face with a young doctor—of average height and weight, brown eyes and a scraggly beard. The man smelled like he hadn't showered or bathed in at least a month.

"Yes?" Blair said.

"I'm Dr. Morgan. Your wife is asleep. I'll take you in to see your daughter. Would you follow me, please?"

Typical of hospitals, they traveled in a semi-maze. Three-quarters of the way along the corridor the doctor said, "I want you to know, there's been a slight complication."

Blair steadied himself. "I beg your pardon?"

"There's nothing to be alarmed about. Your child is doing as well as can be expected. Before I take you into the ICU, you should know that it will appear worse than it actually is. MAS is rather common these days."

"MAS?"

"Meconium Aspiration Syndrome."

Blair was suddenly oblivious to the interns and nurses passing by. "And *merconium* is what exactly?" he asked.

"Meconium," the doctor corrected. "It's an infant's first stool. Among other things, it's made up of mucus, bile, and water. Normally, it's expelled into the amniotic fluid prior to birth or during labor. In the case of your daughter, she ingested the contaminated fluid. This is what caused the respiratory problem."

"You mean, she swallowed her own poop?" Blair wanted to know.

"No, no. Meconium is not poop. Not exactly."

"Oh? So what is it, then?"

"Well, it's poop, as you put it, but unlike feces it's sterile, and has no odor. Mr. Mulligan, your daughter is doing okay. I just didn't want you to jump to conclusions. She is in the ICU, like I said."

Blair's anxiety heightened. He did not associate the intensive care unit with anything good.

• • • • •

There were too many of them. Tiny newborns lying in incubators. He followed Dr. Morgan to the furthest corner where a middle-aged nurse, wearing granny glasses, was seated. She was monitoring various instruments. When she noticed him, she stood and said, "Mr. Mulligan, I presume? I'm Susan Armstrong." She indicated the incubator next to her. "And this is your beautiful daughter, Sandra."

A mop of reddish/blond hair. The correct number of fingers and toes. All overshadowed by the tubes and wires running to and from her mouth and chest.

Suddenly, it seemed to Blair that his daughter's heart was racing too fast. Up and down, up and down. He felt his own pulse picking up, in sympathy. He turned to the nurse. "Her heartbeat doesn't seem normal," he said.

The doctor replied, "It's perfectly normal, Mr. Mulligan."

He didn't know if he should believe him. He bent down to get a closer look. Sandra's chest seemed to bounce with each breath she took.

"Barring any complications," Dr. Morgan said, "your daughter should be released from the ICU before the week is out."

Blair traced a line with his hand along the glass of the incubator. "She's so tiny," he whispered, in awe.

"Tiny but beautiful," the doctor said, obviously trying to cheer him up.

Standing in such close proximity, Dr. Morgan's BO started to get to Blair. He moved away, until he was diagonally across from him. "When will Dr. Sherkin be here?" he thought to ask. Kal Sherkin was their obstetrician and someone in whom Blair had full confidence.

"He's already been," the nurse said. "But he'll be back."

When exactly? he wondered, but knew what the answer would be. Doctors worked to their own schedule.

He remained standing, observing his daughter. He was nervous despite Dr. Morgan's attempts to reassure him. It was just sinking in that he was actually a father. He wanted to bathe in the euphoria, and not have to fear for Sandra's life.

• • • • •

For weeks and months after his daughter was released from the hospital, Blair kept a constant vigil. The least complaint started him wondering—throughout the teething process, the times she came down with a cold, whenever a rash appeared. Every bit of discomfort she displayed sent his mind into overdrive.

Blair had to discipline himself to refrain from pestering their doctor. And it took until her first birthday before he finally believed that Sandra was out of the woods. Then he vowed that he would protect her from harm for the rest of her life.

No matter what...

CHAPTER 56

May passed into June.

Blair sat at his desk, a decrepit antique made of wood, in the basement office arranged especially for him. It was a windowless room with bare walls. A fairly new Dell computer sat at his beck and call. His e-mail address had been inserted and was now operational.

Requests to see his daughter were ignored. He tried every argument he could think of. He even swallowed his pride and begged. It was hopeless.

Blair found it disconcerting that these people were religious enough to feel the call to prayer multiple times a day, yet embraced torture and murder as if they were sanctioned by a Supreme Being.

Khalid Yassin paid him occasional visits, usually at night. Invariably, one of his unfiltered cigarettes would dangle from his mouth. Too often he would boast of how this was only the beginning. How each new strike they planned against the United States was going to get bigger and more bold. How he, Blair, and the rest of the infidels would meet a just fate. Whatever that meant.

Blair dreaded these visits and bore them with a resolve that took all his discipline. Uppermost on his mind was the fact that on September 7th, one hundred thousand pieces of *Cyber-tech* would be released across America. A quarter of consumers, perhaps more, would turn the game on that same night. The numbers were staggering. *Twenty-five thousand explosions.*

Blair thought back to when the concept of *Cyber-tech* was first introduced to him. The Israelis were normally leaders in this sort of product, not followers. Unlike the Japanese and the automobile industry, wherein the best features of German and American cars were often imitated, in the case of *Cyber-tech*, the tables had been reversed. A Japanese product, or a group of products, had been copied by the Israelis and made better.

Unfortunately, rather than a chance at the brass ring, Blair had become a pawn of new-wave fanaticism: Islamic fundamentalists motivated by pure hatred masquerading as philosophical need.

His fault.

This is what it came down to. A realization borne not out of self-pity but the truth. Avarice had thrust him into this situation. His eagerness to hit the big score. *Cyber-tech* was to be his ticket to financial freedom. Instead he would be responsible for mass murder.

• • • • •

He began to type on the computer. He hit each key much harder than necessary. Blair always considered his secretary, Andrea Victor, to be a bright woman. He wondered now why she wasn't getting it.

For the past few weeks he had purposely refrained from giving her the okay to place their orders for the fall season. Without these goods, his company would be in default with many of the major retailers, thereby incurring huge fines.

Andrea knew this. More often than not, she would be the one to remind him of the approaching deadline. What with the requirement of ninety-day lead times or longer, the toy product was either ordered from the Orient now or it would arrive too late.

Blair hoped that by avoiding the subject, Andrea would perceive that something was wrong. It was grasping at straws, he knew. But what else was there? He had racked his brain ever since his capture. Unless his secretary noticed his omission, it would all be for naught.

• • • • •

The image of Sandra's fingernail being extracted constantly haunted his dreams. Tonight it was more pronounced. Giving up on sleep altogether, he sat up in bed and looked at his watch. It was the one piece of personal property that they hadn't confiscated. The time read 3:17 AM.

He stepped to the floor.

His room seemed to be an afterthought, perhaps something added on after the original house had been built.

He rapped his knuckles on the wall. It made a solid sound. As quietly as possible, he continued to probe.

When nothing came of his search, he crawled under the bed. He removed his watch and, cognizant of the noise, began to tap at the space between the headboard and the floor.

It took almost a half-hour before he finally heard something hollow. Too exhausted to continue, he marked the spot with a pencil and vowed to get back to it tomorrow.

CHAPTER 57

The next morning the knock came, as expected, at precisely seven o'clock.

Blair opened the door. The woman was wearing a *hijab*. With her face covered, he couldn't tell if he'd seen her before. He could only go by her size and body language. Neither rang any bells. She handed him a tray of food. He accepted it in silence. The woman turned and he closed the door behind her.

There was a bridge table in the center of the room. He placed the tray on it and took a seat in one of two plastic chairs.

The light in the room came from a lone brass fixture. Unattractive, it dangled like a poor man's chandelier. Blair found its brightness intrusive.

This morning his breakfast was something they'd never served him before. It could have been fish or eggs. It was impossible to tell with the brown sauce that was slathered on top of it.

Blair tentatively dug his plastic fork into the concoction. Ignoring the unpleasant odor, he took a small bite, then practically gagged. He spit out the balance. Then he hurried into the bathroom to rinse his mouth.

• • • • •

Settled in his office, he began to compose e-mail after e-mail. To his secretary, his group of independent sales representatives, Andrew Sciascia, his sister, to Jeremy Samson. No matter how he tried to improvise, to insert a call for help, words failed him. It was truly disheartening to not be able to reveal what was on his mind.

Lunch was a small portion of fresh fruit. It was so much tastier than his breakfast, he savored each morsel as if it would be his last. Then he went back to work. He flailed away on the computer keyboard, but achieved nothing worthwhile.

Dinner resembled chicken but had a foreign texture. White meat on a bone. Blair didn't know what it was and didn't care. His taste buds accepted it and that was good enough for him.

In his bedroom that night, he started on the wall again, taking his time.

When the voice came to him, he paused. Until now he'd been able to ignore it. But it forced its way into his subconscious and reminded him of his options: his daughter or the lives of no less than twenty-five thousand strangers.

He shook his head, desperately trying to clear it.

CHAPTER 58

Blair continued to ask to see his daughter. Yassin was unwilling to let that happen. So for the next few days he stopped working, stopped eating, stopped getting out of bed.

Now it was Yassin who opened the door and stepped inside. "I hear you've been misbehaving," he said.

Blair glared at him. "I want to see Sandra."

"I already told you. That's not going to happen."

"Why not? What harm could it do?"

"No harm. The simple fact is, your daughter is doing well. There is no need to add confusion to her life."

"Confusion?" Blair came to a sitting position. "What the hell are you talking about?"

"Don't raise your voice, Mr. Mulligan."

"What confusion can there be?" he asked more quietly. "I am her father, for God's sake."

"And don't take the name of your lord in vain." Yassin stepped closer, and took a seat on the edge of the bed. "You would think you'd have learned your lesson by now," he said, the voice of reason. "You will do as I ask without any more of your demands. You can starve yourself to death, as far as I am concerned. But only after my operation has been completed. If you dare try something else, no matter how insignificant, you will be made to pay, in a way you will always remember. Have I made myself clear, Blair Mulligan?"

He was fed up with the way the man continued to use both his surname and given name. But he kept his silence.

"Well?" Yassin pushed.

More than ever, Blair resented his own shortcomings.

Yassin rose to his feet. "Do not try my patience," he said.

"At least let me speak to Sandra by phone," Blair pleaded.

Yassin went to the door, opened it and stepped out. He did not bother to look back, let alone offer a reply.

CHAPTER 59

Blair got out of bed, furious that his hunger strike had been a waste of time. He moved the bed aside and dropped to his knees. Carefully, he took hold of the one solid piece of plaster he had been able to extricate recently. It was approximately three-by-two. By preserving it, he hoped to cover up whatever damage was being done to the wall.

Now, he noticed the outline of a crawlspace. Unfortunately, it was surrounded by mortar and insulation. Much of it had hardened and was twinned together. He tried using his watch as a tool again. But very little plaster came loose. He worked for almost an hour before pausing to examine his handiwork. He still hadn't made much headway. And his task remained formidable.

He replaced the piece of plaster in the outer wall and stood, slowly made his way into the bathroom, and took his shower. There was soap but no shampoo. Drying off, he made the mistake of looking in the mirror. His hair was growing long and unruly. For the first time in his life there was significant stubble on his face. He did not find it attractive.

Getting dressed in the same sport shirt and jeans he'd worn since the day he was captured, Blair tried to ignore his body odor. For someone who always prided himself on his hygiene, it hurt not to have the use of something as basic as cologne and deodorant.

With a shrug of resignation, he left his room and headed for the office, located a mere step or two down the hall.

Jeremy Samson's e-mail was waiting for him on his computer:

I'VE BEEN TRYING TO CALL YOU FOR THE LAST WEEK AND A HALF. DID YOU LOSE YOUR CELL PHONE? OR ARE YOU SIMPLY TRYING TO AVOID ME?

Blair paused. By not sending a reply, Jeremy would surely know something was wrong. So he decided to do nothing.

• • • • •

Within minutes, Yassin entered the office with a landline phone. He unraveled the cord and plugged it in. "Here, use this," he said, handing him the receiver.

"What for?" Blair asked, professing ignorance.

"What do you think it's for? Your friend in Israel wants to talk to you. So you will call him. This phone is untraceable and works on a delay. As usual, we'll be listening."

Knowing he had no choice, he took hold of the receiver and nodded automatically. Once Yassin left, Blair began to dial the Tel Aviv number, at the same time trying to think of a way to foil the man's plans.

"*Shalom*," Jeremy said.

Shalom to you, too, would have been Blair's normal rejoinder. Instead, he offered a plain, "Hello," hoping the subtle difference would be noticed.

"I guess you found a phone that works."

"Yes, sir."

"Good. Where are you, by the way?"

"Away," he said. Then quickly added: "On a business trip."

"Oh? It must be a long trip."

"You've got that right."

"The *Cyber-tech* TV commercial's been shot and it's wonderful. I was wondering if I could send you a copy?"

"Please do."

"To your office?"

Blair paused. "Yes," he said, "my office is fine."

"Will you be back soon?"

"I should be."

"You don't sound sure."

"Oh, no, I'm sure," Blair said unconvincingly. And a new thought came to mind. "Jeremy, I was wondering if you'd heard from Ms. Brandt?" he asked.

"Just the other day."

"How is she?"

"She's fine. Why do you ask?"

"Would you let her know that she wasn't wrong? I believe she'd like to hear that."

"Uh-uh, *boychick*. That's something you'll have to tell Lisa yourself."

"You think so?"

"I know so."

Jeremy led the conversation back to *Cyber-tech*. But Blair was hardly concentrating. After his goodbye, he wondered if he'd said enough for his friend to notice.

Almost immediately, Yassin came storming back in. Three of his henchmen were by his side. Without a word, Blair was snatched off his feet. The men bodily carried him out of the room and into the one a few doors down, where he was strapped into the metal chair he'd come to hate.

"I am going to ask you some questions," Yassin began. "And I want your truthful answers."

Yeah, Blair told himself. *You'll get the truth, all right.*

"Who is Ms. Brandt?" Yassin asked.

Blair knew if he didn't act natural, he'd be caught. And Lisa along with him. "A friend of mine," he said, fighting down his panic.

"Who does she work for?"

"I don't know the name of the firm. She's a masseuse."

"Liar!" the man hissed. "I will ask you again. Who does she work for?"

Blair tried to change positions in the chair. The straps were too tight. "I can only repeat what I know," he said. "She works as a therapeutic masseuse, mainly with athletes."

The smack came quickly, once across his cheek.

"What is Lisa Brandt's connection to Jeremy Samson?"

"They are friends," he said.

"Just friends? Not business associates?"

"That's correct."

Yassin's nostrils flared. Then he smacked him again, harder this time.

Blair tasted blood, and knew his cheek had been cut.

"You are lying. Who does Lisa work for?"

"I already told you."

Yassin's hand formed a fist. But before the punch could be thrown, his arm went into spasm.

By the time he recovered, he was furious. "You will tell me the truth," he warned. And he palmed the same remote switch he'd used before, held it up so there'd be no mistaking what it was.

Blair tried to buy time. "Lisa is a masseuse," he said quickly. "Jeremy owns a toy company. That's all I know about them. Why won't you believe me?"

"Because you are not being truthful," Yassin said.

"I am."

"You are not, my friend."

"Listen to me…"

"No, you listen," Yassin said, and he pressed the remote.

• • • • •

The pain in Blair's testicles gradually subsided, but he knew he'd been burned and it would take a long while to heal.

Meanwhile, he wished he could recant his conversation with Jeremy. He cared about Lisa, far more than he'd been able to admit. Putting her at risk was the worst thing he could have done. Getting a message to Jeremy was one thing, not thinking it through clearly, quite another.

"We will talk again," Yassin said.

The straps holding him bound to the chair were undone. He tried to stand but was too weak to do so.

Yassin's men carried him to his room, where he was unceremoniously dumped on the bed.

He lay there, staring at the ceiling, waiting for his strength to return. Thinking of Lisa brought back bittersweet memories. And he was reminded of the mistake he had made in not trusting her, in rejecting her offer to help.

Finally, he made his way to the bathroom. He examined his mouth in the mirror and found the cut in his cheek.

It was a small price to pay, he told himself, for not having caved in.

He tried to urinate. A weak stream came out, but most of it was blood.

A small price to pay indeed, he realized.

CHAPTER 60

Back in bed, he asked himself what was the measure of a man.

His integrity?

His intestinal fortitude?

His ability to act and react in a dignified manner?

By any criterion, he had failed and failed miserably.

Early on, when Khalid Yassin was still John Dalton, the man's behavior should have been warning enough.

It was pitiful, Blair concluded now. The way he had followed orders. He blamed it on his upbringing, the fact that he was taught that anyone of authority automatically deserved respect. Dalton identified himself as a member of a government agency. And he had taken him at his word.

• • • • •

He worked at the wall, doing his best to enlarge the hole. He imagined himself crawling through it and finding freedom. For two hours he chipped away, until the muscles in his arms and shoulders became sore.

He paused.

He was not impressed with his effort at all.

It was just one more indication of his impotence. And this fact was as debilitating as his physical distress.

• • • • •

He settled into routine.

When his secretary advised by e-mail that his ex-wife had charged him with kidnapping, he was encouraged. Apparently, the police had issued a warrant for his arrest.

But an inner voice, playing devil's advocate, warned that the chance of the police finding him was less than nil.

All he could do, he decided, was to will time to slow down, even as it marched, inexorably, closer and closer toward the unthinkable.

CHAPTER 61

It was late a few nights later and he had the bed pushed aside. The piece of plaster guarding the puncture in the wall had been removed. He was on his knees, anxious to get results.

His substantial weight loss had sapped his strength. If he didn't try something now, he feared he wouldn't have the energy for another attempt later.

He reached out to a chunk of insulation and pushed it aside. Then another section and another.

Some forty-five minutes later he was drenched in sweat. Dust seemed to fill every cavity, from his ears to his nose to his mouth. He examined his watch. Its gold-plated sides had been scratched beyond recognition.

His only chance of making progress, he decided, would be to reverse positions. This way he could use his feet as a battering ram. He lay on his back, brought his legs in, then kicked as hard as he could.

If this was to be his last chance, he was going to take it. He used both legs together, then one at a time. Until…

Disbelief threatened to crush him. His right foot had become stuck. No matter how he tried to free it, it wouldn't work. Finally, he leaned in with his upper body and dug at the plaster with his hands. The strain on his back became unbearable. He lay flat for a minute or two before going at it again, this time using his free leg, a frenetic effort, giving it everything he had.

It wasn't working.

He began to imagine the worst case scenario: his foot remaining wedged in place until the morning, when Yassin would walk in and find him.

This image set him off.

But no matter how he clawed at the wall, his foot wouldn't budge. He alternated between his hands and his leg, until he actually considered giving up.

That's it, he teased himself. *Just quit. Show everyone what you're really made of.*

He let his breath out slowly.

No! He shook his head.

He mustn't quit.

He went back at the wall, the noise no longer mattering to him. He grunted aloud and kicked for all he was worth.

• • • • •

When the door to his room flew open, Blair held his breath and waited. He had purposely kept the lights off. The bedspread had been bunched up so it would appear he was beneath it, asleep. The bed may have been moved out of position, but it still blocked him from view.

He remained still.

Unfortunately, the dust that had settled in his nose now began to tickle. He clamped both hands over his face. Instead of muffling the sneeze, it came out as a snort.

In a rush, the bed was jerked aside. Arms took hold, and tried yanking him free.

There was no give.

Yassin's look was one of disgust. "What were you trying to do?" he asked. "This wall doesn't lead anywhere. You were wasting your time." He turned to the other men. "Get him out of there," he instructed. "No matter what it takes."

• • • • •

Blair couldn't say how it happened. The men relentlessly pounded on the wall and on him. One minute he was stuck in the hole, helpless, the next he was strapped back into the all-too-familiar chair.

"I warned you about trying something stupid!" Yassin said, fury masking his face.

Blair knew any comment would be pointless.

The table that was used before to hold the *Cyber-tech* sample was now rolled in and positioned next to him. It contained a butcher's block, masking tape, and a pair of scissors.

"I never should have trusted you," Yassin muttered as if talking to himself. He gripped Blair's right hand, splayed the fingers out on top of the block, and began to secure each digit in place with the masking tape. He trimmed the tape with the scissors.

Blair noticed the machete for the first time.

"I gave you freedom and you abused it." Yassin continued to lecture as he took the machete in hand. "You are not a man of honor, Blair Mulligan. You must be taught a lesson."

What flashed in Blair's mind was a life without fingers. Not being able to write or play golf. Not being able to feel or touch.

Yassin's hand rose above his head. "Do you have anything to say for yourself?"

Blair's thought process had shuttered, rendering him mute.

"I asked you a question."

Say something! Anything!

Too late. The machete came down.

CHAPTER 62

One week prior, Abdul Masri, Yassin's second-in-command, a tall, bearded man in his early forties, had joined Yassin for a cup of coffee. Yassin didn't particularly like the man. But Masri had proven himself to be defiant yet loyal. And loyalty went a long way with him.

When Masri asked if the years of planning were worth it, Yassin hesitated before replying. He was tempted to tell his second-in-command it was none of his business. "Why do you ask?" he said instead.

"Because, if it was me, I wouldn't have the patience."

"Even if you knew the good you were doing?"

"Even then. So I admire you."

"There is nothing to admire. This plot was initiated a few years ago. Paid informants did the research. Arranging the funding was the most complicated part."

"But still worth it?" Abdul persisted.

He nodded. "Absolutely. Look at the impact we will have. The number of casualties. You will go down in history, my friend, along with the rest of us."

• • • • •

When Yassin asked about the final arrangements, Masri acted as if it were an imposition to have to review it with him.

"First," he began, making a show of counting on his fingers, "your airline ticket has been bought and paid for, in cash, in the name you provided. A few of us will be leaving the country by other means. The rest will disperse. Some will return to their private lives, at least for the time being.

"Second, the videotaping of the girl will be completed this afternoon. We will get her to say all the right things, so her father will believe they are to be reunited.

"Third, our group has already been divided into teams as you had instructed. One team will handle luggage and transportation and the like. The other will assure that every piece of furniture, as well as utensils, walls, windows, and lavatories are wiped clean and sterilized.

"Fourth, on the day the retailers put the product on sale, at midnight on September 7th, I will leave New York and drive to Montreal, then fly to Cairo. I will make my way by land back to Palestine. A few others, especially Bishara and Munir, will take circuitous routes but use similar itineraries. They will catch up with us later. Did I cover it all?"

Yassin caught the tone of the question but let it pass. He had either been locked up with Masri too long, or the man simply grated on his nerves. "Seems like you covered it fine," he said. "Thank you."

Yassin now took a digitized electronic receiver out of his pocket and turned it on. Feedback caused it to shriek. He changed positions in the chair and the sound stopped. Sometimes, when he got too close to the transmitting wire, he'd get the same result. "I guess it's working," he said. "Why don't you step into the hallway and say a few words?"

Masri did as he was told.

Yassin found that the signal was clear enough for him to hear the other man's breathing.

"Testing," Masri's voice soon came through. "Testing, one, two, three."

"One week from Friday," Yassin said when the other man returned, "you will take Mr. Mulligan with you to his distribution center. There, you will park opposite the loading dock on the side of the building. Mulligan will be wired. You will listen in as he approves the shipping of *Cyber-tech* to the retailer's warehouses across the country. If he doesn't do this, if anything he says raises suspicion, you will immediately abort your position.

"If he does as he is told, however, as soon as you see him returning to the car, you will call me on your cell phone. Once he gets in the car, you are to kill him, dump his body in the trunk, and call me back.

"Without that second phone call we will assume that something has gone wrong." He paused. "Do you have the cyanide tablet?"

Masri told him that he did, motioning toward his shirt pocket.

"Good. Under no circumstances are you to allow the authorities to capture you. We are too close now to have anything go wrong. Understood?"

"Yes, sir," Masri muttered disdainfully.

Yassin looked at him long and hard, but held his silence.

CHAPTER 63

Blair shut his eyes just before the machete reached his hand. He waited for the pain. Waited for his life to change forever. It was only a matter of a second. Perhaps not even that.

He opened his eyes.

The look on Yassin's face embarrassed him. It was a bluff. The son of a bitch wanted to see him squirm.

Yassin set the machete aside. "Unfortunately, my friend," he said, "I need you in one piece. We still have our endgame to play out. But—"

The punch was unexpected. It caught Blair just below his heart.

"Your little act of rebellion cannot go unpunished," Yassin stated matter-of-factly.

Blair couldn't breathe. He gulped for air.

"What's the matter?" Yassin questioned with mock concern. "Did I hurt you?"

Blair glared at him, doubting he'd ever hated anyone as much.

And Yassin came at him again, his punches thrown systematically, pummeling Blair's chest and stomach.

Blair tried telling himself it was mind over matter.

"Had enough?" Yassin taunted.

The hurt was unlike anything he'd experienced. It seemed to swell without release. Battered, he doubted whether he could take much more.

Yassin's fists were relentless.

The last thing Blair remembered was crying out.

• • • • •

His dream came that night.

His fingers had not only been severed but gangrene had set in. He heard the doctors discussing his case.

"Amputate?"

"Yes."

"When?"

"Within the hour."

"Is there any other way?"

"I'm afraid not."

The scene was so real, Blair shuddered.

• • • • •

It took a full day before he could get out of bed. He pushed the covers aside and sat up. He felt as if he had a fever. Reluctantly, he allowed his gaze to drop. It was a relief to see that his fingers were still attached.

He coughed; blood trickled down his chin.

Blair stood and slowly made his way to the bathroom. Once again, there was blood in his urine. A few of the burn marks on his testicles had formed scabs and were sensitive to the touch.

Getting dressed in the same shirt and pair of jeans, he could smell the sweat in his clothes. There was a *gallabiya* hanging in the bathroom, but the Arab robe was the last thing he'd wear.

Being honest with himself, Blair understood that he was an ordinary Joe, ill-equipped both mentally and physically. Ordinary simply wasn't good enough in his situation. He had no illusions. He felt like a loser. And he was getting a loser's comeuppance.

His insides burned from the physical beating he'd taken as he began to pace the room. His eyes went to the oversized light fixture. Something clicked but he didn't know why. He continued to pace. Then he noticed the bed sheet. And he realized how easy it would be to tie a noose.

Those who wanted to cast stones could do so. His daughter was too important for him to decide against her, twenty-five or even fifty thousand strangers, as the case may be, not withstanding.

It seemed so logical. Why choose at all if a choice could be shunned? He was dead anyway. Hastening this fact by a few weeks made perfect sense. If he waited and Yassin didn't kill him, his conscience would.

CHAPTER 64

It is four o'clock in the afternoon. Blair is twelve years old. He is ice skating with friends in Montreal. They are on a frozen neighborhood pond. It is five below zero. They have the pond more or less to themselves. What bothers Blair is the fact that his skates don't fit. Handed down from a cousin, they are at least two sizes too big. For this reason, his toes are so cold he can barely feel them. Couple that with his constantly running nose and he decides to call it quits.

"Hey, where do you think you're going?" Bobby Harris calls to him as he heads for the spot where he left his shoes.

Bobby is in his class at school. He is heavyset for his age, and was born with a left arm that is deformed.

"I've had enough," Blair tells him.

"Pussy! Get your ass back here!"

Blair hesitates. He doesn't want to appear weak. So he changes his mind. He goes after his friend and challenges him to a race. Despite the ill-fitting skates, he is confident that he can beat him. He has been skating since he was four years old.

Bobby takes up the dare and they start to circle the pond. Each time they pass one of their friends, Bobby makes it a point to push the boy closest to him out of the way.

Each accepts it in stride. Alex Simmons first, then Ivan Chittenden and Felix Beauchemin. But when Bobby bumps Jean Bernier on his shoulder, the boy takes exception and bumps back, using more force than necessary.

Bobby tumbles to the ice.

Instead of stopping, Jean continues to skate as if nothing has happened.

Bobby gets back on his feet and races after him.

Both boys are more or less equal in weight and stature. The fight starts in the center of the pond. Bobby's right arm helps position his left hand in front of his face as a shield. Then his right hand forms a fist and he strikes out. Jean counterpunches. Soon Jean's nose starts to bleed as does Bobby's lip.

Taking this as their cue, Alex and Ivan finally step between them and pull them apart, which is when the insults start flying:

"Fuckin' Frenchman!"

"Maudit Anglais!"

"Screw off!"

"Baise mon cul!"

All five boys change into their winter boots. The fight between Bobby and Jean has already been forgotten.

It is only 5:30, but being the middle of winter, darkness has fallen. The friends live in the same lower-class neighborhood. They cut through a laneway and end up on a street that is snow-laden and quiet.

"Lookee here," Bobby says, pointing at someone coming toward them.

The blind boy is in his early-teens. He is of average height, wearing an oversized parka and baggy jeans.

"Hey, man," Bobby says.

The boy stops. His white cane taps the sidewalk. He is unaware that three of the others have formed a circle around him. "Do I know you?" he asks.

"No," Bobby says. "Though I've seen you before." He snatches the cane from his hand.

"Give that back!" the boy demands.

Bobby flings the cane to the other side of the street. It hits the sidewalk and slides another ten feet. "You have to find it," he says. "But we'll guide you."

"No, you get it for me!" The boy holds his ground.

"Fuck you!" Bobby says. "Go get it yourself!"

The boy doesn't say anything. He brushes past them and continues walking, leaving the cane behind.

Blair admires his courage. And he asks himself why he didn't do anything to help. But his aversion to violence is inbred. He comes to blows only when pushed to the brink, when he loses his temper. Until that point, he does everything he can to avoid it.

• • • • •

Two afternoons later, after their skate, they are taking the identical route home when they encounter the same boy.

Bobby does it again. He strips the cane from the boy's hand and fires it across the street. It embeds itself in a snow bank.

"Sonofabitch!" the boy swears.

"Watch your mouth!" Bobby gets in his face.

"I want my cane back, asshole!"

Bobby seems amused. "Same offer as the other day," he says. "We'll give you directions on how to find it."

The boy tries to step around him.

"Not that way," Bobby says.

The boy is taller than Bobby. He reaches out and grabs the sleeve of his jacket. Bobby brushes the hand aside and punches the boy in the stomach.

Blair is stricken. He runs across the street, digs the cane out of the snow bank, and brings it back. "Here," he says, placing the cane in the boy's hand. "Take this and go."

"Wait a minute," Bobby says. "Who gave you permission to interfere?"

Blair ignores him. "Go on," he says to the blind boy. "Get out of here."

The others form a circle and won't let him pass. Each time he tries, he is pushed back. He taps his cane, invariably touching someone's boot.

Blair takes hold of the boy's arm. He forces an opening in the circle so the boy can pass through.

Silence envelopes the group. Bobby stares at Blair. "You shouldn't have done that," he says. He throws a punch that catches him in the upper chest.

Blair goes down. He splays his legs out, then brings them in to the fetal position.

"Stand up!" Bobby demands.

He doesn't move.

"Chicken-shit!" Jean Bernier pipes in.

"Cunt!" Ivan curses.

Someone kicks him.

It doesn't hurt, but Blair groans, pretending that it does.

Bobby gazes down at him. He tells him to stand up and fight like a man.

He still doesn't say or do anything.

Bobby spits at him.

A wide gob hits his forehead and begins to trickle into his eyes.

Blair remains in that prone position until he is certain they have gone.

CHAPTER 65

His head swam. Reliving that event of long ago, Blair wondered who he truly was. The twelve-year-old with enough courage to help someone who was blind? Or the one who refused to stand up and defend himself against a boy with a crippled arm?

His conscience twitched. It forced him to reflect once more on the bed sheet and the light fixture. The easy way out.

He thought back to the classic novels he had read. One particular character came to mind: Robert Jordan, in Hemingway's *For Whom The Bell Tolls*. Lying injured and facing certain death, the man refused to give up without a fight.

Who am I, Blair wanted to know now. *Robert Jordan? Or someone else? Someone not even worth thinking about?*

• • • • •

In the room they called his office, he turned on the computer and began sending e-mails. One to his sister, one to Jeremy Samson, one to his lawyer, a dozen more to his business associates. Each was a call for help of which only he was aware. The secret words weren't as much disguised as nonexistent.

Blair recognized there was less than a week to go. Less than seven days to decide. If he stopped the shipment of *Cyber-tech* from going out, they would kill his daughter. If he gave the okay for the product to be distributed, as many as twenty-five thousand people would perish. Maybe more. Among the victims would be a large percentage of boys and girls the same age as Sandra.

How could he allow that many children to die?

For the balance of that day, into the next, and the one after that, Blair couldn't think of anything else.

Was there even a choice to be made? he asked himself.

A nervous tic developed in his right eye. Rubbing it only made it worse.

• • • • •

He put a call through to his mother that had been cleared with Yassin beforehand.

They had a problem connecting him at first. Then the caregiver at the hospice in Montreal asked him to hold for a moment longer. When she came back on the line she was apologetic. "I am sorry, Mr. Mulligan; your mother is not able to speak to you at the moment. Is it possible for you to call back later?"

His need to hear his mother's voice was such that Blair felt bitterly disappointed. "Yes," he said. "I'll call back."

CHAPTER 66

By the time daylight broke on Friday morning, the nervous tic in his right eye had progressed and gotten worse. His stomach and chest were still sore, and the pain in his lower extremities seemed amplified.

All night long Blair had relived the various stages in his daughter's life: Proudly displaying what she'd crayoned. Dancing to whatever song was on the radio. Singing to him.

How could he live without her?

• • • • •

Getting out of bed, his body felt like it belonged to someone else. The lump on his shoulders that could have been his head was floating a thousand miles away.

He responded to the knock on his door and accepted the breakfast tray. Then he waited for the woman to leave before closing the door behind her.

He left the food untouched.

Getting ready, Blair was unable to reason logically. Sacrificing his daughter was out of the question, as was sealing the fate of thousands of other children.

A sound escaped his lips, part sigh, part protest. He opened the door and moved into the hallway, where he found a smartly dressed Khalid Yassin standing there to greet him. Gone was his *djellaba*, replaced by a dark-brown suit and matching tie. "I hope you had a peaceful night," he said as if addressing an honored guest.

Blair tried to move past him.

"Where are you going?" Yassin asked.

"To my office."

"No you're not. We have plans for you, my friend. Have you forgotten what day this is?"

He ignored him.

"Mr. Mulligan?" Yassin took hold of his arm.

Blair thought of taking his shot. Right then. Pouncing on him, despite his depleted strength.

Yassin's look became hard, unfriendly, as if he could read what was on Blair's mind.

• • • • •

They insisted he sit in the very metal chair he dreaded. A man began to trim his hair with a comb and scissors. Then he shaved off his mustache and beard.

"We want you to be presentable," Yassin said, once it was done. He handed him a mirror.

Blair disbelieved the face was his own. Sunken cheeks, ultra-pale skin, swollen pockets under his eyes.

"You look wonderful," a smiling Yassin said.

Not only a bastard but a liar, Blair thought. "Where is Sandra?"

he asked.

"Your daughter is busy."

"We had a deal: I head off to approve the shipment of *Cyber-tech* and you release her."

"Not until you return. But I may have a compromise for you…"

• • • • •

Yassin stepped up to the computer. He turned it on and pressed something on the keyboard. "I taped this earlier today," he said.

Sandra was sitting in a chair that was far too big for her, her feet dangling over the front. She was wearing a simple pink dress. Her hair was pulled back in a ponytail. "Hello, Daddy," she said, obviously following a script. "Today is Friday, August seventeenth. I have been treated good..."

Blair felt a chill go up his spine. He had never seen her look so lost.

"I can hardly wait to see you," she continued, her tone reticent and dull. "I've missed you. But the man said that today… Um—he said that today is the day you'll be taking me home."

Blair didn't want the video to end. Sandra muttered something about being anxious. And then she said, "I love you, Daddy."

He wouldn't have known there were tears if not for Yassin handing him a tissue. Blair dabbed at his eyes and watched as the monitor screen went blank.

CHAPTER 67

"Take off your shirt," Yassin said.

He unbuttoned his sport shirt and let it drop to the floor. As if in an alternate state, he watched as the wire was taped to his still-bruised chest. He winced with each touch of the man's fingers.

"Say something," he was instructed.

"I have nothing to say."

Yassin motioned with his head toward the other man standing close by.

The "thumbs up" signal was given.

"We are set," Yassin said.

Blair put his shirt back on. The other man guided him out of the room, along the corridor, and up the stairs to the garage.

"Abdul will be your driver," Yassin explained. "He will take you to the distribution center. He will listen in as you give your instructions, then drive you back here to be reunited with your daughter. At that point, your task will be completed, and you will never hear from us again."

Like hell, Blair wanted to say, knowing he couldn't believe him.

• • • • •

They rode the Westside Highway to the Holland Tunnel, then crossed into New Jersey.

Blair was seated in the back of the Lincoln. The nearer they got to their destination, the more he mentally pleaded for release. He didn't want to make a decision, would give anything to avoid it.

They entered the town of Secaucus and were soon at the sprawling building that Blair knew well. It was one of many in this same neighborhood, of average size, two stories tall.

Blair's heart labored as they drove around to the side and pulled to a stop.

There were six loading bays, four of which were occupied. A few were accepting deliveries. Most had goods that were being shipped out. The drivers and their helpers were concentrating on their tasks.

Abdul turned toward him. "You go now," he said in passable English. "I wait here and you come back. Yes?"

It was cloudy and humid, but Blair still appreciated the fresh air as he stepped from the car.

Choose!

That one command filtered through his brain.

• • • • •

The closer he got to the front of the building, the slower he progressed. Finally, he opened the door, moved inside, and approached the reception desk.

"Mr. Mulligan?" the woman questioned, her mouth flying open.

"Hello, Debbie," Blair said.

"My God, are you okay?" She jumped up, and pointed to the nearest chair. "Here, why don't you have a seat? Were you in an accident or something?"

"No, no. I'm okay. Could you find Mr. Killgallon for me?" The thought of retracing his steps, making a run for it, truly appealed to him.

"Hey you," Larry Killgallon said.

The voice jarred him back to reality. Blair turned.

"Holy Christ!" Larry said, his smile dissolving.

"C'mon." Blair took the initiative and led the way. "Let's go up to your office."

Nothing more was said until Larry was seated behind his desk.

"I'm here to authorize the release of *Cyber-tech*," Blair pronounced formally for the sake of the wire. He removed his shirt and quickly placed a finger to his lips. "Is the paperwork ready for me to sign?"

Larry reeled back in shock.

Blair shook his head, then pantomimed the need for pen and paper.

While Larry fumbled in his desk drawer, Blair asked for confirmation to be sent to him once the shipments of *Cyber-tech* were completed. "I'll need Bill of Lading numbers," he said.

The pen and paper materialized. Blair began inquiring after Larry's children as he quickly scribbled his note:

NO MATTER WHAT I SAY, UNDER NO CIRCUMSTANCES ARE YOU TO RELEASE CYBER-TECH. *THE PRODUCT IS TO BE IMMEDIATELY PLACED IN QUARANTINE. AS SOON AS I LEAVE, YOU ARE TO CALL THE POLICE AND TELL THEM THAT THERE IS AN AL-QAEDA CELL HOLDING MY DAUGHTER HOSTAGE. (ADDRESS AS FOLLOWS.)*

Blair wrote out the address and thrust the note in Larry's hand.

The man's eyes bulged at what he was reading.

Blair waited.

Larry took the pen in hand. He wrote out his own message and handed it to him.

WHAT CAN I DO TO HELP?

Blair put his palms together, showing a need for prayer.

The other man indicated he understood.

• • • • •

It took the walk outside to bring Blair to his senses. And he chided himself for being so discombobulated he hadn't thought of it sooner. There *was* hope. Awfully slim, but hope nonetheless. There was no possible way Yassin could know what he had just done. The script was followed as directed and words spoken on cue. If he hurried, he could pick up Sandra and be out of the house before the police arrived.

He tried to run but his legs wouldn't allow it.

Hope, an inner voice was telling him.

He finally turned the corner and made his way toward the waiting car.

• • • • •

Blair got into the back seat and shut the door. He could feel his heart pounding. An hour more, he figured. Perhaps less, depending on traffic. Approximately sixty minutes and it would all be over.

Abdul slowly pulled away. He drove past the loading dock, then came to a stop. "Must have cigarette," he said by way of explanation.

Blair wanted to tell him to make it quick. His nerves were pumped and he couldn't sit still.

Abdul seemed to be having a problem. Whatever he was trying to get loose—his cigarette package, Blair assumed—was apparently stuck.

Curious, Blair's gaze went to the rearview mirror and he caught sight of the gun.

He panicked for a moment, then swallowed it down. He quickly leaned over the seat, making a grab for the weapon.

The other man fought him off.

He held on to Abdul's arm, not knowing where the strength was coming from.

Abdul lashed out, cursing in Arabic.

Something kept Blair going. He raised one of his legs to get better leverage.

The other man pulled.

A tug-of-war ensued that lasted for several minutes. Blair told himself it was now or never, so he yanked on Abdul's gun hand for all he was worth.

The weapon dropped.

Then both men became caught between the bucket seats. Their arms were pinned between them and neither was able to move. Their chests touched. Blair could feel the other man's beating heart.

Abdul swore again.

Blair made the mistake of moving a fraction of an inch.

It was just enough to give Abdul the advantage. He kneed Blair in the groin.

The shock caused Blair's body to jerk backwards. He caught sight of the gun; it had been concealed beneath him. He tried reaching for it, but Abdul noticed the gun as well.

They went for it at the same time.

Their heads collided.

For a moment, they were equally stunned.

Abdul recovered first. The weapon came into his hand and, as if in slow motion, he took aim.

In a last ditch effort, Blair reached up, made contact.

The gun fired.

• • • • •

Blair waited, holding his breath.

There was blood. Too much of it. Soaking his clothes and the interior of the car.

He turned and caught the sightless look in Abdul's eyes. Numb, he wanted to pause, but he was reminded of his daughter's plight. He had to get to her before it was too late. Abdul obviously had orders to kill him. Logic dictated that his death had been sanctioned, to be effectuated the moment he approved *Cyber-tech's* release. Which meant that everything he'd been told was a lie. Which meant that Sandra…

The thought was too grave to consider.

Adrenaline resurged, he scurried across the back seat, reached a hand out, found the handle, and opened the door.

Removing Abdul from the car was not as easy. The corpse was heavy. He had to maneuver it back and forth.

When the task was done, Blair slipped into the driver's seat, snapped his seatbelt in place, and drove off. Half to himself, half aloud, he asked God to please, please, *PLEASE* spare his daughter.

• • • • •

Typical for a Friday, Manhattan traffic was at a near standstill. Hand on the horn, Blair started to weave in and out, taking advantage of the smallest opening. All that mattered now was staying focused, to get to the house in time.

He finally rounded the corner of the street. He pulled into the driveway and a foreboding set in. The front door was standing ajar. He palmed Abdul's gun that was lying on the seat beside him, and came out of the car on the run.

Caution was thrown to the wind as he hurried into the house. "Sandra?" he called.

He began his descent to the subbasement.

The search only took a few minutes. Finding nothing, he mounted the stairs to the basement level, an area he knew well.

He tried the kitchen first, followed by the room used as his office. There was no sign of life. No sign that anyone had ever lived there. Crouching low, gun in hand, he continued to open doors.

Retracing his steps, he climbed back up to the main floor.

With gun pointed in front, he went from room to room, visualizing Abdul's blood after he'd been shot, petrified of finding more blood, his daughter's blood.

"Sandra?" he called again.

He checked the living and dining rooms, each of the three bathrooms, then circled back to the front door.

Now what? he asked himself.

Blair slowly walked out of the house, moved to the edge of the sidewalk, and wearily let himself down at the curb.

The twitch in his right eye felt like a constant pain. In the distance he heard the sound of sirens. No doubt, Larry Killgallon had come through for him.

But it was far too late, he knew.

PART THREE

SEPTEMBER • NOVEMBER

CHAPTER 68

Transported by the police, he was immediately put under sedation, so for the first few days, he did nothing but sleep. It took until mid-week for Blair to get his bearings and understand that he was in a private room in New York's Presbyterian Hospital on 68th Street.

The FBI questioned him, but he remembered very little of what was said. Mostly, his mind visualized the gun going off. The Arab lying dead. And the copious amount of blood. Then fleeing to the empty house and finding Sandra gone.

Now, he noticed the newspapers for the first time. There were about a dozen of them, stacked in a neat pile on the chair next to his bed. He pushed the covers to one side and positioned the pillow until he was in a more upright position. He took the first newspaper in hand and lay back down. The headline screamed at him:

TOY EXECUTIVE AVERTS DISASTER.

Blair crunched the paper against his chest. Anger seared the wall of his stomach. This sort of publicity was the last thing he needed. Especially with his daughter's life hanging in the balance.

Reluctantly, he unfolded the paper. He skipped some of the words but managed the gist of it. The article described *Cyber-tech's* would-be launch and what could have happened had Blair not stopped it.

He threw the paper to the floor.

• • • • •

By the end of the week he was growing restless. Blair asked the doctor when he could be released.

Olah Marketa was a petite brunette in her late thirties. She had a no-nonsense way about her. In response to his inquiry, she said, "We need to do more tests. Your weight is still far below normal."

"So, how long, Doc?" he asked.

"Today is what? Friday? Another week should do it."

"Another week? I don't think so."

The doctor smiled. "You know," she said, "after the ordeal you've been through, I would think you'd embrace the chance to recuperate." She approached the bed, and touched his forehead. "Is your dizziness gone?" she asked.

"All gone," Blair said.

"And the nausea?"

"That, too."

She took his blood pressure, opened his pajama top, and listened to his heart. "You're a bad liar," Dr. Marketa said.

CHAPTER 69

When Lisa Brandt came to visit, Blair had to hide his emotions. There was so much he wanted to say. But it would have to wait. There were two FBI agents accompanying her.

"Mr. Mulligan," one of the agents took the lead. "Do you remember speaking with us? My name is Bill Prendergast. And this is my colleague—Jim Eathorne."

Blair decided they could be Siamese twins. Young and athletic-looking, but too severe, as if smiling would diminish their stature. He found it ironic that both men would have the same psoriasis problem, their faces dotted with pockmarks. "Is there any word about my daughter?" he asked.

"We want to review what you told us earlier," Jim Eathorne said, ignoring his question. "Can you recall our conversation?"

Blair shrugged and told himself to be patient. He didn't like the man's voice, reminding him the way it did of his history teacher in high school, too solemn by half. "Honestly," he said, "I don't remember much of anything."

"You told us what happened. You mentioned the people involved. Especially Khalid Yassin. We'll want you to spend some time with our sketch artist. Once you are feeling better, that is."

"I feel better now," Blair said, practicing his alibi for a quick release from the hospital.

Bill Prendergast referred to his notepad. "Let me see if I have this right," he said. "A man enters your office back in April and introduces himself as John Dalton, an agent with the bogus BIS. He asks you to go to Israel and convince your colleague, Jeremy Samson, to switch DVD production from one manufacturer to another. You refuse. He starts making threats. You go to Israel but it doesn't do any good. On your second try, after your daughter is kidnapped and Dalton's murder is faked, you are successful. But the promise to release Sandra is a lie. You go in search of the house where you believe your daughter is being held. Instead of gaining her release, you are captured yourself. John Dalton proves to be an Arab living a double life. Worse, your electronic gaming system has been sabotaged. You are given an option, approve the release of the product or Sandra will be killed. On August 17th you arrive at your distribution center where you fake your approval and ask your associate to call the police. You return to the car and the driver tries to shoot you, but you shoot him instead.

"This is what you told us," he concluded, then paused. "I mean, other than a car threat in Montreal and a bombing in Tel Aviv thrown in for good measure."

Blair remained quiet. Having the details of his experience repeated in such a cold, bloodless manner made it seem inconsequential. "Very accurate synopsis," he said caustically. "Now, tell me where Sandra is."

"We have nothing definitive to report at this time," the other agent advised. "With Ms. Brandt's help," He turned toward her, "we have determined that your daughter was most likely transported out of the country."

"Out of the country?"

"Yes, that's right. We are waiting for confirmation."

The next was difficult for Blair. "Is she okay? Does anyone know?"

"We believe she's alive."

"That doesn't sound positive."

"Blair," Lisa jumped in. "Jeremy is on top of it. Has been for a while. He'll be calling me in an hour or so. I'll let you know what he has to say."

He was about to speak, caught her expression, and clamped his mouth shut instead.

CHAPTER 70

The following morning, Blair earned Dr. Marketa's wrath by advising her that he was signing himself out of the hospital. Per their rules, he was transported in a wheelchair. Accompanying him was Andrew Sciascia.

No sooner did they come through the main door of the hospital, however, than a throng of reporters surrounded them. Microphones and cameras battled for position.

"How are you feeling?"

"Any word on your daughter, Mr. Mulligan?"

"What will you do now?"

"Can you tell us where Sandra is being held?"

Speaking on his behalf, Andrew let them know that Blair would have no comment at this time.

"When can we interview him?" a voice called out as if he wasn't standing there.

"Is it true he's already signed a deal for a book?" another wanted to know.

Blair asked to be taken back inside.

Andrew went to get his car and pulled up in front. With the help of hospital security, a pathway was cleared and they were able to make their escape.

• • • • •

The next day he came out of his condo, only to be met once more by reporters. He jogged past them, and kept going until he found an empty cab. An even larger press contingent was waiting for him at his office.

Blair was relieved to make it into the elevator and upstairs. He motioned to his secretary. Andrea Victor followed him into his office, took a seat opposite his desk, and immediately apologized.

"What in the world for?" he asked.

"For not getting it. I went back over your e-mails as soon as the story came out. I could tell something was wrong. That you weren't yourself. I ... should have done something." She was on the verge of tears.

"Listen," he said, "they were reading every e-mail I received or sent out. I racked my brain for a word or phrase I could use to tip you off. I couldn't find anything that would work. This isn't your fault. You did nothing wrong."

"Are you positive?"

He forced his smile to reassure her. "I am more than positive," he said.

• • • • •

Alone, Blair paced his office, thinking only of Sandra.

Al-Qaeda had her. And he knew all too well how merciless they were.

He didn't want his daughter to die.

"Sandra," he whispered aloud.

It helped just to say her name, as if that in itself would bring her closer.

• • • • •

"Jeremy Samson on line one," his secretary advised just after eleven-thirty.

He picked up the receiver and said hello.

"How are you doing?"

"Fine," he said quietly.

"That bad, huh? Look, I wanted to give you an update on your daughter's whereabouts. My contacts here in the Middle East have been put on high alert. If this is where they are bringing her, we will find out. Okay?"

He sighed. "I hear you, Jeremy. Thank you."

"Thanks. *Shmanks.* Don't be so formal. We'll find her, Blair. You just have to give it time."

"Time? I read somewhere that the first twenty-four hours in any disappearance are critical."

"Yeah. Under normal circumstances. This ain't normal."

"I want you to call me the minute you hear something. I'll be booking an open-ended ticket to Tel Aviv. One phone call from you and I'll be on my way."

"Uh-uh. That wouldn't be wise, Blair."

"Why not?"

"You should know better than most what these people are like."

"Then, what should I do?" Mucus caught in Blair's throat and he began to cough.

"You do nothing," Jeremy said. "Wait until you hear from me. By the way," he changed the subject, "the press in Israel has already married the story about what you did in New York to how you saved that girl's life over here."

"Oh, yeah? How would they connect both incidents to me?"

"Moira, the restaurant lady. She noticed your picture in the newspaper. No one knew your identity. Now, people are discussing you by name, talking about your bravery."

Blair tuned him out, embarrassed. "All I care about is finding my daughter. Nothing else matters to me."

"I know that."

"Will you help me, then? I can't go on without Sandra."

"I'll find her," Jeremy said. "I promise."

CHAPTER 71

At home, Blair stripped down to a T-shirt and pair of sweats. He began to mope around his condo, opening and closing drawers, searching for mementos of his daughter, the odd photo, drawings she had made for him at school.

As darkness fell, he left the lights off. He stood in front of the window in the den, staring off into space.

He knew he should have listened to the doctor and remained in the hospital for at least another week. He had a constant headache. Tylenol 3 didn't do a bit of good.

His stomach rumbled. He couldn't remember the last time he'd eaten.

When the phone rang, he checked caller ID and noticed a familiar Montreal number. He almost let it go to voicemail. But what if it was news about his mother? He picked up on the fourth ring and said, "Cyn, how are you?"

"My God, Blair, it's good to hear your voice. You've been all over the news."

"How's Mom doing?"

"I knew something was wrong. I just *knew* it! Goddammit, I'm your sister. You can't hold something like this back." Her tone softened. "Is there any word about Sandra? Where is she? What did they do to her?"

"*Whoa!* That's too many questions."

"I can't imagine what you've been through. How are you feeling?"

"Cynthia, I'm fine. Just a bit tired, that's all." He raised a hand to his throbbing head. "How's our mother doing?"

"Aren't you going to talk to me?"

"Not now."

"When, then?"

"When this is over. When Sandra is back safe and sound."

"Mom is *not* doing well," Cynthia said. "The doctor believes it's a matter of a month or two."

It may have been inevitable, but the news still stung. "Is there anything I can do?" Blair asked.

"Nothing. There's nothing anyone can do."

"Can you handle things, Cyn? I mean, just for the time being?"

"Blair, you don't have to ask. Of course, I can handle things. But keep me in the loop. Okay? Let me know as soon as you hear something."

"I will. Goodbye…"

"Wait. Before you hang up, I want you to know how sorry I am."

"For what?"

"For nagging you the way I did."

"Hey, you can't be blamed. You knew something was wrong."

"I still feel badly. And I apologize."

"Don't. Please, Cyn. You are one person in my life who never has to apologize."

"You mean that?"

"I do. Honest."

"I love you, Blair."

• • • • •

It was past 9:00 PM when someone rang from downstairs. He buzzed in the caller and then turned on a few lights. Moving to the door, he caught his reflection in the hallway mirror. The worry in his eyes gave him the look of someone haunted or possessed.

He opened the door.

When Lisa came out of the elevator, he became self-conscious of his appearance. "Sorry," he said as she neared. "I wasn't expecting anyone."

She stepped inside the condo and closed the door behind her. "If you did expect me, you would have done what?" she asked.

He shrugged. "I don't know."

Her brow creased. "I thought you were feeling better?"

"I feel fine."

"Sure you do. When's the last time you've eaten?" She turned for the kitchen and he followed. She was wearing a plain white top and form-fitting pants. Blair realized she'd look good no matter what she had on.

She opened the door to the fridge and sighed. Then she checked the empty pantry. "My God, this is ridiculous." She retraced her steps. "Give me a few minutes. I'll be right back," she said, and was gone.

Blair hurried into the bathroom and ran a comb through his hair. Then he undressed, and changed into a pair of black trousers. He was so used to wearing suits and ties that it took a while to find the right sport shirt.

Finally, he told himself to relax. As soon as Lisa returned he could come clean with her, talk to her about his feelings, and admit how much he cared about her.

But when she rang from downstairs he grew apprehensive. He buzzed her in, waited until she knocked on the door, and then opened it but remained silent. Every approach he had considered now seemed wrong.

She took one look at him and smiled. "You changed clothes," she said. "I liked you better in your sweats."

"Huh?"

"Just kidding."

He watched her from a seat at the kitchen table as she took charge, turning on the stove, concentrating on his meal.

When she placed the bowl in front of him, she proudly announced: "Chicken soup, just like my mother used to make for me."

He examined its contents. The soup contained not only broth but a variety of vegetables and thick chunks of chicken. He made the effort, slowly swallowing a spoonful at a time. "Aren't you going to eat?" he asked.

"I've had my dinner," she said. "But a glass of wine would be nice."

"I don't think I have any."

"You do now." She brought a bag over to the table. She removed a plastic corkscrew and a bottle of Merlot, which she opened and poured. "Want some?" she asked as she took a seat opposite.

He thought about it. "I better not."

"I read the FBI report," Lisa said.

"And?" he asked, already putting down his spoon.

"You held an awful lot back."

He admired her sagacity. "Nothing was held back," he said.

"Oh? There wasn't much in there about the way your daughter was treated."

"What do you mean?"

"You tell me."

He didn't know where to begin. So he sat, mute, hardly touching the soup. Until Lisa prodded him again.

Blair said: "Yassin believed I might not obey his every command. He said he feared I wouldn't follow his order to approve the release of *Cyber-tech* in the appropriate manner, said he had to teach me a lesson." He paused. "They made me watch as one of the men grabbed Sandra's hand. I think it was her left one. I don't remember." He paused again. "Isn't that awful? Why can't I remember?" His voice rose. "What the hell's the matter with me?"

"Blair—"

He was finding it vitally important that he jar the memory loose. "It was her left," he said. "I'm sure that it was. The man attached something like a dentist's pliers to my daughter's fingernail. He twisted those pliers as if he were prying a staple loose. A vicious pull and Sandra's nail was gone. Just like that."

The scene was too lifelike. Blair found a tremor developing, and was unable to stop it.

Lisa came around the table and held him for a moment.

He realized how much he needed her, wanted her.

She pulled back and began to clear the dishes.

"Leave them," he said. "I'll do it later."

Lisa went to gather her purse. She took out a pen and scribbled on a piece of paper. "This is my private number," she said, handing it to him. "I'm going to be tied up for a while. But if you need to talk, call me."

He took the slip of paper from her.

She hesitated, then said she'd better be going.

Blair sensed her reluctance.

Ask her to stay, a voice encouraged him.

He remained seated, keeping his silence, not moving until he heard the door close.

It was a decision he would regret for the rest of his life.

CHAPTER 72

The following week he found himself in the New York office of the Federal Bureau of Investigation. He had just taken a seat at a square table in a small room that didn't have much to recommend it. Dull, army-green paint. Four chairs. It reminded Blair of the office he had been forced to use while being held captive. And it immediately made him feel uncomfortable.

The sketch artist walked in and introduced himself. He was a man in his late forties, with a narrow face and long, straight hair. He was pallid-looking, as if he hadn't seen daylight in a while.

Were it not for the hair, Blair was thinking, the man could be from the Middle East. And that thought segued into another thought. And another. Until paranoia convinced him that this office was a rogue, not unlike the office of BIS.

He abruptly stood.

"Is something wrong?" the man asked.

Blair could swear he detected an Arabic accent. He glanced at the door, seriously thinking of making a run for it.

"Mr. Mulligan?"

It took an effort to let reason prevail. The agents who had welcomed him here today were the same ones who had visited him at the hospital. Eathorne and Prendergast. Lisa Brandt vouched for them just by their mutual association.

Blair reclaimed his seat. He made a lame excuse about thinking of using the washroom, then deciding it could wait.

The artist, whose name Blair couldn't grasp, gave him an odd look but made no comment. He began to work, asking questions as he sketched.

Some fifty minutes later, Yassin's cold, dark stare was down on paper. By the time the man's nose and lips filled in, Blair was getting antsy again. For all he knew, and despite what logic dictated, this entire exercise could be a sham. Just like everything else in his recent past.

He paused and told himself to get a grip.

• • • • •

Back in his office before noon, the phone calls from the press began, some from as far away as England and South America. He told each of them that he had no comment. When a few persisted, he gave out his lawyer's name and phone number, per Andrew Sciascia's instructions.

Absentmindedly, he began to go through the files on his desk. He'd open one, give it a cursory glance and set it aside. It became an exercise in futility. He couldn't comment on what he'd just read because everything was a blur. Soon he was slamming files down in frustration.

Andrea Victor stepped into his office and asked what was wrong.

"I just can't get into this stuff," he said.

"Perhaps you need more time," she suggested.

• • • • •

When Mandy came to call unannounced a few days later, hope had all but left him.

He ushered his ex-wife into his office and invited her to have a seat. He was surprised by her conservative look. Her blouse was buttoned to the top. Her hair was worn up instead of down.

At first they remained mute, as if they were perfect strangers without any history.

Then Mandy said, “I’ve come to apologize.”

Blair reflected that everyone seemed anxious to apologize to him lately.

“I shouldn’t have reacted the way I did,” she continued. “Shouldn’t have said the things I said. I just had no way of knowing what was going on.”

“It’s not you who should apologize,” Blair corrected. “These people…” He allowed the thought to drift. “They said they would harm Sandra if I told you the truth. I didn’t know who I was dealing with. I thought they were legitimate, part of the government. They played me for a damn fool. I’m sorry, Mandy.”

“You’re sorry and I’m sorry. We make one hell of a team, don’t we?”

He frowned.

“But have you heard anything?” she asked anxiously.

“Not a word. Nothing.”

“Is that true? Or are you holding back on me?”

“I haven’t heard anything. I swear.”

“What are we going to do?”

Good question. “I don’t know,” he said.

“Do you think she’ll come through this, Blair?” Her voice quivered. “Do you think we’ll get Sandra back alive?”

He hesitated, not wanting to expose his own doubts.

“Oh, God,” Mandy said, reading the truth in his reticence. And she began to cry.

• • • • •

Long after his ex-wife had left, Blair sat at his desk, brooding. Mandy didn't cry. It simply wasn't in her nature. Seeing her in tears reminded him of how dire their situation was.

It was late and his employees were gone for the day. For no conscionable reason, he decided to take a stroll through the showroom. With the spotlights off, the toys were not shown to their best advantage. He passed each section with an apathy he'd never felt before. From dolls to board games to radio control cars. No longer creative playthings to him, each somehow represented menace and deception.

Toward the back wall sat a four-foot section of *Cyber-tech*. A working sample of the game was out of its package. Point of purchase material, including signage and shelf-talkers, made the product look important. A motion-activated television set, with a built-in DVD player, was positioned in the center of the display.

Upon his approach, the commercial flashed on the TV screen, catching Blair unawares. He lifted the *Cyber-tech* sample and threw it to the floor. When it didn't break, he bent down and retrieved it, then heaved it against the wall.

There was still no sign of damage.

Anger surging, he took hold of it again and began smashing it into the metal shelf. The product remained unscathed. But a cut had opened in the palm of his hand. The sight of blood sent Blair into a frenzy. He took aim at the boxes in the four-foot section and swept them to the floor. Then he began to stomp on each one until they were crushed. Only then did he head out of the showroom, blood leaving a scarlet trail behind him.

CHAPTER 73

The next morning, he sat in his office, dressed in his customary suit and tie, staring off into space. His company was holding on by the slimmest of margins. His bank had agreed to a bridge-loan until the end of the year. This was all that was keeping them going.

About to stand from his desk, Blair made the mistake of taking a call from Tracey Lambert of Playmart, a four-year-old chain of five hundred stores, prominent in the northeast.

"I must have a meeting with you," the buyer said. "At once."

"At once?"

"Yes, it's important."

Blair grimaced, inwardly furious at this sort of demand. "Could we not discuss this over the phone?" he asked.

"No. I'm afraid not."

He stifled his comment. This is what had become of the business he cherished. It was all one way, the buyer's way, or the proverbial highway. And Tracey Lambert was worse than most. Employed for only six months, she had already succeeded in alienating almost everyone in the industry.

"Look," he tried reasoning with her, "it's difficult for me to get away right now. Can we not put this off for a few days?"

"No, we could not," the buyer said with her usual insolence. "I said it was important."

He sighed, knowing he had no choice.

• • • • •

The drive took two hours. He was using a leased Hyundai until his insurance claim was settled over his lost BMW.

The entrance to Playmart's head office in Wayne, New Jersey was located less than a half-mile from the corporate headquarters of Toys 'R' Us, and the common assumption in the toy industry was that this site had been chosen intentionally. There was no guard station but the impressive grounds were similar, reminding Blair of a sprawling college campus, without the hustle and bustle of professors and students.

He entered the building, registered at the well-lit reception desk, then rode the elevator to the third floor. There, the huge video screen drew his attention, its size representing another obvious jab at its competitor, as if to say, "Whatever you can do, we can do bigger and better."

Now, he confirmed the location of his pre-assigned appointment, headed for the room, entered, and waited.

Within minutes, Tracey Lambert joined him. There was no smile or greeting, and Blair couldn't help wondering if her short, shapeless body and excess girth were the cause of her surly disposition.

The minute they were seated, the buyer thrust a sample of one of his current craft items at him: *Bead-a-licious*.

He spent a minute or two examining the box and was unable to find anything wrong.

"Study the language," Tracey said.

He turned the box from front to back but was still in the dark.

"My God, are you blind?"

He was used to her insults so he didn't say anything.

She yanked the sample from his hands and tapped at a number of lines of print on the box with her index finger. "French and English," she said.

"So?" he asked.

"*So?*" The buyer's voice rose. "How many times do I have to tell you people? I don't want anything but English on my goddamn packaging! This is America, not France!"

You people. Her meaning wasn't lost on him: lowly sales-types. "Tracey," he said, fighting his temper now, despite his resolve, "many manufacturers have gone to English/Spanish packaging, others to multilingual, with French and German added to the mix. It doesn't take anything away from the product. With America's cultural diversity today, it most likely adds to its sales appeal."

"I want it off my shelves!"

"But the expense..."

"I don't give a good goddamn about the expense! You people don't listen! You think you can do whatever you please!"

"It wasn't done to hurt you," Blair persisted. "To save on cost we decided to produce one box for Canada and the United States."

"Well I don't like it. The balance of my inventory has to go back to you. What RA number should I use?"

"I can't authorize a return for something like this."

"Excuse me?"

"I can't do it."

"You can, and you will!"

Blair paused and took a deep breath. "Look, why don't we compromise," he suggested. "You keep the goods in your stores for a period of, say, two months. If every piece hasn't sold by then, you can return the balance, no questions asked."

Tracey Lambert's face quickly became infused with an unattractive blush. "I must be talking funny," she said, "because you obviously haven't understood me. I want every piece of this crap," she slapped the box hard, "removed from my stores!"

Blair stood abruptly.

She seemed taken aback. "Wh—where're you going?"

"I've got to get back to my office," he said, surprised at how meek she'd become.

"What about my RA number?" Her voice had not only softened, it sounded submissive.

He wondered what she was thinking. "Use today's date," he said matter-of-factly. "That'll be your return authorization number." And he walked out.

• • • • •

He took a seat in his car, leaned back, and shook his head. Not all that long ago, the just completed meeting with Tracey Lambert would have driven him to distraction. No matter how well he understood the relationship between buyer and seller, no matter how often he had to camouflage his feelings because his role was, and always would be, subservient, unfairness ate away at him. It was something that normally remained with him for days, even weeks. Swallowing his pride was one thing; being made to choke on it quite another.

But those very feelings were rubbing off him now as if they didn't count. Dealing with temperamental buyers somehow seemed inconsequential.

Ironically, he wished it weren't so.

CHAPTER 74

On Thursday, he arrived at his office a little later than usual. He was just settling himself behind his desk when his secretary walked in and handed him over a hundred message slips. "The phone's been ringing off the hook," she said. "Congratulations."

"Huh?"

"You mean, you haven't heard?"

He tensed. "Heard what?"

"You've been awarded one of the highest civilian honors in the country. The Presidential Medal of Freedom."

"Which means what, exactly?"

"Which means you've been invited to the White House." The woman beamed. "Which means the president himself will be doing the honors." She paused. "Six of those message slips," she indicated the hand still holding them, "are from Andrew Sciascia. He needs to speak to you right away."

The minute his secretary left, Blair picked up the phone and dialed his lawyer. When Andrew came on the line, he explained what needed to be done.

The man's protest was vociferous. "You can't," he said. "No one turns down the president of the United States."

"I'm not turning him down," Blair argued. "You'll be picking up the medal on my behalf."

"Not good enough. I'm not the one he wants to meet."

"Then ask him to send it to us. I'm not going, Andrew."

"It's a mistake."

"I don't care."

"What do I tell the press?"

"The same thing we've been telling them all along. I will not meet with anyone until this is over."

"They're not used to this treatment, Blair. They will not be kind."

"I don't give a shit. Let them find someone else to go after."

"There is no one else. You're the hero of the day."

"Yeah. Some hero. If I were a hero, I'd have my daughter back by now."

"Blair…"

"Andrew, use any excuse you need to make. Just handle it for me. Okay?"

"Wait a minute."

"Please?"

"Okay," the lawyer finally said. "I'll handle it."

• • • • •

There were twelve messages from his sister, all marked urgent. Blair asked his secretary to call and see if this was about his mother. She came back to him within five minutes and advised that Cynthia wanted to discuss something entirely different.

The majority of the remaining messages were from the press. He threw those and the ones from his sister into his wastebasket.

The conversation with Andrew Sciascia came to mind. As usual after the fact, he wondered if he had made the right decision. *How many people get to meet the president?* he asked himself.

It didn't matter.

His decision had been the correct one. Participating in some silly photo-op would not be wise.

CHAPTER 75

The next morning, he came out of the subway and practically ran to his office, only to be disappointed. His instincts had been telling him that there would be news about his daughter today. Not that he understood why. He had simply talked it into himself that this would be so.

He picked up the phone and dialed Jeremy's mobile number.

It seemed to ring forever before voicemail kicked in. "Hey, it's me," Blair said. "I really need to speak with you. Call me back."

After hanging up, he sat quietly, wondering what to do next.

He got on the phone again and tried reaching the FBI agents without success. He left messages for both men.

• • • • •

Later, finally concentrating on his business, he came to the conclusion that without *Cyber-tech*, and with no other potential winner in his stable of products, his company was in trouble.

He made a list of his employees, their salaries, and the role each played. Firing people didn't appeal to him. So he considered changing everyone to a four-day workweek. This way, they would keep their jobs, albeit at a reduced rate of compensation. Not the best solution, but not as discouraging as the alternative.

He stood from his desk and was about to head out for coffee, when his intercom buzzed.

"Your sister again," his secretary told him. "Do I still tell her you're busy?"

"No." Blair sighed. "I'll take it." He returned to his seat.

"I'm really mad at you," Cynthia said before he could say hello. "Didn't your secretary tell you how many times I called?"

"She told me."

"Well?"

"I've had other things on my mind, Cyn."

She paused, then apologized and asked if there was any word about Sandra.

"Nope. I still don't know a damn thing."

"I'm sorry, Blair. Really I am. Mom's condition hasn't changed, by the way. But that's not why I'm calling."

"Oh?"

"I have wonderful news."

"You do?"

"Yes. Hold on to your seat. Or your hat. Or whatever it is you can hold on to."

"Huh?"

"You've won the lottery."

"I beg your pardon?"

"It's true." The joy was back in Cynthia's voice. "Your Loto-Québec numbers came up. Not quite all of them. But five numbers for a cool quarter of a million dollars."

"A quarter of a mil—"

"Yes. Can you believe it?"

He tried to absorb the news and concluded that it was a curse. Like everything else in his life. His obsession with lottery tickets. His preoccupation with *Cyber-tech*. It was all interrelated. His need for the big score, his greed. "Listen to me, Cyn," he said. "I want you to cash it in. Use the money to get help for your hoarding problem. Put the balance in a savings account."

"I couldn't do that."

"You have to."

"Blair, you're not making sense. Can't you use this kind of money?"

"Who couldn't?" he said, thinking of his company's bottom line.

"Then why give it to me?"

"You deserve it."

"I don't think so," Cynthia said. "You're being far too hasty. I think you should sleep on it, at least for a day or two."

"I don't need to sleep on it."

"You *do!* Besides, I can't cash it in. The check will be made out in your name."

"I'll have my lawyer draw up authorization. You should have it before the end of the week. And, Cyn, don't renew the subscription."

"Why not? I thought you liked playing the lottery?"

"Liked. Past tense. I'm cured."

"Cured of what?"

"My bad habit."

"It's not a habit, and it's not bad."

"Bye, Cyn. I'll talk to you soon."

• • • • •

After a quick lunch, Blair revisited his company's financial problem. Putting himself in the shoes of his employees, he perceived the trouble his potential move was bound to create. Losing a chunk of one's salary would surely be a hardship. People might quit. A few would feel betrayed. There had to be another way. He'd already contemplated cutting his own salary in half. But more was needed.

Getting on the phone, he contacted the various presidents he knew at other toy companies. Using what he said was a hypothetical situation, he laid out his financial crunch and ran a few scenarios by them.

Unfortunately, he came away no better off than when he had started.

• • • • •

At home, he considered having a drink to calm his nerves. But he wanted to remain clear-headed, so he decided against it.

At 10:00 PM he tried Jeremy again, to no avail. He found the number Lisa had given him and called it.

There was no answer.

A sick feeling reached the pit of his stomach.

As midnight approached, Blair realized that trying to sleep was out of the question. He moved to the den and took a seat on the couch. Cradling the phone in his hands, he willed it to ring.

CHAPTER 76

It was mid-morning, three days later, when he took a cab to Pigalle at 48th and 8th.

As usual, the restaurant was crowded.

Andrew Sciascia, gregarious as ever, immediately began regaling him with his recent legal exploits.

Instead of acknowledging his friend's comments, Blair took the menu in hand and asked what he wanted to eat.

"Eggs Benedict," Andrew said, smiling. "The only chance I get to have it is when my wife's not around." He patted his paunch. "Although, at this point, do you really think it makes a difference?"

"Not much," Blair said dully.

"Oh, yeah? Last time I ask you."

Blair called the waiter over and placed their order.

"Look," Andrew said, "the press may not be following you around much anymore, but they are still bugging the hell out of me. It might be time for you to come in from the cold."

Blair brushed the suggestion aside. "You wanted to see me?" he said.

"Yeah," Andrew acknowledged. "I have something for you." He pulled out a plain rectangular box from his attaché case and handed it over. "This arrived via courier at my office. I thought you'd like to have it."

Curious, Blair said, "What is it?"

"Your medal, for God's sake. Have you already forgotten?"

The truth was, he *had* forgotten. "Weren't you to pick it up in person?" he asked.

"Sure. Except when the president heard I'd be substituting for you, he changed his mind. Or, his flunkies did."

Blair opened the box. The white, star-shaped medal was larger and more impressive than he had expected.

Andrew waited for his comment.

Blair closed the lid and placed the box beneath his chair.

"That's it?" Andrew asked.

"That's it," he said.

• • • • •

Two more weeks passed. His phone calls and e-mails to Jeremy continued to go unanswered.

The Friday of the third week remained warm, but a September rain was blanketing New York. Unconcerned, Blair walked without the benefit of an umbrella or top coat. Hair soaked, body drenched, he ended up a few hours later at the address he knew all too well in Lower Manhattan. The yellow crime-scene tape was long gone, and there was no indication whatsoever of what had transpired there.

Soon, as if an unseen hand was guiding him, he stepped up to the door of the house. He raised his index finger to the bell. He pressed it once. Twice. A third time.

When no one responded, he pounded on the door with his fist, again as a conduit for a mysterious force not his own … until he began to feel foolish.

He walked away with his shoulders slumped. *What was I thinking?* he asked himself. *That Sandra would actually be here?*

The rain picked up. He could feel the wetness in his shoes and socks. When he spotted the subway station, he decided he'd had enough. He paid his fare, used the ticket in the turnstile, and descended to the platform below, where he paused.

There was a large crowd, and in the thick of it Blair noticed Khalid Yassin. He did a double-take and felt his stomach turning to stone. He looked away, then back. Yes, it was him. He was certain of it.

Blair was just wondering what to use as a weapon, when he got a closer look and realized his mistake. It wasn't Yassin, after all. The man was at least ten years older.

Blair turned, moving as far along the platform as possible. He waited as a train rumbled through the tunnel. He watched it approach as if transfixed. It pulled to a stop and he got onboard.

• • • • •

He arrived home, changed out of his wet clothes, and put on a kimono. He poured himself a Scotch, brought the bottle with, and took a seat in the den.

It didn't take long for his mood to turn sour. The fact that he was mistaking strangers for Khalid Yassin said a lot about his state of mind.

Your daughter needs you to be strong, an inner voice reminded him.

He flashed back to an image of Sandra at the age of three months, her hair turning blond and filling with curls, her bright blue eyes taking in her surroundings and becoming more aware. Then at seven months, holding her milk cup in her hands and eating cut-up pieces of bread and cheese. And at a year old, crawling but in a weird way, more monkey than human, one foot often twisted beneath her bottom.

Blair shot upright.

There had to be something he could do to help rescue his daughter. But what?

He filled his glass to the brim and took a long swallow, relishing the burning sensation in his throat.

Snippets of an idea formed in his head. When his idea finally coalesced, he resumed drinking, guzzling Johnnie Walker as if it were water.

• • • • •

The phone woke him before 5:00 AM.

At first, he didn't know where he was. His head was pounding so badly, the thought of a lobotomy was appealing. Hearing the ring again, Blair cupped both ears with his hands and squeezed. When the phone persisted, he reached over and snatched the receiver.

"Sorry to wake you so early," Jeremy said.

"What's wrong?" Blair shot upright.

"We have a lead. I apologize for not getting back to you sooner. But everything kept changing. Even now, I'm not sure how reliable my information is. You have to understand, we are dealing mostly with informants, not all of whom are trustworthy."

"What kind of a lead?"

"As good a lead as can be expected. I hope to know more in a few hours."

Blair put a hand to his still-aching head. "Don't leave me in the dark," he said. "If you're saying a few hours, Jeremy, then that's when I'll want to speak with you. Not in a few weeks."

"I understand. I'll call you before noon. Your time."

• • • • •

He put on a pot of coffee. When it was ready, he tried a sip. Two cups later he felt as if he could function. Barely.

He took his time showering and shaving. His third coffee of the morning, along with a piece of dry toast, eased some of the pain.

He got dressed and returned to the kitchen.

Jeremy called shortly afterwards.

"I'm sorry," he heard him say. "The lead was bogus but we're working on something else."

Blair asked how much longer it would take.

"I don't know. You can't put a clock on something like this."

Remembering last evening's idea, he paused to gather himself. "Jeremy," he said, "I have a proposal that I don't want you to reject out of hand."

"Which is?"

"Do I have your word?"

"How can I give you my word if I don't know what your proposal is?"

"I'm not talking about the proposal itself. I'm talking about you listening with an open mind."

"I'm listening."

"I want your informants to make an offer to Khalid Yassin. My daughter is of no use to him. I am the one Yassin would like to get his hands on. I'm the guy who foiled his plans. We will do an exchange. Me for my daughter. Yassin will jump at the chance."

The pause was elongated. "Sorry," Jeremy finally said.

"Can't you at least make the effort?" Blair pushed.

"No, I can't. Don't you get it? These people can't be trusted. Negotiating with them is out of the question. The only thing we can try to do is gain Sandra's release by force. Sacrificing yourself would serve no purpose whatsoever."

"How do you know?"

"From my experience; that's how. You're starting to insult me, Blair."

"Is that your ego talking? I'm not trying to insult you. I just don't want my daughter to end up dead."

Jeremy's voice softened. "I know how this is eating at you. And I sympathize. Really, I do. But if you went through with your idea, despite any promises that were made, you'd be murdered along with Sandra. And that's something I can't allow to happen."

"Then what do you suggest?"

"You have to leave this with me. With my organization. We'll find a way to get your daughter back."

"Fine, but I want to be involved."

"You can't be involved. How many ways do I have to explain it to you?"

• • • • •

He knew immediately that he'd ignore Jeremy's wishes. His idea gave purpose to his life. And he wasn't going to squander it.

He turned on his computer and connected to the Internet. The extensive list under "Soldiers of Fortune" surprised him. He made a copy of over a dozen names and their contact information. He was going to make his offer to Khalid Yassin, no matter what.

CHAPTER 77

A meeting was held in the late afternoon on a Tuesday in a contemporary building in downtown Manhattan. Present were Blair, Andrew Sciascia, and Ms. Applegate, a prim and proper forty-something, representing the firm of Rollins and Dunn.

Though resigned to his fate, Blair was disappointed that it had come to this. As a show of his displeasure, he had forsaken a tie. Although he was still dressed in a suit, black in color and his least favorite.

The boardroom was spacious with floor to ceiling windows. The mahogany table could accommodate at least twelve or more. Floral planters sat at either end. A pitcher of water and a half dozen glasses were positioned in the center. A number of eight-by-ten, framed testimonials to the company's success were hanging on the near wall.

Observing Ms. Applegate as she went through her presentation, Blair found it curious that someone of such refined features, short red hair, delicate cheekbones, could be cursed with such a high-pitched voice.

He didn't want to be here, but he waited patiently as she pointed out that the firm of Rollins and Dunn had a proven track record. That unlike their competitors, they specialized only in the toy and sporting good industries. That for a mere fifteen percent off the top they would handle all aspects of the sale of Blair's company, save for due diligence and other legal requirements.

"What about my request for strict confidentiality?" Blair asked.

"That goes without saying, Mr. Mulligan."

"And no approach to companies such as Spin Master, MGA, or JAKKS Pacific?"

"Duly noted." Ms. Applegate attempted a smile.

Blair stood. "What happens if word leaks out?" he asked.

"It won't."

"But what if it does? Do you realize how disruptive that would be? The affect it would have on my staff? The impact on my company's reputation?"

Ms. Applegate stood as well. "Mr. Mulligan, I can assure you that in the forty-some-odd years we have been in business, there has never been one leak, ever."

Blair held his ground. "But if there is a leak, are you ready to confirm in writing that you will offer us compensation?"

The question stopped her cold.

• • • • •

Andrew led the way into the elevator, down and out of the building, to a corner pub. He ordered a beer for each of them. "What's gotten into you?" he said. "I've never seen you so antagonistic."

Blair could only shrug.

"You didn't want to have this meeting. Did you?"

"Not really."

"So why'd you do it?"

"To be prepared. My business sucks. I doubt I can keep it afloat much longer. I … feel sorry for my employees. What can I possibly tell them?"

"Tell them nothing for now. Once your life returns to normal, you'll find a way to salvage your business."

"*If* it returns to normal."

"It will! Christ, you can't continue to wallow in self-doubt."

Blair had the beer bottle to his lips. He stopped himself from taking a sip, wondering if he was really that transparent. "I'm just being realistic," he said.

"Yeah. Realistic, my ass."

"Andy—"

"Blair, you have to be strong. For Sandra's sake, if not your own. You're a good person, dammit, with a lot of admirable qualities."

The comment unnerved him. Recently, his belief in himself had been greatly diminished.

"Cheers," Andrew said.

They clicked bottles.

"I meant to ask you if my will is still in order," Blair said as if he had just thought of the question this minute.

Andrew's concern showed. "Where are you going with this, bud?"

"I just want to know."

"Everything is fine. But why the sudden interest?"

"No special reason."

"Yeah. I'll bet. Well, you can rest easy. The bulk of your estate goes to your daughter. If she should predecease you, your sister inherits it all."

"Okay," Blair said. "That's all I needed to hear."

CHAPTER 78

His first call to Jeremy was made at 1:00 AM, which was 7:00 AM in Israel. He tried his cell, then his office. Not getting an answer, he left a message at each number. Then he went back to the Harlan Coben novel he'd been trying to read. He barely got through a page before losing his concentration.

He continued to try both numbers, every hour on the hour.

When there was still no answer by 4:00 AM, he gave up.

He had last spoken to Jeremy on Friday.

Five days without a word.

• • • • •

Blair had gotten no sleep but didn't feel tired. Mid-morning, he called the first mercenary whose name he'd gleaned from the Internet. It was a number in Philadelphia.

The man spoke in a robotic voice. His words were clipped and to the point. "We don't meet until I get your deposit," he said.

"Three thousand dollars?" Blair wanted confirmation.

"That's correct."

"And what protects my deposit?"

"My reputation does."

"Your reputation? Can you give me some references?"

"What for?"

"What do you mean, what for? So I can get to know who I'm dealing with. So I don't end up blowing my money."

"What did you say your name was again?"

Blair refused to give it out. The more he talked to this guy, the more he sensed a scam. "You'll have my name soon enough," he told him. "After I get a chance to check your references."

"That's not the way this works, mister."

"Well, can you at least tell me about some of the jobs you've done? It said in your blog that you specialize in the Middle East."

"That I do. But I can't divulge any details."

"Why not?"

"Confidentiality. Don't you want someone discreet?"

"Discreet, yes. A bull-shitter, no."

"I beg your pardon?"

"You heard me."

"I've torn limbs off people for saying less than that to me."

"I'm sure that you have. But what's it going to be? Do I get your references or not?"

"I'll think about it. Call me back tomorrow. Or better still, let me have your number and I'll call you."

"Goodbye, sir. It was nice talking to you."

• • • • •

The guy was trouble, Blair realized, and that was something he didn't need any more of right now. He sat at the kitchen table staring at the phone. Now what? he asked himself.

He wondered where Sandra was, at this moment. Was she hurt? Was she suffering?

Was she even alive?

A knock on the door drew his attention. It would most likely be the super or a neighbor, neither of whom he was in a mood to see. But when the knock came again, he reluctantly lifted himself up and went to answer it.

"Someone let me in," Jeremy Samson said, which explained why there was no buzz from the downstairs lobby.

Fear shot through Blair's heart. He placed a hand on the doorframe for support. "Sandra?" he breathed, believing his friend was here for one reason only, to give him the bad news in person.

CHAPTER 79

In Palestine, Yassin, with a full-grown beard, wearing a *kaffiyeh*, waited as the imam poured the tea. The man appeared to have aged far more in the three years that had passed than at any time before. He seemed as fervently determined as ever, but his too-thin body, stooped-over posture, and nearly all-white hair gave him the look of someone frail and well past his prime.

They were seated in the imam's office in the mosque Yassin had prayed at as a child. The room seemed smaller than he remembered: somber earth-tones with a fold-up table, now unfolded, floor lamp, and three wooden chairs.

"Why so glum?" the imam asked as he slowly lowered himself into the seat opposite. "Not every operation can end successfully. This one failed. So what?"

Yassin shrugged off the question.

"You still seem bothered by it."

"Shouldn't I be? We were this close." He held up two fingers pressed together.

"Ah, but time will heal. You just have to be patient."

"I don't think so!" Yassin said heatedly. Patience had nothing to do with it. He was the one to blame, and he would never forgive himself.

"How are your parents?" the imam asked, changing the subject. "I haven't seen them in a while."

Yassin hated small talk. "My parents are fine," he said. "My mother's sister is ill so they went to Norway to visit her. I expect they will return shortly."

"And you? What have you been up to?"

He didn't reply. Admitting that he'd done nothing but brood since he'd returned from America was not something he was willing to reveal.

"I might have another project for you."

His head partially cleared. "You do?"

"Yes. Interested?"

Yassin felt a familiar kick in his gut, the one that gave purpose to his life. "Of course, I'm interested," he said emphatically.

The imam smiled as he took another sip of his tea. "You know a man by name of Taher Ramli?" he asked.

Yassin rubbed his chin for a moment. "The name is familiar…"

"Taher looks after another part of the world, one you haven't been involved with yet."

"And?"

"He has a few personal problems he has to attend to. But this couldn't have come at a worse time. We have something going on that is close to completion. I was hoping you could replace him."

The buzz in his chest shot to his head. "What's involved?"

"Another trip to a foreign country."

"How soon?"

"A few more weeks, maybe a month at the most."

"I'm ready."

"This can't turn into a mission of revenge, Khalid. What happened in New York is over with and done."

"It won't be revenge," Yassin lied.

CHAPTER 80

Blair waited.

"Sandra's alive," Jeremy said as he stepped inside the apartment.

He wondered if he'd heard right. "She is?" he asked.

"Yes."

"Then what are you doing here?"

Jeremy's smile was forced. "Don't I at least get a cup of coffee?"

"A coffee?" He paused. "Yeah. Sure. Where are my manners?" He went to make it, Jeremy following on his heels.

"Let me ask you something," Blair said, once the kettle was plugged. "You flew all the way here from Israel just to tell me that Sandra is alive?"

"Yes. Why? Do you want me to go back?"

"No. I'm surprised, that's all. You caught me off-guard, showing up like this, to tell me something you could have told me over the phone. What's really going on with my daughter, Jeremy?"

"I told you."

"Yeah…" He let the thought hang as the kettle came to a boil.

• • • • •

Once Jeremy had his coffee in hand, he took a seat at the kitchen table.

Blair remained standing. "Tell me why you've come to New York," he insisted.

Jeremy hesitated. "Pull up a chair."

"I can hear you very well from here."

Jeremy took a sip of his coffee. "A couple of days ago we almost broke your daughter free," he said. "We had her in our sights, only to have our plans foiled once more. We were so darn close."

"How did you find her?"

"Through our contacts. I told you we would. It was just a matter of time."

"What exactly did you do?"

"It wasn't me."

"What do you mean, it wasn't you?"

"I supervised a team of very good people from the sidelines."

"Bull! Weren't you the one in charge?"

"That's what a person in charge does."

"So who was it, then, if not you? Who actually handled the physical attempt to rescue my daughter?"

Jeremy turned introspective. "Lisa," he finally said.

"Lisa?" Blair couldn't hide his surprise. "How did she get involved?"

"She was always involved. Didn't she tell you?"

He tried to recall what was said. "All she told me was that she would be busy for a while. She gave me a phone number. I tried it a few times but could never reach her."

"No wonder."

"Yeah. So, where is she now? I'd very much like to talk to her."

Jeremy stood from the table.

• • • • •

Outside, Blair noticed that New York was experiencing a beautiful September afternoon.

"Lisa did more than take the lead in this operation," Jeremy said, his gaze dropping.

"And?" Blair pushed.

"She actually put her life on the line."

"Okay. So that means what, exactly?"

"It was a joint operation between my team and the FBI. The two agents you met, Prendergast and Eathorne, they were also in on it."

"And Lisa?"

"I'm afraid she didn't make it, Blair."

"Huh?"

"Lisa didn't make it. She was killed."

• • • • •

One minute he was looking out the window, admiring the sun-filled day; the next his vision blurred.

"Blair?"

"How do you know she's dead?" he asked, half speaking to himself. "Have they found her body?"

"No. Not yet."

The answer gave him hope. "Then how do you know, with any certainty, that you are correct?"

"We know, Blair. The other people involved confirmed it."

"Maybe they are mistaken?"

"They're not mistaken."

He didn't believe him, didn't *want* to believe him.

• • • • •

He stood in one place, eyes clamped shut, as if keeping them open would defile Lisa's memory.

The chill he felt was implacable.

When he finally moved it was zombie-like—from one room to the next, hands shaking, unable to keep them still.

His mind traveled back in time, to when he had first met Lisa. The immediate attraction he had felt, the love they had shared. Recollection after recollection filled his head, each hurting a little more, until the guilt manifested physically into a vicious headache, like an anvil pressing into his brain.

CHAPTER 81

Jeremy flew back to Israel. Blair could hardly recall him leaving, or even saying goodbye.

Over the following weeks, a melancholy settled in. He wished he had the wherewithal to enact revenge on those responsible. But he knew that justice was a misnomer, intended to confuse, to deceive the gullible.

He could also see how hatred could consume someone, turn them into a person they never thought they could be. Self-hatred was its worst form, destroying one's confidence, ruining whatever hope still remained

Time did not heal. This was another falsehood, promulgated by those who never experienced loss.

He missed Lisa with every fiber of his being.

• • • • •

Getting Sandra home safely was his only priority. Lisa's sacrifice could not be in vain. Without apology, he reached out to Jeremy by phone and e-mail, no less than once, often two or three times a day.

"Any news?" he would ask. "Are you getting any closer? Is there something I can do?"

The answers were always the same: Jeremy and his Mossad team, along with the FBI, were doing all that could be done.

It wasn't enough.

Blair's frustration got the better of him.

• • • • •

At home on a Monday evening, he poured a Scotch over ice and took a seat in the den, his favorite room.

Absentmindedly, he picked up the *New York Times* and read the feature story. It involved al-Qaeda and a foiled attempt to explode a bomb near the White House.

Even without Osama bin Laden they continued to push, Blair concluded. And eventually they would succeed. Evil had won in the past; it would triumph again in the future.

Whoa!

Was this who I've become? he asked himself. *Mr. Doom and Gloom?*

He went to sip from his glass, then paused.

Andrew Sciascia's words came back to him, something about his wallowing in self-doubt.

Self-*pity* was more like it, Blair realized. And he cringed.

CHAPTER 82

More and more, Lisa's face would flash before Blair's eyes, often co-mingled with Sandra's, to the point where he couldn't separate the two. And he knew, for obvious reasons, that they would be linked forever.

It was this realization that made him want to do something meaningful. But what? What could he do, he wondered, that would serve Lisa's memory?

His need became obsessive. He considered one idea after another, only to discard them all.

It took almost a week to find something.

But it was one thing to formulate a plan, quite another to implement it.

• • • • •

"Uh-uh," Jeremy said over the phone.

"Why not?" Blair asked.

"Because. It won't accomplish anything."

"It will."

"It won't!"

"Look, I am going to do this, with or without you."

"Blair— "

"No, I won't let you win this argument, Jeremy. I've already booked my flight."

"It's a goddamn mistake!"

"I don't care. I don't look at it as a mistake. I feel that it's right."

Jeremy's sigh was a long one. "When did you say again?"

"Next week. On Wednesday."

"And I can't talk you out of it?"

"No one can talk me out of it."

CHAPTER 83

Time passed interminably. Blair started to wonder if he was doing the right thing.

But changing his mind was out of the question.

He had spent hours weighing the pros and cons. When it came down to it, he felt it was far better to do something than nothing, even though there were not many options to choose from.

And he felt, with some certainty, that this was the best one.

• • • • •

Jeremy was not pleased when he picked up Blair at Ben Gurion Airport. He hadn't been in favor of setting up this meeting with Lisa's parents. And he had tried everything in his power to dissuade Blair.

They were no sooner on the road, when Blair wondered aloud why Lisa had been picked for the mission in the first place.

"She insisted," Jeremy said.

"As her boss, couldn't you have dissuaded her?"

"I tried. She wouldn't take no for an answer. Said she wanted to help you. To show how much she cared."

"Christ!"

"You mad at me or at yourself?"

They rode the next few miles in silence.

"She lied to me," Blair stated miserably.

"About what?" Jeremy asked.

"She said her parents were American."

"Yeah. So?"

"They aren't American. Never lived in the United States, as a matter of fact."

"So?"

"So nothing, I guess."

"Be prepared for a cold reception, by the way."

"Why?"

"Her parents haven't adjusted very well. Lisa's their only child. They didn't want to have this meeting. They are angry."

"At me?"

"At you. At me. At everyone."

"They don't even know me."

"They don't know me, either. At least, not very well. But it's human nature to want to blame someone. Her parents won't listen to reason."

"So, what are you saying?" Blair asked.

"It's not too late to turn around."

"Huh?"

"It's up to you."

"I'm not turning around."

"Okay. Can't say I didn't try."

• • • • •

It took another twenty-five minutes to reach the southern suburb of

Ra'anana. Jeremy parked, then led the way to a small bungalow at the tip of a cul-de-sac. They were met at the door by a maid or housekeeper and ushered inside.

Blair felt the modern furniture was out of place, especially in a country as steeped in tradition as this one. Even the Judaic knickknacks, including an acrylic *Mogen David* positioned in the center of a bookcase lining the far wall in the living room, had a too-new look to them.

Lisa's parents remained seated in individual chairs next to the bookcase. They wore grim expressions. Neither went out of his or her way to be polite, even after Jeremy made the introductions.

Mrs. Brandt was in her late fifties. Tall and statuesque, she had similar facial features as her daughter, with hair that was just as blond, but perhaps a little less full. Lisa's father was slightly older than his wife. He had an impressive physique for someone his age, a bald pate, and eyes an unusual shade of greenish-blue.

Blair followed Jeremy's lead and took a seat on the couch opposite them. Self-consciously he placed the small box he had brought with him by his feet. No sooner did Jeremy begin to speak in Hebrew, than he was filled with trepidation.

Jeremy paused, then translated his words into English, telling Blair that he had apologized for the intrusion. "I mentioned that the reason why you are here is to explain your involvement with their daughter."

Blair knew this was his cue. But he hesitated. And he asked himself what his real reason was for coming here.

What do I want? he wondered.

Understanding?

Absolution?

"Blair?" he heard Jeremy say.

Finally, he began to speak, his voice low and as unemotional as he could manage. He explained when he and Lisa had met, omitting how and where this happened. And he went on to describe how they fell in love.

He told them about the horrible situation he had found himself in, how he was tricked into believing that he was dealing with a legitimate government agency, and how his own daughter had been used as a pawn to ensure his cooperation.

Every few sentences, he paused in order for Jeremy to handle the translation. The Hebrew seemed to take forever. And through it all, he noticed Mr. and Mrs. Brandt refrain from looking his way.

"When I learned of Lisa's connection to Mossad," he went on, "I felt as if she had deceived me. I knew I was in love with her, yet I believed she had lied about loving me.

"So you see, I am to blame. I should have given Lisa the benefit of the doubt. If I had, she would most likely be alive today..."

The house became deathly quiet.

Jeremy did not offer a translation.

Blair had been in situations before where he had felt intrusive and embarrassed. This felt worse. Without the translation his guilt could not be expunged. Yet, he asked himself if this was something he truly wanted.

He glanced at the box by his feet. And he hesitated. But he had no other way of expressing himself.

He bent down and lifted the box. Then he stood and approached Mr. Brandt.

He opened the box. "This is the Presidential Medal of Freedom," he explained. "It is the highest civilian honor issued by the Government of the United States."

He placed the medal in the man's hands.

"I want you to have this," Blair said. "I know it won't bring your daughter back. But I hope it will act as a reminder to you and your wife of Lisa's bravery."

Mr. Brandt did not hesitate.

In one abrupt movement, he came to his feet—proving to be taller than Blair realized—and took him in his arms.

He began to rock him, gently, as if he were a child. Behind him, Blair could hear Lisa's mother crying.

CHAPTER 84

He was quiet during the ride back to his hotel, unable to get the meeting with Lisa's parents out of his mind. Their pain was like a disease, insidiously infecting anyone who came near them. He wished he could have said or done more.

"I want to tell you something," Jeremy said, breaking the silence. "I heard what you said to Lisa's parents. How you are to blame. Which is utter nonsense. This all happened because of circumstances beyond your control, Blair. Your behavior throughout this ordeal has been exemplary."

"*Exemplary?*" he scoffed.

"Tell me one thing you could have done differently?"

Blair knew of more than one thing, from his initial acceptance of Dalton/Yassin at face value, to turning aside Lisa's offer to help. But he held his tongue.

"I'm concerned about you, *boychick*," Jeremy said. "You can't keep this angst, this guilt, bottled up inside."

• • • • •

They decided on an early dinner at his hotel. Over a glass of Chardonnay, Blair began to question Jeremy about his past. "I mean, how did you make the transition from toys to working undercover for a government spy agency?" he asked. "It seems ludicrous."

And his friend smiled. "Suffice it to say that during my compulsory army stint, my superiors discovered I had a knack for the—uh—physical. And an analytical mind to boot."

"So they did what—conscripted you?"

"In a manner of speaking."

"But you had a reputable business, did you not?"

"That's what they liked. The fact that my business took me to many parts of the world. Especially North America. Anyway, I can't tell you anything more. It just is what it is."

• • • • •

The night ended early and Blair went up to his room. Without consciously knowing why, he turned on the television set. An old movie starring Shirley Temple was playing.

The curls in her hair brought back memories of how Sandra had looked at a younger age. He took a seat on the edge of the bed.

No reminder was necessary of the promise he had made to himself. The incident with Meconium Aspiration Syndrome at Sandra's birth was past. And Blair had vowed that no harm would befall her again.

Rather meaningless as far as promises go, he reflected now.

He stood. And for a moment, he didn't know what he wanted to do with himself.

Sandra was his pride and joy. Someone who brought meaning to his life. An innocent little girl.

"So why is she being punished?" he wondered aloud.

He went into the bathroom, washed his face and brushed his teeth, then got into bed.

Instead of sleeping, however, his mind went into overdrive. Jeremy had arranged to pick him up in the morning and take him to the airport. But he had no intention of being here when Jeremy arrived.

In New York a few days ago, Blair had Googled "Soldiers of Fortune" in this part of the world. Out of all the names he had found—and there were quite a few—three prospects seemed legitimate.

He remembered his discussion with the man from Philadelphia, how phony he turned out to be. And he realized the risk he was taking. But he was not going to be dissuaded. Appointments with all three men were already set.

CHAPTER 85

Just before 5:30 AM he rushed into the shower, then shaved and hurried downstairs for a quick breakfast. No longer trusting cabs in this city, he had arranged with the concierge for a private car and driver. He was on his way before seven o'clock.

It was a beautiful morning: clear sky, eighty degrees. As they drove, Blair felt a nervous excitement. Just being here, in this country, helped him feel closer to his daughter than he had in weeks.

The driver, a good-natured gentleman in his mid-fifties, gave a running commentary about each town that they passed.

They had left Nablus twenty minutes ago and were approaching the site of Blair's first prearranged meeting. He couldn't see it, but the driver told him that off in the distance sat the separation barrier, manned by Israeli army personnel.

Self-consciously, he fingered the envelope in his pants pocket. Twenty thousand dollars in cash, seven of which was from his personal savings account. The same seven thousand he had offered to Jeremy as a bribe in what felt like ages ago. The balance was a loan from his bank, having used his condo as collateral.

Suddenly, the driver swerved and came to an abrupt stop. All four doors of the car were yanked open. Blair counted no less than six men in their early twenties. There were no guns. No weapons of any kind. At least, none that he could see.

"Step out of the car!" one of them barked.

Blair hesitated.

"Mr. Mulligan, I will not ask again." Voice guttural, sounding angry.

The fact that he was addressed by name frightened him even more. Blair slowly came out of the car. "What is this about?" he asked.

The same man indicated toward a black Jeep, its motor running. "Get in!" he demanded.

Blair looked around for a means of escape.

Too late, one of the men took hold of his arm and led him forward. He was pushed into the back seat without pause or ceremony.

• • • • •

There were no blindfolds, no attempt at subterfuge. Three of the men had gotten into the Jeep with him. The remainder had commandeered the driver and car Blair had contracted at his hotel.

It was slow going as they wended their way through traffic. Blair was sandwiched in-between a man on either side. He turned to the one on his left and asked where they were taking him.

He got no answer.

A few blocks later, he tried again: "Look—I'm an American citizen. You can't treat me this way." It sounded lame and ridiculous, but he forged ahead. "I deserve some answers."

The silence only continued.

• • • • •

They pulled into the underground entrance of a nondescript building. From his knowledge of the city, Blair guessed they were somewhere in central Tel Aviv.

They entered a lobby with a bank of elevators. The men chose the stairs. Blair considered his options. One of the men had taken the lead; two were positioned behind him. No options at all.

The door leading to the third floor was opened and they stepped into a drab corridor, now deserted. Blair was ushered into a small room that resembled a prison cell. Poor ventilation and a vague, unpleasant odor. There was a wash basin and toilet. And a steel-framed, single bed.

He froze.

His suitcase was standing beside the bed.

He glanced at the men, then back at the suitcase. Only Jeremy could be behind this, he realized. And his anger surged.

The men left without another word. He heard a click as the door closed. He knew it was hopeless, but he tried the handle anyway.

It was locked.

He took a seat on the bed and cursed.

• • • • •

The same three men greeted him the following morning. One carried his suitcase. Another led the way downstairs and back toward the same Jeep.

He had spent a miserable afternoon and evening. The only break in his solitude came when his meals were brought in.

And even then he was ignored.

Blair recognized the road they were on, so he knew where they were taking him without being told. There were only so many flights from Israel to New York. Thus his confinement yesterday. It was simply a matter of waiting for an airline seat to become available.

• • • • •

They checked him in at the El Al desk, then accompanied him through security. Instead of stopping at the gate, however, the men led the way a few hundred feet further along, through an unmarked door and up a short staircase.

A key was used and they entered a windowless room, painted off-white, with five or six chairs lining the walls.

Blair took a seat in the one nearest him and looked at his watch. He knew that he had over three hours before his flight was due to depart.

He waited.

No one spoke to him.

• • • • •

Ten minutes later Jeremy strolled in with his usual swagger.

Blair scrambled to his feet, so upset with his friend he actually cocked his fist.

"Sandra's been freed," Jeremy said casually.

Blair pulled up short.

"It's true," Jeremy said. He indicated with his head.

The other men fled the room.

"She's here," Jeremy continued, once they were gone. "I asked her to wait in the hallway. I wanted to prepare you. She's been through a lot. She's lost weight. She looks—" He paused. "Haunted is the only way I can describe it. But its best if you don't act surprised. Understood?"

Blair's heart was pounding so fiercely he could barely nod.

Jeremy held the door open.

Nothing happened.

"Sandra?" Jeremy said.

Her hair had been cut ultra short, like a boy's. Her limbs appeared skeletal. She had a blank stare as if she were lost. And when she moved, it was with difficulty.

Blair felt sick. She looked worse than Jeremy had described. Frail and fatigued. He swallowed the acid down, then held out his arms.

She went to touch his cheek but quickly pulled back.

He noticed the ugly scab where her fingernail should have been. And he wished he could have the excision reversed.

"She'll need a little time," Jeremy said.

His friend's voice startled Blair, so engrossed had he been in seeing Sandra again.

He reached out once more.

She turned away.

Blair wondered if she was being reticent because of him. Because he was the one who got her into this situation. Because she now associated him with the bad guys. "I've missed you so much," he said.

She hid behind Jeremy as if she were shy—or worse, afraid.

Blair felt an incomparable need to hold her, to vanquish all her demons.

"Daddy?" Sandra questioned as if finally realizing who he was.

"Yes. It's me, darling."

She left Jeremy's side and took a slow step forward. Then another and another, until she was standing in front of him.

He held his breath.

She turned from Blair to Jeremy. And back again.

"It's okay," he said as softly as he could manage.

Tentatively, Sandra wrapped her arms around his waist. Then she squeezed. Gently at first. Then tighter.

And Blair's world stood still.

EPILOGUE

The man's Air Canada flight arrived in Toronto a few minutes early from London, England, and he now stood in line at Canada customs at Lester B. Pearson Airport. He had not been able to camouflage his height, of course. But everything else about him was different: black wig, hazel-tinted contact lenses, blackish-brown mustache.

When his turn came, he handed the agent, a woman around thirty years old of East Indian descent, his customs card and fake passport, and waited.

The agent checked his passport, then gave the card a cursory glance. "Here on vacation, Mr. Carter?" she asked.

"Yes," he said with a forced smile, accent all but hidden. "For five days."

"I hope the snow doesn't derail your plans."

"Snow?" he repeated.

"Yes. Haven't you heard? Very unusual for November. But you know what they say about Mother Nature." The agent used a red ink pen to scribble her code across the card. Then she handed the passport and card back to him and wished him a pleasant vacation in Canada.

The man proceeded along the corridor, then rode the escalator down to the arrival's hall. At carousel seven he waited to retrieve his luggage, which had still not made an appearance. When it did, some fifteen minutes later, he noticed his bag was slightly wet, no doubt from the snow the customs agent had mentioned. He picked it up easily, having packed light, and headed for the exit line.

A second agent—another East Indian girl, older than the first one—accepted his card and waved him through with hardly a second glance.

Stepping outside, he was caught unawares. His British topcoat was no match for the chill in the air. Most of the snow had been plowed, but more was falling. He was aware of Canada's foul weather, although no one had ever mentioned that it could start this early.

The lineup for taxis was a long one. In order to keep warm, the man hopped from one foot to the next. Finally, his turn came. The driver, a middle-aged Trinidadian with dreadlocks, asked his destination.

"The Stanfield Hotel," the man said, then added, "In Yorkville," hoping he sounded like a native.

The drive was a slow one: south on Highway 427, east on the QEW, which connected to the Gardiner Expressway. Traffic was backed up for miles. They progressed at a snail's pace. A normal journey of a half-hour took an hour and a half.

By the time he arrived, the man was ready to throttle someone. He was not appeased by the hotel staff's politeness, finding it instead to be cloying: "Good evening, Mr. Carter. Glad to have you with us, Mr. Carter. We hope you enjoy your stay, Mr. Carter."

While he was checking in, the clerk, a brunette of twenty-five or so, turned over the package that he had been expecting. "This arrived for you earlier today," she said.

He took it in hand without comment.

Once in his room, he unpacked and removed the contents from the package. Then he headed out, taking the elevator to the lobby floor. Less than a block from his hotel, he reached in his pocket for his throw-away cell phone. When he couldn't find it, he realized he must have left it in his bag upstairs.

Frowning, Alan Carter, aka John Dalton, aka Khalid Yassin, reversed his steps.

• • • • •

Avenue Road, a normally busy thoroughfare, especially as it neared Yorkville, was quiet this early in the evening. And the man realized that remaining inconspicuous would be difficult, what with the wait lasting longer than expected.

The cold was also getting to him, especially with the way it affected his hands and feet. Thick snow flakes were obstructing his vision. As he paced back and forth, he disparaged environmentalists everywhere. He deplored their decision to call the world's changing weather patterns "Global Warming." A misnomer if ever there was one. In a science of endless possibilities, why they would be so obtuse was beyond him. "Global *Warning*," was more like it.

Finally, his target made an appearance, disguised as he'd been instructed, replete with wig and mustache.

The man, going by the name of David Wells, watched as Khalid Yassin reached into his coat pocket, then brought his hand out empty. And he cursed when Yassin returned to his hotel.

Mr. Wells found it ironic that he would be here at all. But fate had shined down upon him. Once word reached him that Yassin had taken over this operation in Canada, he wasted little time in involving himself.

Now, the wait continued for another seventeen minutes. During this time, David Wells regretted not following protocol. By contacting the Royal Canadian Mounted Police, the Ontario Provincial Police, as well as the head of the Metropolitan Toronto Police Force, he could have had any number of personnel at his disposal. At least then he wouldn't be the one standing out here, freezing.

• • • • •

Yassin used the cell phone, got directions, and left the hotel a second time.

He arrived at Jane and Finch. Many of the mid- and high-rise apartment buildings in this particular neighborhood were in disrepair. Most of the residents were black, law-abiding and poor. A minority belonged to gangs or were involved in nefarious undertakings too numerous to count.

Yassin had the cab driver let him off at the southeast corner, from which he only had to walk a few blocks.

He entered a red-bricked building that had graffiti running up and down its walls. The lobby was in shambles: there was a black couch, torn in various sections, with stuffing sticking out. Ninety percent of the mailboxes had been ripped open.

He took the stairs to the second floor and knocked at 217.

Four men were waiting for him. Each was dressed in a long-sleeved shirt and jeans. *Kaffiyehs* covered their heads. Each was thin with a look of desperation in his eyes. One wore glasses. Three were tall, while one was of average height.

"*Asalaam alaikum,*" they welcomed him in unison.

"*Walaikum asalaam,*" he said in reply, embracing each man in turn.

He stepped inside. The tiny apartment was no bigger than seven hundred square feet. Everywhere he looked he noticed stained wallpaper, the original color of which was deeply obscured.

One of the men served tea. In the background, Yassin could hear a baby crying, then the sound of a woman's voice trying to soothe it.

The leader of the group, a boy with a pock-marked face, took the initiative. He handed a crude map to Yassin and drew his attention to the target areas that had been circled in pen. "*Triple-B* awaits your go-ahead," he said.

Triple-B, Yassin thought to himself. *How appropriate.* "Bathurst Bloody Bathurst" had been coined by one of the men. It stood for Bathurst, of course, a major north/south street long associated with its Jewish residents.

"There are five targets," the boy pointed out. "Each a synagogue, as you had requested."

"Estimated number of casualties?" Yassin asked.

"Well over a thousand."

"Excellent."

"So we have your blessing?"

"You do."

"Good." The leader said. "And when can our date be confirmed?"

Calmly, Yassin removed the Luger from his shoulder holster. It had been concealed in the package collected at his hotel when he had first checked in. "As soon as the traitor in our midst is identified," he said.

• • • • •

Mr. Wells was staying at the same all-suites hotel as Yassin. His spacious room was situated at the far end of the corridor on the fifth floor. He had requested this location for its lack of foot traffic.

Earlier, once Yassin's destination had been verified, he had seen no need to continue his surveillance and had returned to the hotel. But he'd been back for nearly two hours and there had been no phone call. He wondered why.

Months ago, his man inside had apprised him of the plot, code-named *Triple-B*. All that remained was for the date to be confirmed. Then they could put countermeasures into effect.

He looked at his watch. It was almost 8:00 PM. He went to the hall closet, took out his suitcase, and entered the code for each of two locks. He removed the equipment, relocked the bag, and replaced it.

Footsteps in the corridor drew his attention. He stood to one side, and quickly attached the suppressor to his Beretta. Then he watched as a legal-sized envelope was slipped beneath the door.

There was no indication that the person was leaving.

He moved along the wall and lifted the folded luggage rack. He approached the door but kept clear. Then he used the leg of the rack to nudge the envelope toward him.

Once he had it in hand, he tore the envelope open…and immediately felt faint.

There were six photographs of his contact—Ibrihim—a twenty-one-year-old naturalized Canadian born in Lebanon. The boy was a devout Christian doing an extremely competent job posing as a Muslim extremist. Each picture was three by five, in vivid color. It hurt Wells to the core to see the puncture wounds to the boy's face. His body was covered with cuts and burns, especially to the genital area. Nothing was left to the imagination.

Wells let the photographs drop to the floor. Then he reached for the equipment he had removed from his bag.

Months ago, Ibrihim had supplied details not only of what Yassin had planned, but exactly what he and his group had in their arsenal. This included a gas identified as CO449, a product used to incapacitate but not kill.

Wells knew that Yassin's cell consisted of himself and three others. It wouldn't be long now before they fired a blast of this same gas into his room. The door would be forced and they would take him captive, have him suffer a fate equal to Ibrihim's, perhaps worse.

But thanks to Ibrihim, he was prepared. Scientists in his home country had developed a gas to counteract the other gas, a gas that would impregnate Yassin's group's gas masks but not his own, and render them unconscious in a matter of seconds.

David Wells, aka Jeremy Samson, knew he had only a few seconds left to prepare.

• • • • •

Khalid Yassin was enjoying the moment. A number of months ago he believed that Jeremy Samson was a simple business associate of Blair Mulligan's and nothing more. There had been no indication of Samson's connection to Mossad. This bit of interesting news only came to him today, once they had made Ibrihim divulge the name of his handler. And Yassin could not believe his good fortune.

Yassin was only here as a replacement for the man normally in charge of Canadian operations. So the thought of taking down a prime enemy of al-Qaeda was too good to be true.

He indicated to the other men—boys, really—that they should prepare for the assault. As prearranged, he would stand guard against any interlopers before joining them.

Positioning himself at the opposite end of the corridor, Yassin attached the silencer to his pistol. He confirmed that no one was coming. Then he gave the signal to proceed.

They filtered the gas beneath the door. A moment later the lock was blown.

Yassin watched as the three men, with masks attached to their faces, made their way into the room.

• • • • •

Jeremy had his mask in place and released his own gas canister. Then he dashed into the bathroom and waited.

In less than sixty seconds all sound died.

He opened the bathroom door a smidgen. The haze was thick. He had to hold on a bit longer for it to dissipate.

When he came out, his stomach constricted. There were only three unconscious bodies where there should have been four. Quickly, he went from one to the other. He removed their masks and discovered who was missing.

Without hesitation, he fled the room. He dropped the moment he reached the hallway and went into a roll, holding on to his gun with both hands.

Noise from the stairs drew his attention.

He removed his mask and got back on his feet. He opened the door leading to the stairwell and bent low with the intention of making himself as small a target as possible. He looked up, believing the noise he'd heard had emanated from that direction.

The quiet was ominous.

The first bullet barely missed his scalp. The second grazed his left arm. The force of it threw him to his knees. It was just a flesh wound but it stung nevertheless.

Shit! The bastard was below him, not above.

He had to pause until the pain subsided. Blood was flowing but not sufficiently to require a tourniquet. He moved his arm; it was uncomfortable but still functioned. He wiped the film of sweat from his forehead.

Descending the stairs two and three at a time, he gained some ground. The minute he got Yassin in his sights, he fired off a round.

Yassin returned the gunfire.

Jeremy had to cling to the wall of the stairwell to avoid being hit again.

Yassin reached the lobby level. He burst through the door, then disappeared.

Jeremy was right behind him. He realized that without prudence, it could all end here. Badly. He slipped to the cement floor and flattened himself. He opened the door from his lying position. The corridor was brightly lit. He couldn't see anyone.

He came to his feet.

Taking the narrow corridor, he reached the lobby barely in time to see Yassin pushing his way through the crowd.

Throwing caution to the wind, Jeremy went after him, keeping his gun hidden, his gaze pointed straight ahead.

"Hey, you're bleeding!" someone called out, as if he wasn't aware of it himself.

There were too many people in his way.

Yassin sailed through the revolving doors.

He followed him outside.

Yassin was wearing a white shirt and trousers. Jeremy wasn't dressed any warmer. But Yassin's shirt was like a beacon in the dark. Jeremy was easily able to keep track of him. The man was less than half a block ahead, going north on Avenue Road.

The snow was falling again. The wind had picked up and the cold was sufficient to cut to the bone. There were a few pedestrians on the sidewalk. Vehicular traffic, while not as heavy as usual, was steady.

On the run, Jeremy began to close the gap.

Before he could take aim, however, Yassin began to fire at him, showing a disregard for the pedestrians.

Jeremy understood he could no longer remain on the sidewalk.

Yassin followed his example and moved onto the road.

Having been to Toronto before, Jeremy was aware of the average driver in this city. Most were ill-equipped to drive in rain, let alone snow. Too often they either went too fast or too slow. Tonight, the streets were especially slippery.

Seeing Yassin dart through traffic, he quickened his pace. Once he was close enough, he waited for a car to pass, and he fired his weapon.

Yassin ducked.

This went on for several minutes, with each man trying to gain the upper hand.

The cold was getting to Jeremy. He could especially feel it in the flesh wound in his arm. It was affecting his reflexes.

Suddenly, a woman slipped on the icy sidewalk.

Her cry distracted Yassin.

Taking advantage, Jeremy bent low and began to run alongside a fairly new Honda Civic. The driver was a woman in her late sixties or early seventies. Her hair was more white than gray, and she looked stricken.

He held up a hand, trying to indicate the need for calm.

The woman slowed down.

This perfectly served Jeremy's purpose. Popping up at the approximate spot he expected Yassin to be, he called his name.

Startled, Yassin backed up, straight into the path of a fast-moving car—a white Audi—coming from the opposite direction.

There was a horrific sound.

Yassin's body flew into the air, then came down with a thud.

Jeremy rushed to his side. He felt for a pulse but was unable to find one.

Pausing, he checked again.

"Dammit!" he swore aloud. Yassin deserved to suffer, not to succumb to what was practically a merciful death.

Standing, Jeremy caught sight of the distraught driver of the Audi making a beeline toward him. The man was elderly and heavyset, wearing an overcoat, scarf, and gloves. "It wasn't my fault," he was babbling. "You saw it. There was nothing I could do."

"Easy—" Jeremy started to say, when he spotted the man's *yarmulke*.

And he burst out laughing.

"What's so funny?" the driver said, growing angry.

"What's your name?" he asked.

The question seemed to unsettle the man even more. "Ch... Charles," he said.

"Charles?" Jeremy repeated. "You did good, Charles. You have no idea how good..."